SLEEP NO MORE

SLEEP NO MORE

APRILYNNE PIKE

HarperCollins *Children's Books*

First published in hardback in the USA by HarperCollins *Publishers* Inc. in 2014
First published in Great Britain by HarperCollins *Children's Books* in 2014
HarperCollins *Children's Books* is a division of HarperCollins *Publishers* Ltd,
77–85 Fulham Palace Road, Hammersmith, London, W6 8JB.
www.harpercollins.co.uk

Sleep No More
Copyright © Aprilynne Pike 2014
All rights reserved

Aprilynne Pike asserts the moral right to be identified as the author of this work.

ISBN 978-0-00-756996-0

Printed and bound in Great Britain by Clays Ltd, St Ives plc.
Typography by Ray Shappell

1

FSC™ is a non-profit international organisation established to promote
the responsible management of the world's forests. Products carrying the
FSC label are independently certified to assure consumers that they come
from forests that are managed to meet the social, economic and
ecological needs of present and future generations,
and other controlled sources.

Find out more about HarperCollins and the environment at
www.harpercollins.co.uk/green

To the survivors of Newtown

TEN YEARS EARLIER:

I sit on the itchy couch and stare at Mommy's eyes, wishing for them to open. Everyone tells me she's going to wake up, but it's been two days. Aunt Sierra promised and the doctor said so.

But Daddy's not coming back. Ever.

In my vision, it was Sierra who died. I was just trying to stop that.

But things didn't happen like I thought.

Sierra's alive. And Daddy's not.

A lady came in to talk to her. They've been outside in the hall for a long time. I look at Mommy and then slide down from the couch and sneak to the door. They're quiet, but if I put my ear right where the door isn't quite closed, I can hear them.

"It was supposed to be *me*," my aunt says in an angry whisper, and my stomach starts to hurt. I didn't want her to know. Now she'll figure out I changed things.

"You?"

"Yes, it was supposed to be me and I did nothing. Give me some credit."

"Then who?" the other lady asks.

I cross my fingers, but Sierra still tells on me. "It must have been Charlotte. It would've terrified her."

"You know how severe of an infraction this is," the lady says, and I don't know what *infraction* means, but her voice doesn't sound like it's something good.

"She's six!"

"She broke the rules," the woman says. "You're one of us, Sierra. And hopefully someday that girl will be as well. But only if you get her under control."

"I've been working with her since she was three!" Sierra argues.

"Then you're going to have to work harder, aren't you?"

Sierra says something but it's so quiet I can't understand her. Then I hear the loud click of high heels. The lady's going away. Sierra's coming back.

I run across the slippery floor and jump onto the couch again just as Sierra pushes the door open and pokes her head in. "Hey, sweetheart," she says. "Are you hungry?"

I'm not, but when I said no all day yesterday, Sierra got mad. So I nod.

"Let's go get a snack," she says, holding her hand out to me.

But she doesn't take me to the cafeteria. She stops at a vending machine and buys a package of M&M's and we go to a dim, quiet room with a big cross at the front. It looks like a church, but it seems weird to have a church in the hospital. I guess everyone else thinks it's weird too, because the room is empty.

Maybe that's why Sierra brought me here.

"Charlotte," Sierra says, "you had a vision about this, didn't you?"

My bottom lip quivers, and tears overflow when I nod.

"And you tried to stop it."

I nod again, even though the way she said it wasn't really a question. It's bad to see the visions at all. Sierra's been teaching me how to fight them off since I was three.

But it's hard.

And sometimes it hurts. This one hurt a lot.

"I tried to save you," I whisper, but I can barely get the words out through my tears. My chin drops to my chest and I feel her pull me onto her lap, where the curled ends of her pretty, blondish-red hair tickle my face.

"I'm going to come live with you," she says, and I'm so surprised my tears stop with a loud sniff. "Your mom will need a lot of help, and . . . I'm going to keep an eye on you for a while," she says, and it sounds like a bad thing.

She lifts my face and rubs my wet cheeks with her thumbs. "Your mom *is* going to wake up," she says, her voice very serious. "And when she does, you cannot tell her what happened. You can't tell her *anything*."

"But you said—"

"I know. I hoped that someday we could. But this accident has changed things. We can't *ever* tell her now."

"Why not?" I ask.

"Because . . . because she might be angry. With both of us," Sierra says after a long silence, and my chest hurts at the thought of Mommy being mad at me.

"Charlotte, I'm afraid the time has come for you to act much more grown up than you are. It's going to be difficult, but you have to work very, very hard at following the rules from now on. Do you understand?"

I nod, even though I really don't.

Sierra glances at the door that leads into the little church place. "Tell me the rules," she says.

"You know the rules," I say, rubbing my eyes with my fists.

"Tell me again," she says, and her voice is very soft and gentle now.

I stare at her, not sure why I have to do this here, but I start to recite anyway. "Never reveal that you are an Oracle to anyone except another Oracle."

"Good. Two?"

"Fight your visions with all your strength. Never

surrender. Never give up. Don't close your eyes."

"Three?"

"Never, under any circumstances, change the future." Sierra nods and a single tear shines on her cheek.

Then I understand.

I did this. Daddy is dead because I didn't follow the rules. I bury my face in my aunt's shirt and start to sob.

ONE

What I wouldn't give to live somewhere without snow. Not that there's any snow actually sticking on the ground yet. Just dead grass and bitterly cold winds. Ugly cold.

Until I open the front door to the high school and am blasted with a mixture of heat, moisture, and noise. The hall is swarming with bodies and music and cell phones chirping, but I put my head down and wander through it like a winding maze.

The space in front of my locker is crowded with people and for a moment I indulge the fantasy that they're waiting to talk to *me*. But I know better. Robert Jones is one of the most popular guys in school and his locker is on my right—thus the majority of the crowd.

On my left is Michelle.

We used to be friends. Now we have this wary sort

of acquaintanceship. Michelle glances in my direction and even though I see her catch sight of me—that slight widening of her eyes—she gestures to the two girls with her and they walk off together toward the cafeteria.

Whatever.

I bodily shove some big guy talking to Robert out of my way so I can get into my locker.

Unfortunately as I touch the scratched metal surface, I feel a tickling at the edge of my brain.

A vision.

Fan-freaking-tabulous. Just what I need before school even starts.

Now it's a race to get my locker open so I can crouch down and lean against it and look like I'm doing something. Something *else*.

I spin to the last number and yank up on the locker handle. It doesn't budge.

Damn it! I start to try the combo again, but it's too late. I'm going to have to sit on the floor. My legs bend, almost too easily, and I drop hard to my knees. I lean my forehead against the cool metal and breathe slowly, trying not to draw attention to myself.

The visions themselves aren't that big a deal; they're usually over in less than a minute. But I hate getting them in public because in those seconds I'm blind to the world. If no one speaks to me I'm fine—no one notices, the vision eventually dissipates, the world starts turning again, and life continues.

But if anyone tries to get my attention it's a little hard to miss the fact that I'm completely unresponsive. After that, I suffer mockery for days. Or I used to. It's a little better now that I'm in high school. People already know I'm a freak and just ignore me. The trade-off is, of course, that everybody knows I'm a freak.

Can't think about that now. I suck in air slowly, like I'm breathing through a straw, and stare straight ahead. I visualize grabbing a black curtain and pulling it over my inner eye—my "third eye," as Sierra always calls it—to block out the vision. Mental visuals seem to help.

I'll be affected by the foretelling no matter what, but if I black out my mind, fill it with darkness, then I won't *see* it.

And if I can't see, I won't be tempted to do anything about it.

As an added bonus, when I fight it, the vision generally passes more quickly. Which, when I'm at school, is the number one goal.

Sierra spent years trying different methods to help me block out my visions: a big, black paintbrush; turning off an imaginary switch; even covering my third eye with imaginary hands. The black curtain works best for me.

But no one can see what I'm doing on the *inside*; they only see the outside. And on the outside I'm some girl, kneeling on the dirty floor, my head against my locker, completely still with my eyes wide open.

I can't close them. Closing your eyes is a gesture of surrender.

I cling to the words I used to resent:

Never surrender.

Never give up.

Don't close your eyes.

I say them over and over, focusing on the words instead of the force of the vision fighting to get into my head.

An incoming vision feels like a huge hand squeezing your skull, trying to dig its fingers into your brain. You have to push back as hard as you can—with every ounce of concentration you have—or it'll find a soft spot and get in. The pressure grows to a fever pitch, and then, just as it gets truly painful, it starts to fade. That's when you know you've won.

Today, as usual, I win. It's so normal, it doesn't even feel triumphant. As the sensation ebbs away, my body belongs to me again. My lungs cry for air and even though I want to gulp it in, I do the breathing-from-a-straw thing so I don't hyperventilate. Made that mistake once in fourth grade and passed out. Not my finest moment.

A few more seconds and I'll be able to see again. Hear again. The noise filters in like turning the volume up on a radio and, as soon as I have the strength, I straighten my spine and let my eyes dart carefully from side to side to see if anyone noticed.

No one's paying attention. I reach for my backpack and my hand covers a shoe instead. I look up to find Linden Christiansen towering above my head and holding my backpack.

Mortification and delight fight to drown me.

He reaches out a hand and I wish it meant anything other than that he's a nice guy helping a girl up. But as soon as I'm on my feet, he drops his arm. "Migraine coming on?" he asks, handing over my backpack.

The lie that rules my life. "Yeah," I mumble.

He's looking at me and I let myself meet his gaze—and thus risk turning into a babbling moron at the sight of his light blue eyes that remind me of a still pond. "I t-took some new meds this morning," I stammer, "but I guess they haven't quite kicked in yet."

"Do you want to call your mom?" he asks, his forehead wrinkling with concern. "Go home?"

I force a smile and a shaky laugh. "No, I'll be okay. I just need to get to class and sit down. They'll start working soon."

"Are you sure? You want me to carry your backpack or anything?"

I'm tempted to let him. Anything to buy a few more minutes. But the vision has passed—I'm completely fine now. And my ego rebels against faking weakness for a guy.

Even Linden. Who I've liked since before my age reached two digits.

It'll never happen. Even if by some miracle he were interested, there're those stupid social lines that are practically stone walls separating us. I'm in the Artsy-Semi-Nerd pen. Linden is in the Super-Popular-Don't-Even-Try-It pen. Despite the fact that he's so nice. And talks to me sometimes. In choir class mostly. When he's bored. He doesn't actually sing very well, he just needs an arts credit.

But he wouldn't ask me out or anything.

And what would I do if he did? I can't date *anyone*. What would I tell the guy when he asks why I'm always so tense and jumpy? That I'm always on guard for unwanted foretellings of the future? Yeah, *that*'ll break the ice.

How about why I don't want to go to a movie? *Ever.* Somehow telling someone I don't like dim places because—like closing your eyes—they make the visions harder to fight, feels even more embarrassing than the lie that I'm afraid of the dark. Which is what I had to tell friends who used to spend the night—only *once*, of course, before they realized how weird I was—when they asked why I sleep with my bedside lamp on.

Not night-light. *Lamp.*

"You're positive?" Linden asks, and I nod, hating that I want to cry inside. He throws me a grin—a real one, a nice one—and says, "I'll see you in choir then."

I wave lamely and watch him walk away. I wish I could just be normal.

But I'm not. I'm Charlotte Westing and I'm an Oracle. The kind you've read about who once imparted wisdom and advised great kings and queens and assisted brave knights on their quests. But *those* Oracles existed a long time ago. When they could actually reveal their foretellings and use them to make lives better.

The world is different now. And our role is different. Oracles once worked with the leaders of civilization to mold, shape, and change the future for the good of mankind. But corruption led to several disasters like the fall of the Roman Empire and the Mongol invasion of China, so the Oracles withdrew their power. From then to present-day, the Oracles have followed an ancient vow to allow the future to unfold as it will. Now, Oracles believe it's best that no one sees the future. So that no one's tempted to change it.

So that no one dies because an Oracle doesn't have the strength to resist that temptation.

A hollow sadness fills my chest and I force it away. The past is gone. No one, anywhere, can do anything about what has already happened.

But the present? That's what *I* have to deal with. The visions are part of my life—have been since my first at age three. As soon as I was capable, my aunt Sierra started teaching me how to resist them.

A child should never be burdened with knowledge of the future, she told me, and I tried to believe her even though at the time I was excited that I could "do magic."

I know better now.

TWO

I'm more than ready to be finished with the day when I head into my final class—trigonometry. We're going over a review test and I'm having trouble paying attention. My external senses feel oddly muffled, the subtle feeling that generally precedes a foretelling.

But I just had one this morning; twice a day is pretty unusual. And this foretelling is being weird. I never like weird. Weird is unpredictable. Usually, once I get the feeling, the vision follows within minutes, max. This time, the sensation has lasted almost half an hour and still nothing.

Class is nearly over when the blackness starts to descend around the corners of my eyes and it's almost a relief to lay my forehead on my arms so I can get it over with.

Even though all my muscles are tensed and ready, it's more forceful than usual and I try not to shudder as a painful weight settles on my body.

It feels different this time. It's a vise that envelops my entire head. Squeezing, squeezing. A moan builds up in my throat and I push it away.

An Oracle never loses control. My aunt's voice echoes through my head, but her words blow away as a storm thrashes within my brain like a physical thing, battering against my skull until I honestly fear the bones are about to shatter. *What is this?!* Distantly I feel my fingers grip the edges of my desk and I hold statue-still, scrolling through every tactic my aunt taught me and new ones I've come up with on my own throughout the years.

But this vision is too strong. It tosses aside my defenses as though they are tissue paper trying to hold back a stampede.

Within seconds, the formless presence of the foretelling pulses around me. I can still kind of hear Mrs. Patterson answering a question about the radius of convergence, but her voice is getting further and further away as I struggle against a pull that feels like a river, carrying me away in a whirling current. Inside my mind, shadows are emerging. Then I'm spinning, falling.

No, no, no! I shout in my head, trying to grip my desk harder, breathe even shallower.

None of my tricks are working.

I've *never* had a vision this strong. Even when I was

younger and didn't know how to control them, they didn't overwhelm me quite this way. Some tiny part of me knows that I'm in school, sitting in a classroom surrounded by other sixteen-year-olds, but in the midst of the vision, those facts seem as fantastical as stories of princesses and dragons.

Then, with a brilliant flash of light, the falling sensation stops and my stomach feels like it flips upside down.

My feet are on solid ground.

I'm at the school football field.

It's dark.

Cold.

Goose bumps rise on my arms, and the air is clammy and damp like I'm standing in a thick fog. The vision pulls me forward, forcing me to walk, bending me to its will as though it were a living thing.

I fight every step even though I know it's too late. Still I fight. Because I'm supposed to. Because Sierra would expect it.

Because I owe it to my mom and dad to at least try.

I see her feet first.

Clearly a *her*—small feet clad in maroon ballet flats with little bows over the toes. I focus on those bows. I don't want to see the rest.

But even where I look is out of my control and my gaze moves up her body. Legs, torso, shoulders. Face. In my mind, I gag and I hope my physical self doesn't too.

Her eyes are open, sightless and a vivid blue. The splatter of blood across her cheeks is so fine it almost looks like glitter. But deep-red liquid pools under her neck, still dripping from her unmoving body. The puddle spreads as I watch, and the slice across her neck gapes in a grotesque display that makes my whole body rebel.

Get away!

I want to run—*need* to run—but the vision isn't finished with me yet. I focus on the rest of her body, taking in the smaller injuries I missed the first time around. Her shirt is torn across her midriff and a long, bloody scratch decorates the skin there. A knife? Fingernails? I can't tell. Her ankle is twisted at an unnatural angle and her hand is covered in blood starting at the fingertips. Her own? Her attacker's? There's no way to be sure.

Charlotte.

The voice is almost singsongy.

Chaaaaarlotte.

"Charlotte!"

I jerk my head up and air rushes into my nose. With a dull shower of sparks, my physical sight fades back in.

"Yes, Mrs. Patterson," I say as soon as my throat stops convulsing long enough to let me speak. Croak.

"Number twenty-three," she says, her hand on her hips, her voice heavy with annoyance.

How many times did she call me?

I make my neck tilt down; my eyes have trouble

focusing as the numbers swim on my paper.

"One hundred sixty-seven point six eight," I say, finally locating my answer. I look up and meet her eyes, hoping she'll just move on. I don't even care if I got it right. She stares at me for a moment. A beat. Too long? Too short? I don't know.

"Jake? Twenty-four."

Thank you.

My breathing returns to normal but my fingers are still clutched around the edge of my desk, pressing so hard they're white all the way up to the second knuckle. I force them to relax, one at a time, but when I pull my arms back and tuck my hands into my lap, they ache from the tension.

A sheen of perspiration prickles on my forehead and catches the breeze from the heater, making me shiver. More sweat is trickling down my spine, gathering under my arms. I feel gross and worn out and all I want to do is go home and take a nap.

And some ibuprofen.

And something that will make me forget.

Even before I was better at blocking foretellings, the things I saw didn't *always* happen—the future is fluid and the glimpses Sierra and I get are simply that: glimpses of how the future is currently set to play out.

But my record is pretty solid. Because unless you do something to *change* the future—which I would never do again—it's *probably* going to flow down the foretold path.

My heart speeds as I try to recall every detail. But it almost hurts to remember. The stark image of the thick, syrupy blood still pouring from the slash across her neck makes my stomach churn. It may not technically have been a real body, but unless something changes, it will be.

The bell rings—shrill and piercing—loud enough to distract me for the tiny second I need. I pull my mind away and take a deep breath, pushing back some of the nausea.

I have to get out of here, I think as I shove my books and papers into my backpack. Get out of this classroom and I'll be okay. I can go home. Take a nap. Forget about all of this.

I yank the zipper closed and spin toward the door in the back of the classroom, hoping I can walk some semblance of a straight line.

Then I freeze.

Bethany laughs and touches her friend's shoulder.

I didn't think about her face in the vision. Didn't worry about identifying her.

All I saw was that cut. The blood.

She's alive.

For now.

But she's wearing those maroon ballet flats.

THREE

"I'm home," I call as I walk in the front door.

"Office," Mom hollers back.

I'm almost afraid as I approach the converted bedroom where she does medical coding from home. Does it show on my face how stressed I am? I hope not. I can't talk to her. Not about this.

She doesn't know what I do. She can *never* know.

I peek my head around the doorway and smile, taking in my mom's shiny brown hair that falls into perfect waves—unlike mine, which is the same color but frizzes no matter how much product I use. She's slim and has long arms that reach for a file in one direction, a red pencil in the other, all fluid motions that flow almost like a choreographed dance rather than an entry-level job she never expected to work.

She looks perfect, always has. If you didn't notice

her wheelchair, you'd assume she was about to jump up and give me a hug.

But that hasn't happened since the accident that left her paralyzed.

The one where I traded my aunt's life for my dad's.

I suck in a breath and push that thought away, the same way I do twenty times a day. At least. But it's harder today after having a foretelling I couldn't fight. About another death. Those are the worst. People like to laud heroes. The ones who rush in, risk their lives to save someone. And I'm not saying they don't deserve it; they do.

But you know what's harder? *Not* doing anything. Standing back and letting bad things happen. Letting people die because they're *supposed to*.

I remember asking Sierra once, soon after she moved in, *why* we didn't act. "We could be superheroes," I argued with her. "We should *help* people. Isn't that the right thing to do?"

"Look what happened when you tried to save *me*," she said so gently I couldn't be angry.

Just sad.

In the end, it's not the right thing. Ever. And so I stand back.

Before I gained control—when I saw my visions more often—I foresaw a few deaths. Usually it was something like car accidents, heart attacks, that kind of thing. Things I probably couldn't stop even if I did try.

But *murder*? Just a word of warning to Bethany. To be careful. How much could it hurt?

Especially when the other option is to let her die a terrifying death.

"You've got your thinking face on, Char," my mom says, pulling my mind back into her well-organized office.

I make myself smile. "Lots of homework," I lie. Not that I *don't* have a bunch of homework. Just that it isn't what I was thinking about.

She pauses and glances up at me, her face so soft and caring it makes me want to cry at the thought of all the lies and half-truths I tell her on a daily basis. "You work so hard," she says quietly.

I bite the tip of my tongue. The last thing I deserve is her sympathy. I don't take advanced math and science and every AP class the school counselor will let me into because I'm some brainiac who's all self-motivated and ambitious. I do it because if I tire my mind out enough, I don't have time to think as hard. About the visions, about my utter lack of social life, about the fact that I ruined my mother's life and now we'll grow old together, two lonely spinsters.

Three, if Sierra stays with us.

"Gotta get into Harvard," I say in the lightest tone I can manage. It's another lie. I'll go to Rogers State in Claremore, about twenty miles away, so I can live at home. For a million reasons. Because Mom needs me and I'm responsible for her. Because it's dangerous for me to drive to Massachusetts, at least semi-irregularly, on the freeway, where I can't pull over at the first sign of a foretelling.

Because I could never live with roommates.

But Mom doesn't need to know any of that. Not yet.

"Is Sierra home?" I ask, changing the subject. Even though Mom's basically self-sufficient now, Sierra's never left.

And even though I hope it's not because she thinks she still *has* to babysit me, she kinda does anyway. I don't mind. Much. It means she's there to talk to, and the three of us all get along really well. Like *Gilmore Girls* plus one.

And a big-ass secret.

Mom often reminds Sierra that, although we love her and she's welcome to stay as long as she wants, we don't *need* her anymore and she can go out and have a "real life."

But Sierra and I know the truth: Sierra's an Oracle too, and her "real life" is inside her head. There's not really a possibility of anything else for Oracles. Getting married? I'm pretty sure a spouse would notice all of the weird things we aren't allowed to explain. I've always hoped that maybe someday Sierra would find that perfect person who she could trust enough to confide in. But even assuming Sierra would be willing to go against the rules, would finding out the truth chase someone off? And if it did, would they keep their mouth shut about it? Not likely.

Or, let's say they *did* believe her—it would take a pretty big person not to start prying about *their* future. Everyone thinks they want to know the future.

Everyone is wrong.

So it just . . . wouldn't work.

Similarly, there's no perfect soul mate in my future either. Only a lifetime of hiding. I didn't choose this. I *wouldn't* choose this. But it's the hand I was dealt. The hand Sierra was dealt. Some people are short, some people have freckles, some people see the future. It's all genetics.

"I think so," Mom says, and I've forgotten what it was I asked.

Oh yeah. Sierra.

"But you know how she is; she sneaks in and out and I don't hear a thing." Mom grins at me over her shoulder before turning back to her work. "Check her office."

I pull Mom's door closed and walk down the hall to the room Mom always refers to as "Sierra's office"; but it's really her room/office/work/life. When Dad died, we didn't have the money to move—especially not with all the medical bills—but Mom couldn't handle sleeping in the master bedroom anymore, so she gave it to Sierra. It's a big room with a small sitting area and private bathroom and . . . well, Sierra doesn't leave it very often.

At least not when I'm home.

Her desk is set up in the sitting area and about half the time I bring dinner in to her so she doesn't have to stop working. The walls are covered with shelves full of books about history and mythology and other Oracle stuff that she is constantly pulling out to use as references. When I was twelve, I asked what she would do if Mom came in and *really* took a look at her books but Sierra shrugged and said, "I'd tell her it's research."

Then I asked what she would do if *I* started coming in and borrowing books. She said she'd start locking the door.

Two days later when she caught me with *Oracles of Rome*, she started doing just that.

She always knows more than she's willing to tell me. She says too much knowledge makes what we can do excessively tempting and that she only trusts herself because of years of resisting as she researches. I'm not even sure what that means. I guess we might be tempted to change the future, but she talks like there's more.

And I desperately want to know what that *more* is.

I don't think it's fair. I can't really believe any other sources; they're legends at best. But Sierra's library is the real deal. Ancient books and manuscripts that don't exist anywhere else in the whole world. I keep trying to sneak glances at them, but Sierra's not stupid—she notices. That's why she does most of her errands when I'm at school.

And if I *am* home, the door is always locked when she leaves.

I try not to resent it. After all, she's devoted so much of her life to me. She taught me everything she knows about fighting foretellings, and she's always patient. I've actually never seen her lose her tempter.

But all those books . . . She says she'll let me read more when I'm a member of the Sisters of Delphi. Like her.

Sierra is an author of several texts about Greek mythology and the unseen world. That's what she does to pay the bills. And while her books are probably really great—I can barely understand the few paragraphs I've read, but she wins awards all the time—it's just camouflage for her real job: the historian of the Sisters of Delphi.

The Sisters is an ancient organization of Oracles that basically monitors all of the Oracles in the world. All twenty or so of us. Sierra won't tell me much about them. Which seems weird to me since there are so few of us. Shouldn't we all share our information? But Sierra says that when I'm eighteen and it's time to join them, I'll be ready to know more.

Always the promise of more. But not now. Drives me crazy.

I knock softly on Sierra's door. She must be home; her door is not only unlocked, but open an inch or two.

"Come in."

Sierra's work space is bright and inviting. The curtains are pulled back, letting in the sunshine, and there are two tall, standing lights flanking each side of her desk, which are on as well. The surface of her desk is a jumble of stacks of papers and books and about six coffee mugs, but there's no dust, and certainly no darkness.

Darkness is our enemy.

Sierra doesn't even look up until I've been standing beside her chair for what feels like a very long time. "Charlotte," she finally says, pushing wisps of hair away from her face with a smile. Her hair is a shiny brown—just like mine and mom's. At least it is *now*.

I remember when it was strawberry blonde, when she curled the edges and it danced around her face. Now she dyes it. I don't know why anyone would opt for brown over that gorgeous strawberry. But when I asked her about it a few years ago, she looked so sad I've never asked again.

That was back when she always looked pretty and dressed up. Not anymore. No makeup, no fancy hairstyles. A single ponytail, a braid down her back, sometimes a bun. *I* glitz myself up more than Sierra does, and that's saying something.

She's staring at me, eyebrows raised, waiting for me to speak, and my mind vacillates. *Confess or keep quiet?* I honestly don't know what the best thing to do is. I'd like advice, but I feel like a kid again, confessing that I wasn't able to block a vision. Despite the fact that Sierra and I are close, she's still my mentor, and she expects a lot of me.

"When was the last time you saw a vision?" I finally blurt out.

That gets her full attention. She slides her reading glasses up onto her forehead and pushes her office chair back. "The last time I *fought* a vision or the last time a vision won?" she asks softly.

"Both," I say after a moment of hesitation.

She waves her fingers in the air almost dismissively. "I fought one this morning. It was small. No big deal." She removes her glasses now and sticks the end of one earpiece in her mouth, her teeth worrying the plastic with audible clicks. "The last time a vision beat me was ten years ago," she whispers as though confessing to a crime.

"Ten years?" I echo in the same hallowed whisper. And I thought I was doing well going on almost six *months*.

"It gets easier," Sierra says, reaching out for my hand. "You'll grow stronger."

I nod, though my throat feels tight and I can't actually speak.

"Hard one today?" Sierra asks, and her thumb makes circles on my hand.

I look at her and I know she can see the answer in my eyes. I always come in to see her on tough, draining days when blocking a foretelling takes everything out of me. Some days we don't even talk; I simply sit and share the same space with the only person in my life who understands the struggle I face every day.

She hesitates and I'm afraid she's going to ask if I won my fight or not. I don't know how I'll answer her. "Your teens are the hardest time," she finally says, her thumb still stroking the back of my hand. "Life is so full of things to pull your attention away from your defenses, your body is still changing, hormones are raging."

Oh yes, please talk about puberty right now, I think, forcing myself not to roll my eyes. I do pull my hand back though, and cross my arms over my chest.

At least she didn't ask. She usually assumes I won. Because I almost always do. Maybe she trusts that I would tell her if I didn't. And she *should* be able to. More guilt.

But ten years? I really am crappy at this.

"Things will calm down once you finish college and can withdraw from the world more," Sierra says calmly, evenly. Like she didn't just sentence me to a life of seclusion.

"Sierra," I say after several long seconds of silence.

"Would it really be so bad if we just let them come?" Her eyes narrow slightly, but I continue. "Not all the time, just, like when I'm alone in my room at home." I don't remember a lot from when I didn't fight, but the foretellings I did get were mostly little things. Things I didn't care about. "If I don't *do* anything about it, of course," I add when Sierra's lips tighten.

She leans forward, looking up at me with dark brown eyes that look so much like Mom's. "I know you *think* you can do that, Charlotte, but believe me, the temptation will become too great. You'll want to change things. And that's not a bad thing; it's because you're a good person and you have a desire to help people." She furrows her brows and then she's not meeting my gaze anymore. "You don't know how bad the visions can get. Not even you."

Not even me? Not even the girl who got her father killed trying to save her aunt? How much more devastating than *that* could it possibly get?

But then, maybe seeing a murdered teenager is worse. It makes me wonder what Sierra has seen that puts that haunted look in her eyes.

I want to ask more, but I'm not sure how I can without revealing what I saw today. And I just don't want to. Don't want to admit how much I suck.

I stand there silently for so long that after a few minutes, Sierra squeezes my hand, turns back to her computer, and resumes working.

I wander over to the shelf that houses the oldest books. With my arms folded, I scan the spines and titles—as close as Sierra ever lets me get. My eyes catch on a cracked leather spine printed with the words REPAIRING THE FRACTURED FUTURE.

Air slips slowly out between my teeth with a tiny hiss. This. *This* is what I need. I glance at Sierra, but she's as focused as she was when I first came in. My fingers walk slowly forward, sneaking the same way I might tiptoe down a hallway. Closer. Closer.

My index finger hooks around the top of the spine and I pull slowly, tipping the book down. A whisper of the leather covers rubbing together makes me freeze, but after a few seconds I let the spine lean all the way into my palm.

Now I just have to pull it out and—

"Charlotte."

Disappointment wells up in my throat. She didn't snap—she never does—but that edge of "you know better than this" in her voice makes me want to melt into a puddle of shame. With my teeth tightly clenched, I push the book back where it belongs—at least she won't know *exactly* which book I wanted—and turn to look at her.

Sierra sighs and rises from her chair. She comes close and puts an arm around my shoulder, deftly steering me toward the door. "You know you're not ready," she whispers.

"I think you're wrong," I say defiantly, proud of myself for voicing what I've thought for at least two years.

"I'm erring on the safe side this time," Sierra says, leaning her head close enough to touch mine. "The last time I didn't watch you closely enough, this entire family paid for it. You don't need more temptation in your life."

And without another word, she pushes me the last few inches through the door.

By the time I turn around, the door is closed and even as I raise my hand to turn the knob, I hear the unmistakable sound of the lock turning.

Great.

Maybe I should have told her. Now I have to decide what to do all by myself.

And I don't even know where to start.

FOUR

It's all over the news the next morning.

Her body is covered with a white drape, and the reporter is rambling on about her injuries, but even his gruesome descriptions can't compare to the actual sight. The one I saw only yesterday.

Mom's hand is clenched around a mug of coffee, but she hasn't lifted it to her mouth since she turned the television on ten minutes ago. "Who could do this?" she finally whispers after what feels like hours.

Unfortunately, despite the vision, that's a question I can't answer. Visions are fickle that way—sometimes they give you the important information, and sometimes they simply . . . don't.

Sierra walks into the noticeably tense kitchen. "What's going on?" she asks, looking between Mom and me and not seeming to notice that the TV is on despite its high volume. She's like that, totally unaware of some things while being hyperaware of others. Probably because she's constantly on guard for visions.

I guess I'll be like that someday too.

"A teenage girl was killed at the high school last night," Mom whispers, still staring horrified at the television. "Throat sliced right open."

Sierra's head swings to me and she stares with questions shining in her eyes. I feel like I did when I was six. I don't know how she knew then, but she did.

And she knows now.

Her expression evokes the same awful guilt, even though this time I did nothing. Which makes me feel even *more* guilty.

Sierra fills her coffee cup with marked carefulness. She begins to leave the kitchen, but just before she disappears around the doorway she flicks her head, gesturing for me to join her.

I stall. I've got about five bites of now-soggy cereal in the bottom of my bowl, and I lift them to my mouth slowly. But I can't put it off long—I have to leave for school soon.

Sierra is waiting for me just outside her bedroom door. "This is why you were asking questions yesterday, isn't it?"

There's no point in denying it.

"You didn't tell me you *actually saw it*. I assumed you fought." Even though her voice is soft, I can tell she's angry. Angry that I didn't confide in her? Maybe.

"I *did* fight!" To my dismay, tears are starting to build up in my eyes. I didn't expect it to actually happen so soon. I wasn't ready. "I fought so hard," I continue, pleading now. "It was different from anything I've ever experienced before. I *couldn't* stop it."

She stares at me for a long time, but then her eyes soften and she simply says, "I wish you'd told me."

"Why?" I shoot back. Not mad exactly, but very helpless. "So you could *do something*?" Her jaw tightens but I continue. "What good would it have done to tell you?"

Sierra looks down the hall toward the kitchen where I can hear the news continuing about the murder. She steps close and lays a hand on my shoulder. "Charlotte, the life of an Oracle is very solitary; we're lucky to have each other. Please don't push me away because I have high expectations of you. I don't think you failed—these things happen. But that means it's time to be even more vigilant."

Her steady gaze makes me weirdly nervous and I pull out my phone and light up the clock on my home screen. "I gotta go."

After getting dressed, I walk into the kitchen and pick up my set of house keys from the basket beside the back door. Surprisingly the soft jingle is what finally distracts Mom from the gruesome scene on the screen. "Where are you going?" she says in a rather irritated tone.

I blink at her, confused. "School?"

Her hair looks almost wild around her face as she shakes her head. "You can't go to school today."

"Why not?" The words are out of my mouth before I realize how stupid they are. Of course my mother is worried about my safety; a girl who's in a couple of my classes just got murdered *on school grounds*.

She doesn't know that I'm completely safe.

It's kind of an open secret among Oracles; we all know how we're going to die. Or, like me, we don't *yet* because it's too far in the future. The more personal a foretelling is, the harder to fight off. And *nothing* is more personal than one's own death. I managed to get that tidbit out of Sierra once when I asked why she didn't try to change her own death in the vision we both saw when I was six. But then she clammed up and wouldn't tell me anything else.

I've never had a foretelling about myself. I'm pretty sure that means my death is years and years and years in the future. My lonely, eccentric future.

And that means I'm safe today. But Mom doesn't know that.

"I know this is awful," I say, "but I have a test in trigonometry today. I have to go."

Mom fixes me with a dry look. "I have a feeling the test is going to be postponed."

As though she can control the television, the silence between us fills with a voice announcing, "Due to the fact that William Tell High School is a crime scene that has not yet been released by the police, classes have been canceled. Principal Featherstone hopes to open campus as early as Monday, but until then, please keep your teenagers home, where they're safe."

Canceled or not, a quick shot from the news camera shows that the teenagers of Coldwater, Oklahoma, are certainly *not* at home. The football field fence is lined with students and adults alike, most in tears as they watch from behind bright yellow barriers of police tape fastened across the chain-link.

"The police haven't released the name of the victim yet," the news reporter continues, catching my attention again. "Only that she was a student attending this school." She indicates the crowd of people, many on their phones. "You can imagine the panic these kids must be feeling as they call and text their friends and wait anxiously for responses. For channel six, this is—" But I tune her out; I don't care what her name is.

My eyes are glued to the draped body that's now being lifted onto a gurney bound for a waiting ambulance. They do a good job of keeping her face covered, but a gust of icy December wind wrenches the drape free from one foot and a maroon ballet flat comes into view.

A scream sounds from offscreen and, as though drawn to the agony, the camera swings toward the fence and shows a tall brunette crumpling to the ground, surrounded by a handful of other girls.

Rachel Barnett. She's Bethany's best friend. The one I saw her with yesterday. She would know instantly who those shoes belong to. Sobs shake her body as the news camera zooms in, invading her private grief. I can't help but feel like a voyeur as Rachel wails and shakes her head. I don't even realize I'm crying until I'm gasping for air.

I turn and leave the kitchen, ignoring my mom when she calls after me. I swing the door to my bedroom closed as fast as I can without slamming it, and lock it. My room feels too dark even with the sunlight pouring in through the window, so I turn on my overhead light, and then add my bedside lamp for good measure. After kicking off my shoes, I dive under my comforter, wishing something as simple as a fluffy feather blanket could hope to chase away the frost inside me.

I could have stopped this.

No, that's not exactly true. I *might* have been able to stop this. And I didn't even try. Even though I can hear my aunt's voice screaming in my head that I did the right thing, I feel like a terrible person.

And what's worse is that I hadn't actually decided what to do yet. I thought I had more time. I was going to make the for-sure decision this weekend. And now the choice has been torn away from me.

I did nothing.

Not because I *chose* to do nothing, but because I didn't make a choice at all. The thought sickens me. I wish I'd never seen the vision. I wish I'd fought harder. Assuming I even *could* have fought harder. The memory of how drained I felt after the foretelling makes me doubt it, but maybe there was something else I could have done.

Even without a vision, the whole idea of a murder would have seemed surreal. Coldwater is the kind of place where stuff like this just doesn't happen. We're not teeny tiny; there are, like, ten or fifteen thousand people in the community. Lots of farmers, people who say hi at the grocery store even though they don't exactly know who you are. Half the town goes out to the high school football games Friday nights without fail. That kind of thing.

Our idea of a crime-filled night is some couple getting drunk and causing a "domestic disturbance," or maybe a high schooler attempting to steal a bottle of tequila from the liquor store on a dare.

Not killing people. Not killing *kids*.

I should have warned her. I shove my head under my blanket in some long-forgotten instinct, and then tear it off again to escape the darkness.

As light flashes across my eyes, I have a terrifying thought: maybe that was the reason the vision overwhelmed all of my defenses—because I was *supposed* to help her and I failed.

But what if I *had* done something? If I'd warned her to be careful she might have taken Rachel with her. Then two people would be dead. And that second death would have been entirely my fault.

This isn't about choosing between right and wrong; it's about trying to predict the line between wrong . . . and *more* wrong.

FIVE

Monday is pure hell. Even worse than the torture I've been putting myself through all weekend. There's a huge pile of flowers and candles and stuffed animals in front of the school. Not just from other students—from the whole community. The sense of security that permeated Coldwater is gone.

People are afraid. Sad and afraid.

News vans have come in from Tulsa. I'd like to think it's because they care—and that's certainly the façade they're trying to sell—but it feels intrusive. Like strangers attending a strictly family funeral. I want to chase them away and tell them this isn't *their* loss.

But I can't. I have to attempt to blend in—act like I'm as surprised by this horrific act of violence as anyone. That I'm as normal as every other kid floating aimlessly through the halls today.

Standing in front of my locker, I almost don't notice

Linden. Of course, he's not drawing any attention to himself. Maybe he's even consciously trying to avoid it. I pretend to be sifting through the stuff in my backpack as I study him. The light and spark in his posture and expression that generally define him are gone. His eyes are red rimmed. He looks broken.

I forgot that he was one of Bethany's friends. I want to go to him, to say something to ease that awful look in his eyes. It makes me hurt to see him this way.

I probably shouldn't, but I do anyway.

I approach tentatively, not wanting to screw this up and make it even worse for him. "Linden?" I say softly. He turns and for just a second it's like he's too deep in his grief to even recognize me. Then his face softens.

"Charlotte. I didn't see you."

"That's okay."

We're both silent for a few seconds. "I'm so sorry about Bethany." And somehow, just saying the words— apologizing to *someone*—makes me feel better. "I know she was your friend," I add in a mumble.

He nods stiffly.

"If I can . . . if you ever need, I don't know, someone to talk to or something," I blurt, half mortified at what I'm saying.

He stares at me for several long seconds before a ghost of a smile touches his mouth. "That's really nice of you. I—" He hesitates and for a moment I think he's actually going to say something—something meaningful.

"I'll remember that you offered. Thanks," he says, and then wanders away with a small hand flutter instead of saying good-bye.

I watch him go with an ache in my heart. Somehow, seeing Linden hurt like this makes my remorse even worse.

He doesn't show up to choir.

When school gets out, I know I should hurry home. My house is literally within sight of the front gates of the high school and though I finally convinced my mom to let me walk to school this morning, she wheeled out to the front porch and watched me the entire way.

She'll stress until I walk back in the door.

But I need a few minutes.

I slump against the worn metal door of my locker, letting my back slide down until my butt hits the floor. I rub at my temples. I've been in a blur all day, but my head feels downright cottony now.

Oh no. My eyes fly open. "I'm so stupid," I mutter to myself. I've been so distracted by my own guilt and pain I didn't recognize the signs. The very last thing I want to do right now is to fight another foretelling; it's harder when I'm feeling emotionally vulnerable.

And there's something else. Something new: fear. After the horror of the last vision a tiny quiver clenches in my stomach at the thought of losing a fight again. Of seeing something like that again.

I briefly wonder if I can make it all the way home and into my bedroom before it overtakes me, but even if the pressure in my head weren't already starting to build, I suspect my mom won't let me get past her without at least five minutes of talk—she hasn't been able to focus on anything except Bethany all weekend.

Fine, it's gotta happen here in the hallway. I can handle this. I can do it.

At least I don't have to worry about anyone looking at me funny. *Everyone* is out of it today. I brace my forehead on my knees and stare steadfastly at the tiles on the floor, forcing a black veil over my second sight. Bracing myself to hold it there the way Sierra taught me.

A savage storm rips it away.

Not again! In my head, I grasp for the blackness and for just a second the imaginary drape slides into place and I think I've won.

Maybe I even *could* have won if I weren't already exhausted. But the last dregs of my mental strength aren't enough when a fistful of fingers reaches forward and rips the curtain away again and the same vise from last week squeezes my skull until I want to scream in agony.

I can't erect a strong enough barrier to block it, and then the fingers are pushing into my mind, taking over, and I'm tumbling down the river. Then falling. Falling.

45

The darkness flees, leaving me standing in a strange grayness.

It's snowing. Those thick, heavy flakes that fall silently and feel like a blanket being laid over the earth. My vision self breathes a sigh of relief. We haven't gotten our first real snow yet. Whatever I'm about to see, good or bad, I should have some time. Not like Bethany.

As the vision forces my feet to walk, I start resisting again. Fighting with every ounce of strength I have left. Not because of Sierra or the rules.

Because I'm terrified.

I've never been so afraid of what might be waiting for me. I know what a vision this strong can bring and I don't ever want to see something like that again.

But my feet keep striding through the cottony snow. There's a large, dark shadow in front of me. Not a person, a thing. *A truck,* I realize when I get closer. The truck is sitting on a dirt road, but there are no streetlights. The sky is cloudy, so I can't tell how full the moon is—*that* would have been helpful; maybe I could have looked it up. The filtered moonlight and distant lights from town are reflecting off the pure white snow and the billowy clouds above, giving the night air a strange orangey glow that always comes with this kind of thick, silent snowfall.

The door of the truck hangs open, and at first I don't see anyone inside. But there's something. . . . I gasp as

I realize the dark stain I'm seeing on the far side of the windshield is blood. A huge spatter of blood decorating a spider-webbed crack in the glass.

I swallow hard as dread eats at my stomach, but I can't stop my legs from continuing to carry me to the truck, my neck from peering around the open door. And even though I squeeze my eyes shut, only my physical eyelids close.

My foretelling eyes *have* to see.

He's draped facedown on his stomach across the bench seat, with his hand wrapped around his phone. Trying to call for help, I suspect. I try not to see the rest, but bile rises in my throat as I force back a sob and take in the details. It's gunshot wounds this time, instead of a knife. One, two, three, four, five of them up his back before the veritable crater in his skull that makes me sway on my feet. Each wound is a gaping hole in his skin—through his coat. Five ripped circles stained with still-wet blood that looks shiny black.

His head . . . I can hardly focus. It's too much. His hair is sprinkled with fragments of bones and small bits that I'm pretty sure belong *inside* his skull. The bullet must have done this, then kept going through the windshield on the far passenger side—making the bloody star I saw first.

He never had a chance. I swallow hard and remind myself to observe. I have to be brave enough to face this horror—figure out where he is, *who* he is. I can't move my feet to where I want them to go, but if I crane my neck I can see just a little bit better. I force myself to look past the bloody mess of his hair and try to make out his profile in the dim light.

I throw my hand over my mouth. He's one of the basses in our performance choir. A sophomore, younger than me.

Matthew. Matthew Phelps. He was in one of my art classes last year too.

With my fists clenched, I whirl around, trying to take in my surroundings. I don't know if I can do anything to save him, but figuring out *where* we are is definitely the first step. Coldwater is a pretty spread-out community with a forest on the west end of the city. I think that's where we are now. I'm surrounded by bare, spindly trees, but I'm not in the middle of nowhere. Just off the paved road. There're a bunch of rich-people houses, up on what passes for mountains in Oklahoma, that don't have paved roads leading to them. Maybe Matthew lives there.

Maybe he was just going home. And some guy asked him for directions. Then he turned his back and . . . I don't know. I look at the trees as the vision begins to darken and force myself to stare, to memorize, as the vision fades.

I have to find out where this is. And more important: *when*. I don't care what Sierra thinks—I have to do something. I'm not sure my conscience can handle another disaster. Not something even more bloody and violent than Bethany's death.

The school hallway slowly comes into focus and I'm shivering uncontrollably. I huddle beneath my coat. It takes a couple of minutes before I have the strength to stand. This vision was even harder on me than the last one and my legs are quivery. With Bethany's, I felt like I was put through a punishing workout—today I feel like I flat out got beat up. Bruised from head to toe.

I limp home and, sure enough, my mom's wheel-chair is sitting out on the porch and she's bundled up in her warmest coat, staring at the screen of her phone.

"There you are!" she says, reaching out for me.

"I'm so sorry," I say, squeezing her hand before I wheel her into the warm house and down the hall to her office. "We had a choir meeting after school," I lie smoothly, "and I thought it was going to be, like, five minutes and it just kept going and going. I should have texted you."

She gives me a tight smile. "Yes, you should have. But the important part is that you're here now, and you're safe."

I sit on the chair in her office that's always left empty for me and just watch her. She's working, but the smooth rhythm from last week is gone. She writes a few things, then turns to stare at a small TV she's set up on a stool beside her desk. It's muted, the news reporters mouth-ing words I don't need to hear anymore to understand.

Bethany's body, her delayed funeral, interviews with her parents, her teachers, her friends—when they can hold their tears back long enough to speak. I've seen it all, but they keep replaying it like some terrible CD skipping over and over.

I've got to go find that forest. I can't let this happen again.

"Can I borrow the car?" I ask.

Mom turns and fixes me with a surprised gaze, clearly shocked that I would even ask.

"I just want to go for a drive. To think."

She's already shaking her head.

"Mom, please," I beg, trying to hide how desperate I am. "I'll be careful. I'll keep the doors locked and I won't stop for anyone or get out of the car or anything. I'll just drive." *Up some dirt roads that may or may not lead to a future murder site in the middle of nowhere.*

"I don't want you leaving the house," my mom says.

"We can't let this make us paranoid," I protest irrationally.

"It's not that," Mom retorts. Then she pauses and amends, "It's not *just* that." She turns back to the silenced television beside her desk. "The forecast is calling for snow tonight."

SIX

There's nothing on the news the next morning. But that doesn't make me feel any better. The location looked remote; they might not have found him yet. My mom held firm last night and the weather guy was right. So I sat at my bedroom window until the wee hours of the morning, helplessly watching that thick, muffling snow cover the ground, certain I was too late.

I sit at the breakfast table, pushing my food around on my plate and waiting for the time when I have to leave for school. I keep expecting a hint of *something* on the news, but it's all still Bethany. People are starting to get angry because the medical examiner hasn't released her body. It's been five days and as far as anyone can tell, there are zero leads.

I wonder if the discovery of another body will make them keep her longer or let them move on.

I feel like all of my insides are twisting around each

other and squeezing. I wish I could fake sick. But then the news of Matthew's death will come through and Sierra will know why I stayed home. I can't risk it.

I considered telling her this morning—coming clean before the body was found—but when I got to her room, her door was locked. I thought about knocking—lifted my hand even—but I couldn't make myself do it. I feel like the lamest Oracle on earth.

I leave the house with a quick glance at Sierra's still-closed door, and Mom wheels onto the porch to watch me again. Tomorrow, she won't let me walk. After today, I'll be lucky if she ever lets me out of the house again.

I'm grabbing my trigonometry book from my locker when I see him, standing there with no idea he's supposed to be dead.

The heavy book falls from my hands and lands on the linoleum floor with an ear-splitting *crack* that echoes through the hall. People turn to look at me, but I'm already staggering toward Matthew, ignoring everything else.

"Hey," I say lamely, realizing I'm so focused on the fact that he's not dead that I don't have any idea what the hell to say to him.

"Hi, Charlotte." He studies me, furrows his brow and then asks, "Are you okay?"

Better now. "Um, yeah, I just, I . . . I forgot my music for 'Winter Wonderland.' Do you mind if I borrow yours and make a copy of it real quick?"

"Oh, sure. Of course," he says, the concern erased from his face so easily I want to cry with relief. He's alive, he doesn't suspect, and no one is looking at us anymore.

He hands me a piece of music. "Just bring it to choir with you. No hurry."

"Thanks," I reply, taking the music I don't actually need. I hesitate, but the hellish hours I spent last night aren't something I can live through again. I banish Sierra's voice from my head and say, "Matthew, you live kind of out in the middle of nowhere, right?"

"Sort of. I mean, there are, like, four houses in our little neighborhood, but it's up on the hill west of town." He's confused again.

"Be careful," I say, hurrying on before Matthew can say anything. "Maybe I'm just paranoid because of Bethany, but that guy is still out there somewhere and . . . be careful, okay?" I spin away and flee before he can reply.

Before he can ask any questions.

There. I did *something*. Who knows if it will be enough? But I warned him. Being careful can't possibly hurt. And considering last night's snow, there's a chance he *was* going to die, but that the future changed and it's not going to happen at all.

The future is funny like that.

I return to my locker—which I left open with my

trig book on the floor in front of it—no wonder every-one thinks I'm such a freak—and gather my stuff. I know I ought to feel guilty. But I can't bring myself to be anything but glad.

As I pick up my trig book, my phone peals out my text chime and I drop the book again, winning myself more startled looks.

It's a number I don't recognize.

You're the only one who could have helped her.
Why didn't you?

The world spins, and I suddenly can't breathe. *Who the hell could have written this? Who knows my secret?*

The emotional roller coaster I've been on this morn-ing proves too much for my nerves and a stabbing pain starts up in my head. The first bell rings and everyone starts shuffling toward their first-hour class, but I can't take trying to listen to American history right now. Just . . . no.

I head to the nurse's office instead. One of the perks of being weird is that the nurse has been informed that I "get very sudden migraines." I don't like the lie, but when I do actually get a tension headache, it means I can have a prescription-strength naproxen instead of the two Tylenol that most kids get.

The nurse takes my temperature and though she frowns at the thermometer in a way that tells me my temp is normal—I could have predicted *that* without any Oracle skills—she lets me lie down in the last available bed and gives me a well-worn but soft blanket before tugging the privacy curtain around me.

I should tell Sierra; I know that. But can I tell her the truth about the vision I saw with Matthew and still hide that I told him to be careful? That I broke the all-important rule of Oracles? *Never, under any circumstances, change the future.* She can read me so well—I swear, she'll just *know.*

Why didn't you? The words from the text swim through my aching head until my stomach starts hurting too. I've got to figure this out. Maybe it was another Oracle. Maybe she had the same vision.

I squint through the small crack in the privacy curtain and see the nurse sitting in front of her computer. I turn my back to the gap and carefully pull out my phone. I find my aunt's number and then text her:

Are there any other Os in Coldwater?

I hit SEND before I can think too hard about the consequences of what I've just done.

My phone buzzes and I clench my teeth at the sound, hoping no one else heard it.

No.

Helpful, I think sardonically.

I send my reply with shaky fingers:

Are you sure?

A little while passes.

Completely. No bloodlines within 500 miles of us.

Oracles are not only always female, but the ability is genetic. So you don't just have Oracles pop up out of the blue. It can skip a generation—even two or three sometimes—but there's always a connection. And one of my aunt's jobs is tracking genealogy for the Sisters. She of all people would know.

There goes that idea. I mean, technically it *could* be someone from far away, but if they *know* about me and saw what I saw, I have to assume they're somewhere close.

So . . . *probably* not another Oracle. But then how . . . ?

My phone buzzes again.

Why?

I scrunch up my face and try to think of a reasonable answer.

I just wondered if we should reach out and be supportive. That's all.

I hold my breath and hope that satisfies her. Luckily I come to Sierra with Oracle questions all the time— even if she doesn't always answer them very often. It's not like I can go to anyone else and besides, she knows more about Oracles than . . . probably anyone else on Earth. Literally.

Rolling over again, I flip back to the other text. Not to read it; I know what it says. The words are burned into my mind. More to convince myself it's real. I clench my fingers around the phone and hold it against my chest as I curl my spine and clutch my aching stomach and try to ignore the slowly softening pounding in my head.

Everyone thinks they want superpowers. To be magical and more important and special than everyone else. To be extraordinary. But they don't really. They don't understand. I would give *anything* to be normal.

SEVEN

Despite my stress and guilt and worry and paranoia, I do manage to get one uninterrupted night of sleep before I find out Matthew is dead.

My mom is crying in the kitchen, and fear squeezes my heart so tightly I'm pretty sure it stops beating for a few seconds. I can't help but feel a smoldering of anger as I watch the news report. What could he possibly have done to get killed like this—stopped to pee in the snow? Everyone's been on their guard—why would he get out of his car?

I *told* him to be careful. It wasn't enough. I failed.

I'm almost deaf to the sound of the newscaster when one detail worms itself into my head.

"We have been informed that the male minor—who police have identified but whose name has not yet been released—was shot with a gun that, though registered to his father, was engraved with his name. The gun was left at the crime scene and hopefully holds a key to this killer's identity."

Shot with his own gun.

My knees won't hold me and I collapse into a chair as questions race through my head: *Why did he have a gun in his truck? Did he start carrying it because of Bethany's murder? Or because I told him to be careful?*

I feel a strong hand wrap around my upper arm and pull me into the hallway, but the message doesn't reach my legs in time and I stumble and stagger after Sierra. Momentarily out of my mother's sight, Sierra stares at my face, studying me. Not studying—scrutinizing. I don't have the energy to try to hide anything. I simply look back, tears coursing down my trembling cheeks.

Sierra straightens, appearing satisfied. "This one surprised you," she whispers, her hand rubbing my upper arms. It would be comforting if I didn't already feel so guilty.

I nod. It's the truth. I had just started to believe—to almost hope—that he would live. That I had changed his fate. I *was* surprised.

"You didn't see it."

I close my eyes and start to cry in earnest now. She takes my sobs as an answer and gathers me against her chest. "This is always the hardest part," she murmurs in my ear as her fingers stroke my hair away from my damp face. "Seeing innocent lives snuffed out and thinking there was something we could have done."

She pulls back and looks down at me. "Charlotte, listen. There is *nothing* you could have done. Not for him, not for that girl. Not without setting into motion uncontrollable ripples of consequence. You're innocent."

Innocent? I'm anything but. If I had said nothing, would Matthew still be alive? Was it something he did in the name of caution that led to this? There's no way to know for sure. But I took action and now, to some degree, I bear responsibility. I am *so* far from innocent.

But I nod. Because I have to. Because she won't let me go until I do, and I need to get back to the news—to hear anything they might have discovered. My own method of torture, perhaps.

When I flee, Sierra doesn't bar my way and I go right back into the kitchen. I eat a type of cereal I couldn't have identified five minutes later and listen to the news, hungering for some tidbit of evidence that might exonerate me.

Or condemn me.

After an hour, I push my still half-full bowl away and go to my room. As fast as I can, I pull on yesterday's jeans and shirt and jam my bare feet into boots. I'm back in the hallway in less than a minute, headed toward the front door.

My mom can tell what I have in mind the second her eyes fall to my boots. "Charlotte, no. You are *not* going to school today."

I ignore her and grab my coat from the row of hooks by the front door. There's a crash from the kitchen and I know Mom's trying to maneuver her wheelchair down the barely wide-enough hallway. I'm a terrible daughter for taking advantage of her handicap to get away, but I do. I fling the door open as my arms slip into the sleeves of my heavy coat, then slam it shut and take off.

I'm almost half a block away before I hear Mom reach the porch and start shouting my name, but I duck my head and hurry onward, taking the first corner I reach to dart out of her sight.

She won't chase me in her wheelchair; she knows she'd never catch me. There's going to be hell to pay when I get home, but I had to get out of there before I choked.

I didn't even think about the fact that I headed in the direction of the school. The "corner" I whipped around isn't a corner at all; it's the edge of the parking lot. Now I'm walking through the middle of a huge square of white snow. If I were younger—more ignorant, less guilty—I would lie down and make a snow angel. Or run around in circles full of giddiness at being the first person to mar the perfect blanket of pure whiteness.

Instead, I stand in the middle of the lot, the snow untouched except for my single line of tracks that lead halfway across.

It's almost time for school to start. But no one's here. Well, there's a sprinkling of cars right by the front doors that probably belong to teachers. I wonder if school will be canceled again.

My phone chimes in my pocket. My mom. I stare at the brightly lit screen as it continues to ring and it occurs to me why this day is different from the day they found Bethany. That morning, a crowd gathered around the crime scene and word of who had been killed leaked out like wildfire as soon as Rachel saw those shoes.

Matthew was killed in a remote area. Even the few people who were there were kept far from the scene by both officers and the trees.

I'm the only student who knows the name of the victim.

I can imagine exactly what's happening right now in hundreds of homes around Coldwater. Students are frantically calling each other; checking on their friends one by one. I can picture the texts.

Are u ok? Text me back RITE NOW!

U didn't answer. Call me the SEC you get this.

Or even something as simple as:

Another kid is dead. Please let me know it wasn't you.

The only person who called *me* was my mom. And I didn't answer.

I text my mom a simple:

I'm at school. Sorry.

and shuffle forward. I'm halfway up the steps when my text chime pings again.

"I'm sorry, I'm sorry, I'm sorry," I mutter as I dig my phone out again.

A sinking swoop envelops my stomach when I see that it's not from my mom, but that same unknown number as before. I look around but see no one.

Which is stupid because there's no reason someone should need to *see* me to *text* me. With shaky hands, I unlock my phone. My hands are so cold I can hardly manage it, then I huddle into the corner of the entry-way and force my eyes to look down at the screen.

Your attempt was admirable, but it obviously didn't work. I can show you how to stop it from happening again. Call me when you get desperate enough. Do it for that poor boy's sake. Please.

I suppress the urge to fling the phone to the ground as my lungs suck air in fast, loud gasps.

Whoever this is, they *know*. But how *much* do they know? Are they watching me?

They know I saw the vision of Bethany, and that I tried to warn Matthew.

And that I failed.

I shove my phone into my pocket and duck back into the early morning wind. I'm not sure where I'm going.

I can't go home. I just can't. I'm not ready. Not to face my mom or Sierra. I head past the school, walking down more unshoveled sidewalks and marring more perfect sheets of snow. My sockless feet are starting to tingle with cold inside my boots, but I ignore them. My mind tosses questions and possibilities around and around my brain.

After half an hour, I've circled the same block three times and I'm out of new snow to walk on. I feel similarly trapped in my head as my mind grows weary. It leaves the wild theories, the guilty scenarios, and instead focuses on the two pictures that won't leave my eyes, even when I scrunch them closed: the bleeding gap across Bethany's throat, and the hole in Matthew's head.

And I realize I can't live with myself if it happens again.

EIGHT

When I get back to my house, I'm shivering and stiff
and fairly sure my toes are frozen. I took the long way
and avoided the school, so I honestly don't know if I'm
technically ditching or not.

I guess I'm the empty desk today.

I'm certain I look pathetic when I come in the front
door and go right to my mom's office to apologize.
But she takes one glance at my face and I know words
won't be needed. She helps me shrug out of my coat
and kick off my boots. I murmur that I'm sorry as we
go out to the great room, where I lay on the couch
while my mom rubs my back. It's something she's done
for me when I was sick for as long as I can remember.

I'm not physically sick today, but *heartsick* is a word I
really understand now. Eventually my mom has to get
back to work; I assure her I'll be fine. That I just want
to go to sleep.

Which is absolutely true.

But ten minutes later, I hear footsteps click down the hallway and the jingle of keys before the front door opens and closes. My heart pounds in my chest as I rise silently from the couch and peek out the window to see Sierra driving away.

My fingers tingle with both fear and anticipation as my gaze travels down the hallway.

Her bedroom door is closed, but that doesn't necessarily mean anything. I don't think she knows I'm home.

With a quick glance toward the corner that leads me to my mom's office, I creep down the hall and lay my fingers on the doorknob. I take a breath, cross my fingers, and try.

It's unlocked.

I have no idea how long she'll be gone.

And if she catches me, she'll be so angry.

But it's a chance I'm going to have to take. I hurry in and leave the door open a few inches so I can listen for her to come back. As though pulled by a magnet, I go right to the ancient copy of *Repairing the Fractured Future* and pull it out, feeling like the worst niece in the world even as my mind tells me I'm completely justified. *Why* shouldn't *I be allowed to know what Sierra knows?*

I need this.

Sierra has told me that knowledge is dangerous, that

she has a very risky position as the historian for the Sisters. But that sounds remarkably like all the arguments people give for censorship and banning books and stuff. I don't agree with that either.

I know that the Sisterhood has the basic functions of finding Oracles, training them, and protecting them in ways I don't really understand. But as far as I can tell, the main purpose they have—at least in my life—is to suppress all knowledge of Oracles. And not just from the world, but from the Oracles as well.

Shaking away my dismal thoughts, I carefully open the book. The title is stamped onto the leather cover with gold embossing, but to my surprise, the book is written by hand. The handwriting on the yellowed pages is full of loops and curlicues and as cool as it looks, it's going to take *ages* to decipher. My heart sinks. I'd need days at the very least and there's a pretty good chance Sierra just ran out for a cup of coffee from her favorite local café.

I start reading as fast as I can and I've worked my way through less than two pages when I realize I'm being stupid.

There's a camera on my phone.

Isn't that how the last Harry Potter book got leaked?

I pull my phone out of my pocket and crouch down to lay the book out flat on the floor. Focus, take the picture, flip the page. Again, again, again. My concentration is laser sharp as I continue to page through the book, cursing under my breath when the camera phone has trouble focusing on the blocks of cramped handwriting.

When the sound of a door opening echoes in from the front entryway I'm so intent I almost forget what it means.

Sierra. Home.

Shit!

With a sharp pang of regret, I slam the book closed and shove it back into its gaping space on the bookshelf. I hear Sierra greeting my mom as I slip out her door and pull it closed behind me as silently as possible. On quiet feet, I sprint down the hallway and duck into my bedroom. I count to five and then poke my head out like I'm casually saying hi.

"I didn't know you were here," Sierra says, startling a little when she sees my face.

Or I wouldn't have left, I finish her thought in my head.

I bite my lip, but my mom's voice trickles in from her office to save me. "It's bound to be a rough day," she says. "I let her stay home."

"Oh. Oh yes," Sierra says as though only just now remembering that another teen was murdered less than two miles from this house.

She turns and heads down the hallway to her room and as she turns the doorknob, I stand frozen, gripping the wall to keep my fingers from shaking. I'm waiting for something to happen. *Why the hell did I think I could get away with this?*

But Sierra's door closes with a soft *click*. My mom clatters on in her office. The world keeps turning.

I just can't breathe.

NINE

The next few days pass in a blur and by the time the end of the semester arrives, the worst of the shock has passed. Not that anything's back to normal. But we're starting to remember how to function again.

Today's the last day of school before winter break, but I don't feel festive. No one does. I'd never have believed that the social walls in the school would crack, but something about one of the Populars and one of the Nerds both being killed within a week of each other has splintered that unbreakable stone. Everyone mourns together and though I'm sure it can't last, this blending of all the cliques feels like a fitting way to honor them both.

Except for me. I drift through the hallways as much a ghost as Bethany and Matthew might be. No one in the entire school knows what I know—no one else feels the weight of such a blend of emotions. Even in the face of this united grief, I'm alone. Two deaths in the school apparently doesn't make me any less of a freak.

The one silver lining in this whole catastrophe is that, oddly, Linden's talking to me more. Not every day, and generally he just asks how I am, but it's a bright spot in my very dark world and it helps keep me centered.

At this point, the cops aren't fully convinced the two killings had anything to do with each other. One girl, one boy. One with a knife, one with a gun. One Popular, one Nerd. One white, one black. Although everyone was certain in the beginning that they *had* to have been killed by the same person, there's nothing to actually link the two teens except for their ages and the fact that they're both from our small town. People are starting to hope that it was two bizarre but isolated incidents and that everything will go back to the way it was.

I'm not letting that stop me though. I've put a password on my phone—just in case—and each night, after I've closed my door, I pore over the pictures I took. I got about forty of them, but after almost two weeks I've barely made it through twenty. Not only is the handwriting hard to read, it simply doesn't make sense. It talks about jumping into a supernatural plane, and there's a drawing that looks like a domed room. I don't know what that means, but apparently once

71

you're there, you can see multiple visions—multiple futures—and maybe even change them?

But there's nothing about *how* to do this. Or even if a normal Oracle can. I mean, if I had a power like this, wouldn't I know *something* about it? Or this supernatural plane place? I'm starting to wonder if this is one of those legend books that doesn't actually have any truth in it, but that Sierra bought because it was a cool, old, handwritten text.

I keep reading anyway. I risked so much to get these pictures, and there might be something more helpful in the rest of the pages.

There haven't been any new messages from the mysterious texter either. I read the two I've already received at least ten times a day. I haven't gone so far as to call, but the number is always there. Just in case.

The parking lot at school is still covered with snow. It starts to melt in the afternoon sunshine, only to freeze again in the bitter cold of the night. So it's not soft, fun powder anymore, but sharp, unforgiving ice veiled by a thin layer of fluff.

I'm only halfway through the lot when I feel the familiar tingling of a foretelling. After shaking off the terror of what might be coming, I glance around and then crouch beside a big truck and let it come.

Since the vision of Matthew's death, I haven't fought a single vision, and I've had a good ten or so. It seems pointless—the murder visions I had about Bethany and Matthew bowled me over anyway, and the others are so insignificant that resisting them isn't worth the effort. And despite that bubbling fear each time I feel one coming on, every vision since the one about Matthew has bordered on boring. Who cares that Mr. Johnson's car is going to slide off the road on Christmas Eve? He'll be fine and it's an old car anyway; he *wants* a new one. And there's some lady I don't know who's getting ready to serve her husband with divorce papers. What the hell would I do? Find them and tell them to get counseling?

It's just tiny glimpses into the lives of people in Coldwater—most of whom I don't know. So I let the foretellings come and then forget about them almost as soon as the vision is over. Although I wouldn't dare tell Sierra, I'm glad I've stopped fighting. It's all so much easier now.

Eas*ier*. Not easy. I'm still doing the same things I've always done—throwing myself into my classes and studying my brains out so I'm too tired to think when I lie down to sleep at night. But at least I'm not trying to conserve energy to fight visions on top of that.

The blackness starts to encroach on the edges of my physical sight and I close my eyelids before it even starts. Give up. Let it wash over me and suck me in.

I'm standing in an open field at night and soft, powdery snow is falling lightly. Like lace, not the heavy muffling snow we've been getting lately. This is the kind of snow they always have in movies right before the main characters kiss.

I look around and see nothing. Confused, I wait for the vision to pull my feet in the direction they're supposed to go, but after several seconds, I'm still standing there.

With nothing else to do, I try to take a step on my own but my feet are glued to the ground. Okay, there's *something* here I'm supposed to see. Instead of looking forward, I look down and realize the lumpy surface a few feet to my left isn't, in fact, a snow-covered patch of bumpy ground.

It's a cream-colored coat.

I suck in a freezing breath and even in my vision the sudden cold makes me want to cough. I lift my foot and it obeys me now. With terror pounding in my heart, I walk forward one step. Two. Three.

Whoever this is is lying on their back so peacefully he looks like he's sleeping. I choke back a sob and hope with all my heart that it's just some drunk guy who fell asleep and froze to death. Not that I would wish anyone death but it would be better than . . . better than . . .

Better than a teenage face looking up at me with vacant eyes and skin covered with a tiny layer of lacy flakes. A gust of wind clears some of the snow and then I see the bruises.

It's another victim.

His coat is unzipped halfway down his chest and his scarf has been untied and pushed to the side as though to display what the murderer has done. Deep purple swatches cover his neck, almost black against his pale skin made even whiter by death. I stand there shaking, shivering, even though I can't feel the cold anymore. He looks so serene that it's almost worse than the gory scenes I witnessed with Bethany and Matthew. So incredibly dissonant.

I force myself to focus—the vision won't last forever—and I lift my eyes to his face.

"Jesse." My words are lost in the wind. Jesse Prince. He was in my art class last semester and we ended up being partners on a project. He had all the talent; I had all the discipline. The final result was subpar at best.

I suck in a ragged breath and look around again. It's an empty space—a parking lot?—and I'm standing underneath a tall lamppost with only one light functioning. Maybe a park?

That's it. A park. And now I can see the dim outline of a row of houses just out of the circle's light. There's a sign. It's some kind of development. But as I lift my feet to get closer, the vision starts to fade. I try to run, to get there before everything goes black, but I can only lift my foot an inch or two and, within seconds, it's all gone.

I blink slowly, carefully, bright sunlight invading my

eyes and making them sting after the pure blackness. Unfortunately because I was sitting on a slippery patch of ice, I'm now lying full out on the ground beside the rusty truck. My head sits right next to a puddle of slush and I can feel moisture soaking into my hair and dampening my scalp.

I sit up, but don't bother to look around. It doesn't matter if anyone saw me; nothing matters now. Damp strands of hair fall into my face but I shove them away and push my hands into my pockets, grasping for my phone.

I don't stop, don't think, and don't let myself reconsider. My icy-cold fingers dial the number and, as it starts to ring, I get to my feet, hanging on to the truck for balance.

"Hello?"

A man.

I was expecting a girl.

A woman.

Despite what Sierra said, deep inside I was certain it had to be another Oracle. "Hello?" My voice cracks as I answer and I have to clear my throat a few times before I can speak clearly.

The man on the other end says nothing, just waits.

"It's Charlotte," I say once I can speak again.

I hear a long, slow breath and he whispers, "Finally," so softly I barely hear it. "Did you see the next one?" he asks in that same, calm voice.

"Yes," I whisper, tears stinging my eyes.

"I need to meet with you."

I swallow hard and force my emotions back. "How do I know *you* aren't the killer?"

He laughs now, a soft, bizarre sound considering the circumstances. "Charlotte, how stupid would I have to be to try to kill an Oracle?"

Every muscle in my body stiffens.

Never reveal that you are an Oracle to anyone except another Oracle.

He pauses and when I don't say anything he continues: "You know you're not going to die today, don't you?"

My silence is answer enough.

"If it makes you feel better, you choose the place. It can be as public as you want so long as it's somewhere we can talk without being overheard."

It's still so soon after the vision that my brain and my body are moving at half speed. I should have waited to make the call until after I had recovered.

But then I might have changed my mind.

"The food court," I finally decide. "At the mall."

"When?"

"I'll head there now. How will I recognize you?"

"I'll find you. I know you."

The way he says "I know you" makes a trickle of fear shiver up my spine. But I chide myself for it. Of course he knows me. He knew me well enough to

77

learn my cell number. He's been watching me closely enough to know that I warned Matthew.

Of course he knows who I am. But the words make it real.

"Ten minutes," he says, and then the line goes dead.

What have I done? But my fingers clench and I push my phone into my pocket. "Something," I mutter to myself as I duck my freezing and still-damp head and turn in the direction of the mall. "I'm doing *something*." Of course, the last *something* I did might have made things worse. But I shove that thought away. I can't be afraid.

It only takes me about twenty minutes to walk to the mall, which is plenty of time to feel thoroughly frozen. Coldwater's mall is more like one hallway of a real mall, with a mini food court stuck onto the end. There are about ten tables spread out around an alcove with several skylights that are quite pretty in the summer, but make everything feel even colder in the winter. I pick a table at the edge farthest from the stores and restaurants. Everyone can see me, but the nearest seat is about ten feet away. It'll work.

I sit there like I'm just ditching school to meet a college boyfriend. Like I'm sneaking off for some typical teenage mischief, not supernatural lifesaving. At least I hope it's lifesaving. If this guy can really show me how to stop this, then it's all worth it.

Because I'm not sure my mind can handle another

kid dying. A kid pretty much just like me.

I sit alone for a few minutes before I realize someone's looking at me. I raise my head to get my first look at the man who thinks he can save our town from this monster.

TEN

I'm not sure what I was expecting—not really certain if I was expecting anything at all. But he's so nondescript my eyes slid right past him the first time I glanced his way and he only caught my attention when I realized he was looking at *me*. He's basically average: average height, average build, average age if such a thing exists. *Maybe midthirties,* I decide as he gets closer. But his hair is prematurely peppered with gray, so at first he looks much older. He's wearing nice jeans—the kind that are almost as dark as slacks—and a black peacoat that looks like half the coats in Coldwater. He's neither handsome nor plain, but has a strange kind of in-the-middle face.

I expect him to smile when our eyes meet. For him to try to put me at ease, get me to trust him. But the somber expression stays there as he drops into the seat across the small table from me.

"Hello, Charlotte," he says, and I instantly recognize the voice from the phone.

"I don't know *your* name," I say. It's kind of a rude way to greet him, but since *he's* ignoring the meaningless niceties of meeting someone for the first time, I follow suit.

"Call me Smith," he says. "No, it's not my real name," he adds before I can scrunch my face up into a look of suspicion, "but you'll forgive me if I'm not inclined to give true information to an Oracle whose aunt has such close ties to the Sisters of Delphi."

I pull back, staring at him with shock and fear. It's one thing to know about Oracles, it's another to know about my relative and the role she plays in a secret society. A secret society *I* barely know anything about.

"Don't do that," Smith says, holding up a hand. "People will start looking at us. Stay neutral."

"How do you know about my aunt? And the Sisters?"

"I know a lot of things. And let's just say your Sisters of Delphi wouldn't mind at all if I ceased to exist because of it."

I sit silently, my nerves crackling.

He doesn't speak again, doesn't rush to fill the silence, and I realize he's not going to offer up information. I'll have to ask. "How did you know about me?"

"I learned the signs of an Oracle a very long time ago, Charlotte."

It's disconcerting the way he keeps using my real name when we both know the one he gave me is fake. "How?"

He loosens his scarf—like he's settling in for a long chat. I'm not sure if that's a good thing or not. "When I was very young, I lived a few houses down from a girl who was an Oracle. We were best friends and when she started having foretellings, she did what any kid would do: she told her buddy, Smith." The start of a smile lifts the corners of his mouth for about half a second, but the haunted look in his eyes cancels it out. "Her mom was an Oracle too, and took her in hand as soon as possible, teaching her the same things I imagine you were taught." He waves his hand toward the table as though there were a pile of items on display. "Fight the visions, don't ever tell anyone who isn't an Oracle what you can do, never ever, ever change the future. And she was very dutiful. With one exception."

"You?" I say after a long pause.

He nods. "I watched her suffer through the same kind of things you probably go through—spacing out in the middle of class, everyone thinking she was a weirdo, feeling like she could never have friends."

I swallow, empathy filling my chest as I compare that to my own solitary childhood. My solitary *life*: it's not like that part ended along with scraped knees and cooties.

"I did what I could," he says, looking out at the food

court again. "Shielded her when she had a spell. Took her to prom when no one else would. Supported her lies when she told people she was epileptic. But her senior year something happened. I suppose the Sisters got to her. Threatened her somehow. She staged a huge fight in the middle of school. I knew it was forced, of course—I knew her better than anyone else in the world—but afterward, she wouldn't speak to me. Not even on the phone. When I left for college, I sent her letters and they were all returned unopened. For several years, I thought our friendship was just over."

"Did she come back?" I ask, knowing the end of this story isn't "happily ever after" and wishing it was anyway. Not for Smith's sake, necessarily, but for this other Oracle girl. But I know better. We don't get happy endings.

Smith swallows visibly and shakes his head. "No. But the accidents started." He runs his fingers through his already tousled salt-and-pepper hair and looks decidedly uncomfortable. "I don't have any proof, of course, but I think that when I kept trying to get in touch with her, the Sisters decided that if I wasn't going to go away on my own, they'd *make* me go away."

I want to tell him he's lying. That an organization my aunt would belong to wouldn't actually kill someone, but I can't get the words out. "What does that have to do with me?" I ask.

His head jerks up almost like he'd forgotten I was

there. "At some point, I realized I wasn't going to last very long if I didn't disappear. So I started traveling. Bounced from town to town. Eventually I came here. Sometimes I wonder if I was drawn to this place. I'd been around a couple of weeks when I was walking past the playground at your school. You must have been nine or ten. I wasn't watching *you*—I was just seeing kids out playing and remembering the times I had with my friend. And then a girl fell off the monkey bars."

He looks me in the eye now and I know what's coming next.

It's where everything with Linden first started. It's one of my most precious memories and it makes me feel sick to hear it coming out of someone else's mouth.

"She lay there, staring off into space. And I knew that look on her face. I'd seen it hundreds of times before. The scene played out just like I knew it would. All of the kids walked away, trying to avoid the freak." He leans forward, elbows on his knees, fingers knit together.

"I probably would have run again, right then," he says. "Disappeared—found an Oracle-less town to live in. But I saw a boy sit beside you and help you up, right before the teachers realized what was happening and intervened. It was me and . . . and *her* all over again. I couldn't look away." He shrugs and clears his throat. "I've watched out for you from a distance ever since."

I stare hard at him, trying to decide how much of

this is true. Obviously some of it is; how else could he know that story? And know exactly what it *meant*. But the idea that some stranger has been watching me since I was ten creeps me out. "Why don't I recognize you?"

"What do you mean?"

"If you've been *around*," the word comes out a little mockingly, but Smith doesn't seem to notice, "shouldn't I recognize you?"

"I'm good at blending in," Smith replies. "Besides, it's not like I'm some sick stalker who scopes you out constantly. I see you every few months. Very casual."

It doesn't quite ring true. "But you knew I saw Bethany's death. And you knew I tried to warn Matthew. Those aren't exactly casual observations," I say, getting a little heated now.

"I didn't actually know you saw Bethany," he says, looking chagrined. "I guessed."

"You texted me!"

His jaw tightens. "I shouldn't have. I was angry. But by the time I thought better of it, it was too late." He looks up and meets my eyes again. "I've watched you more closely since her murder though. I just pretend I'm someone's parent at the high school." He points at his hair. "I look older than I am. And no one questions strangers in the hall right before and after school hours; a lot of parents are walking their kids all the way inside the building these days. I . . . I saw the look on your face when you talked to the tall, black boy. Matthew.

You can't hide that desperation. I knew something was going to happen to him. And after the murder, when they reported that it was a teenage boy, well, it wasn't hard to put the pieces together. I should have gone right to you that day, but I was afraid I would freak you out."

And he would have.

"I want to end this, Charlotte. Otherwise I'd have let you continue on your little Oracle life doing what every other Oracle in the world does."

"You said you could help me stop it."

"I can."

The strength of those two words—his confidence as he says them—strikes me into stillness. "But . . . but you're nothing special." I don't apologize for my rude words. It's the truth. He's not an Oracle; he's just a guy.

"No," he says, without flinching at my insult. "I'm not. But I knew someone who *was* special and we used to experiment and explore. More than that. We learned things no one else in the whole world knows." He takes a deep breath. "I'll teach you—*if* you'll stop this."

I stare at him for a long time. I can't just jump at false hope. "You're a stranger who knows all about me. Not to mention you know an awful lot about these murders. I have to say, that doesn't inspire trust."

He rakes his fingers through his hair, looking as harrowed as I feel. "I know. I *know.* How else can I convince you?"

The desperation in his eyes is so deep, so startling that I almost want to believe him right then and there. But this is too important a decision to make based on ten minutes of acquaintance.

"I just, I have to think. I have to plan. I have to . . ." My voice trails off. It's not like I know what the hell I'm doing either.

He nods shortly, but looks nervous. "I can give you time if that's what you want. But before we do this, you have to promise you'll keep my secret." He meets my eyes, intensity glowing from his dark-brown irises. "You *cannot* tell your aunt about me. Or about anything we do. My life is at stake here. If the Sisters figure out—" His voice cuts off and he leans back abruptly, clearing his throat. A heavy silence lies between us for a long moment. "They can't find me again," he finishes in a whisper full of terror.

"I won't tell," I assure him. "Even without you in the picture, Si—my aunt would be furious that I was doing *anything*. Even *thinking* of doing anything." I don't want to think about the Sisters. About what they might do. A coldness that comes from inside me makes me pull my coat tighter and shiver. "How exactly do you think you can help me?"

He licks his lips and then pulls his chair closer to the table, leaning his head in close to me. "Have you ever revisited a vision?"

I just stare at him, not sure what that even means.

He reaches into his bag and brings out a small glittering stone, strung on a silver chain so tarnished it's almost entirely black. "This is a focus stone. Have you seen one of these before?"

I shake my head, but I'm mesmerized by the glinting gem that seems to be colorless and every color in the world all at the same time. It's the size of a large grape and cut into a teardrop.

He caresses one of the large facets of the stone as he continues. "It has no power by itself, really. It helps enhance your abilities."

"What abilities?" I say, but I have to force myself to breathe steadily. Maybe this is what the pages of *Repairing the Fractured Future* are talking about. What I always suspected was possible. Abilities beyond simply the visions.

He hesitates. "There are so many things that an Oracle can do. It's not just about seeing the future; you can have an active role in *creating* the future."

I hold my breath now, my eyes fixated on the stone, but I say nothing.

"This stone will allow you to revisit a vision you've already had, and change it."

"Keep Jesse from dying," I whisper, understanding now. I hold out my hands. "May I?" His nod is a bit jerky, but he places the stone in my hands.

It's warm. Warmer than a few minutes in his hands should have made it. It frightens and exhilarates me all at the same time. "Where did you get this?"

"I didn't. Sh—she never told me how she got it. Thought it was too dangerous a secret for even me to know."

"Your Oracle friend?"

He nods.

"What was her name?" When he hesitates, I raise my eyebrow. "You want me to trust you to teach me forbidden powers and you won't even tell me her name?"

"Shelby," he whispers, like it hurts him to say it.

I stare at him, wondering if he's telling the truth. About any of this, really. "I can't do this right now. I need to think."

Smith looks disappointed, but he doesn't argue. "Don't wait too long," he says.

"I want to take this with me," I say, curling my fingers around the stone when he reaches out for it. His hand clenches into a fist for a second before he pulls back and slips it under the table again.

"I'm not sure you know what you're asking." He inclines his head toward the stone. "That is one of the most powerful items on the face of the Earth. I've spent over a decade of my life hiding it. Protecting it, really. If anyone finds it—if your aunt sees it—both of our lives are at stake."

"If you want me to trust you, you need to trust me too. Let me take the necklace, and I'll make a decision." My voice comes out much more steady than I feel. "And either way, I'll give it back." I can tell he doesn't like it, but I've put him in a position where he has no choice. Not if he wants any shot of working with me.

Still, he hesitates. Then he reaches into his bag again and holds up a small velvet bag. "Be careful with it," he says, his voice low and serious. "And I don't recommend trying anything. I'll teach you everything I know if you decide to trust me, but you could mess up a lot of stuff if you dive in on your own."

His words chill me because they ring with such truth. Powerful and dangerous. That's what this thing is.

Unless, of course, he's completely crazy. Then it's just a shiny piece of costume jewelry.

That's what I need to figure out.

ELEVEN

Despite hurrying back from the mall, I'm going to be late to my second-hour class. I'm rushing down the hallway toward choir when I hear someone calling my name.

"Charlotte, wait."

I turn to find Linden breathing hard after running to catch up and everything inside me melts and freezes all at the same time. Maybe it's because Smith was just talking about him. About *us*.

It's a story I think about almost every day, but that I'm sure Linden has forgotten. Why would he remember? To him it was just a minor playground accident.

To me it was everything.

I still remember his eyes looking down at me in concern as my sight came back. He had said, "I got the wind knocked out of me last week when I fell off my bike. It's okay." Then he reached out his hand. And I took it. Teachers arrived about ten seconds later, but for those brief moments it was just him and me. My little ten-year-old heart fell in love that day.

I guess I forgot to fall out again.

"I just wondered if you're leaving town over Christmas."

I shake my head, trying to remember how to make my mouth form words. "W-we're staying here," I finally manage.

"I thought maybe we could get together sometime during the break."

Breathe, breathe, breathe.

"Sure," I say, pulling out my phone. We exchange numbers and I focus really hard to make sure I don't screw up and enter any of them wrong.

"I hope you don't think this is weird," Linden says, pocketing his phone, "but it's nice having someone I can chat to about something—anything—other than . . . you know."

"Yeah, it is," I agree, although I'd have talked to Linden about anything in the world.

The bell rings, startling us both. "I'm sorry; I made you late."

"Trust me, no one's going to care," I say, a lump in my throat.

"Oh yeah," Linden says, and then is quiet.

"Hey, Linden," I blurt, as much to change the subject as anything, "do you remember the day in fourth grade when I fell off the monkey bars?"

He grins. "No." Then he sobers. "I didn't push you or anything, did I?"

I laugh at the idea. "No, you rescued me." I shrug. "So, yeah, call me anytime, okay?"

"Thanks," he says sincerely. "I appreciate it."

I turn and head toward class, but only until I hear his footsteps heading the other way. Then I pause and look over my shoulder and watch him walk away, a simmer of joy warming me from the inside out. Talk about a roller-coaster day.

That afternoon when I get home, I call out a hello to Mom, then slip quickly into my room and lock the door. I've got to get through the rest of the pages on my phone before I can decide whether or not to trust Smith. It's two hours of squinting before my tired eyes make out the words *focus stone*. I sit up straight and zoom in on the scrawled paragraph.

Though the ability to enter the supernatural plane exists within all Oracles, the use of a focus stone will almost certainly be required to invoke it.

Focus stone. That's what Smith called the necklace.

But this part of the book isn't about revisiting visions, it's about going to an entirely different place. I'm not even sure if it's somewhere inside an Oracle's mind or an actual physical location. The text talks about jumping, but I don't know how literal that is.

Still, it's something.

Maybe there really is more to being an Oracle than I ever imagined. Maybe even more than Smith knows.

But does that mean I should use the stone? That I should trust Smith? Ultimately even if I found a full explanation in this text of everything Smith talked about, that wouldn't tell me whether or not I should trust him.

I have to decide that on my own.

I rub my tired eyes and turn off my phone, even though I've only managed to get through a few pages. I'm exhausted and starving and that's having some severe consequences on my attention span. I wander out to grab a soda and then head into Mom's office.

"Hey, Beautiful," Mom says. "Have a seat; I'm just wrapping things up."

We sit quietly for a few minutes before I say, "Linden's been talking to me."

Mom's hand pauses. "*Linden* Linden?"

"Yeah."

She smiles. "Still head over heels for him?"

I shrug.

"Then this is a good thing, right?"

"I think so. He was close friends with the girl who died and maybe he just wants to distance himself from that. I don't really have any connection to her."

She shrugs. "Friendships have certainly had worse beginnings."

"I just wish he liked me for *me*."

"You don't know that he doesn't."

"I guess not," I murmur. "But—"

"Don't underestimate yourself. You're very good at that."

I let a few more minutes go by in silence. "What if he doesn't call?" It feels a bit silly to be thinking so far ahead—I mean, he only got my number this morning. But this is the first good thing that's happened to me in weeks. So I'm already overanalyzing it. Of course.

Mom turns to look at me squarely now. "Then you're no worse off than you are now."

"But I'd be so disappointed."

"Is he worth the risk?"

"Duh," I say with a grin.

"Charlotte, we never know what's going to happen in the future," my mom says, and I mentally cringe. "Look at me. Even the day before the accident I would never have believed that your dad would be gone and I'd be in a wheelchair."

The guilt that fills me is like knives slicing my stomach.

"But I wouldn't change a thing."

My head jerks up.

"The time we had was worth every second of heart-break since." She's quiet, her eyes unfocused as she loses herself in a memory. When she snaps back to attention, she does that forced smile that tells me she's trying not to cry. "Some things in this world are so amazing, you have to risk everything to get them."

I don't feel like we're talking about boys anymore.

"Besides," my mom says, sounding more genuinely cheerful, "even if bad things happen, when the moment comes, you'll be strong enough to handle it." She strokes my hair. "You come from good, hardy stock."

I raise my eyebrow at her, but at that moment I feel the niggle of a vision coming on. "Thanks, Mom," I say, rising to my feet. "You're probably right."

"I'm *always* right," she corrects playfully. "Dinner's in the oven. It'll be ready in five minutes."

I nod wordlessly and then retreat back to my bedroom, closing my eyes and flopping down on my bed, hoping it's something small that passes quickly.

But this one feels really weird. Off, maybe.

It's only when I find myself standing ankle deep in the snow that I realize why.

It's my vision of Jesse.

Again.

I've never had a vision twice. Something must have changed.

Maybe he'll live.

But no, there he is, lying in the snow beside me.

Seconds pass and I keep waiting for something to be different. But nothing is. When the light in the foretelling dims and the scene disappears, I blink until my physical sight registers the murky twilight in my room again.

I don't get it. *Why would I have the vision again?*

A thought I've been trying to stamp out wriggles its way to the surface and this time I let myself dwell on it.

Maybe I'm *meant* to do this. If there's more to being an Oracle than I ever suspected, maybe we *are* supposed to help. Is it so far-fetched to wonder if I'm destined to stop these deaths? If that's why the foretellings I have about them are so strong? And why this one has come to me twice?

Believing in destiny and fate kind of goes hand in hand with being an Oracle. So why shouldn't this be *my* fate?

Still conflicted, I reach into my backpack and pull out the necklace I borrowed from Smith. Again, it feels too warm. I cradle it in my hands and stare at the stone that seems to be all colors and no colors all at the same time. I hold it up to the light, but that doesn't make the colors clarify at all. If anything, it looks even more multihued.

Is it really a focus stone? Can it help save people?

There's only one way to find out.

And one person who can show me.

My mom's words echo in my mind: *Some things in this world are so amazing, you have to risk everything to get them.*

What could be more amazing than saving someone's life?

I picture Jesse's face in my mind. Alive Jesse. Working together at my house on our art project—one of the only classmates who's ever come here.

And then I picture him dead in the snow. I see the purple bruises on his chest and wonder how excruciating it must be to have the life literally choked out of you.

Maybe I won't succeed, but I have to try.

TWELVE

I'm nervous. Like, meeting-a-first-date nervous.

Not that I actually know how that feels.

I decided we should meet somewhere more private this time. So I chose the library, which has private study rooms that you can reserve.

I should have realized Smith would be there before me.

"Do you have it?"

Not *hello*, not *I'm so glad you made this decision*. "Yes," I reply with more than a little *duh* in my tone. When Smith doesn't look convinced, I pull the pouch out of my pocket and hand it over.

And he *still* unfastens the drawstrings and looks inside to check.

"Maybe you need to learn to trust *me*," I say dryly.

He doesn't meet my eyes as he nods. "I know. I *know*," he says, almost to himself. "I've just spent so many years . . ." His words trail off as he slides the necklace onto his palm. "We should get started."

A jolt of fear races through my whole body, but the decision is made. Whatever he has to teach me, I'm determined to learn. "I had the vision again last night," I offer after I close and lock the study-room door and jiggle the blinds shut. "The one about Jesse."

"Exactly the same?"

"I think so."

"Tell me about it."

Despite the closed door and thick walls, I lean forward and lower my voice to a bare hush. I tell him about Jesse, the strangulation marks, and what I remember about the scene. Smith tents his fingers and lifts them to his lips, contemplating for a few seconds. "I can teach you to change the scene on your own—and I will," he adds. "But I think for this first one I should come into your vision and coach you."

"What do you mean, '*come into*'?" I ask, the fear returning with a vengeance.

"With both of us in contact with the stone, I can enter the vision with you. I have no power there, but I can help."

It sounds so bizarre.

"You're really going to have to trust me."

"Okay." He must hear the hesitation in my voice.

"Not just with your secrets. I need you to trust me to . . . get into your head, essentially. It'll only be for a few minutes, max, but you have to open yourself entirely. Hold *nothing* back."

"You can save him?" I ask, letting that last drop of doubt seep through.

"I can show *you* how to save him."

"You're sure?"

"Yes."

"Then I trust you." I'll *make* myself trust him. For Jesse.

"Okay," Smith says, pulling his chair closer until our knees are touching. "We both need to be in contact with the stone. You, so you can return to your foretelling, and me, so I can come with you."

Again my stomach clenches at the thought of anyone else seeing my visions. My life—my already bizarre life—has turned completely upside down.

"Shelby and I did this hundreds of times," Smith says when I don't reach out for the necklace. "I promise, it's safe. Strange, but safe."

I nod and then lay my hands on top of his so we're cradling the stone in between our two palms.

"No, no," Smith says, moving my hand. "It's easier if you can see the stone."

I adjust and we start again.

"Okay, gaze into the stone and bring forward the scene you saw with Jesse. Then put yourself back in it."

Back in it? Back into one of the most terrifying experiences of my life? But this is how I can change it. No risk, no reward. *Here goes nothing.* I look at the stone—it seems pink now—and picture the scene. When I'm sure I have it fixed in my head, I say, "Okay."

"No. You're using your mind. Your mind is not your . . . um, you probably call it your 'third eye'? Maybe 'second sight'?"

I look up at him, my forehead scrunched. "I know the words, but I don't know what you mean."

He sighs. "It's hard to describe something you've never actually experienced. Okay, when you have visions—not the ones you've fought off, the ones you've actually experienced—you keep your eyes open, but *inside* you . . . you go somewhere else and darkness covers your physical sight, right?"

I nod, oddly frightened that he has described *exactly* what happens. Like some stranger telling you in detail what your underwear looks like even though you're fully clothed.

"Stare at the stone again, and, um . . . *will* that darkness to cover your physical eyes. And do you . . . when you fight, do you have something you throw over the vision so you can't see it?"

"A drape," I say, still trying to push back the horror at a conversation that feels so suddenly intimate.

"Good! Perfect!" he says, latching on to that. "Once your physical sight goes dark except for the stone right in the middle, pull the drape aside. Don't just peek behind it, you need to yank it away. Be committed.

Your mind will sense if you have doubts."

"Okay." I try again with only the barest idea of what I'm doing. This time, instead of remembering the scene with Jesse, I picture the blackness in front of my physical sight that a vision always induces. As soon as I do, I almost lose concentration entirely when it appears right at the edges of my vision, but without the muffled sensation that always accompanies a foretelling. *Okay,* I think, trying to calm myself down, *I just imagine it and it happens.*

When I concentrate again, the blackness advances unnaturally, beginning at the edges of my peripheral vision, a slowly—so slowly—shrinking circle of sight surrounded by darkness. I widen my eyes and, oddly, that seems to help. The circle of light shrinks, smaller, smaller, until only the gem, shining purple now, remains. A tiny, tight center in the middle of sheer blackness.

An odd instinct kicks in and I know I need to raise my hands—not my physical hands, but the hands I rarely have control of in the visions. I lift my arms and reach for the dark veil that covers my third eye. It's as though these hands weigh twenty pounds each, but I lift them anyway. After a few seconds, my fingers find the edge and pull it back.

I'm standing in the snow again, and Jesse's body lies covered in a thin layer of flakes beside me.

I did it! I want to yell, to cheer, but even though

I've managed to enter a foretelling on purpose for the first time in my life, there's still a dead teenager on the ground beside me. Nothing about *that* has changed.

I glance around me, and everything feels familiar and foreign at the same time. I've been here before—technically I always come here during the visions I don't fight—but it's not somewhere I *know*. Not somewhere I was even aware I *could* know. It's somewhere I fight against coming to almost every day—well, used to fight. To be here now feels wrong and strange. But even so, there's a sense of possessiveness that's welling up within me.

It's my *second sight; why shouldn't I come here?*

"You're there, I can tell," a soft voice says in that faint, faraway pitch that all outside noises take on when I'm either in or fighting a vision. Smith. "Now comes the hard part."

The hard *part?* I'm nearly shaking from the effort of having done this much. "What do I have to do?" I ask, but the wind sweeps my voice away. I realize I've never tried to speak while in a vision before. There's never been a reason to. Does my physical mouth talk when I'm in this other plane? Can Smith tell I'm speaking?

"I'll talk you through it," Smith says. "And don't try to ask questions; you're only talking inside your vision." *Well, that answers that.* "First I'm going to place my fingers on one of your temples. It's going to feel very jarring, like you're in two places at once. Your

104

mind won't like that and will want you to pick one or the other. *You can't let it send you back*. We'll have to start all over again."

I say nothing, just brace myself for his touch.

As soon as his skin comes in contact with mine, I gasp. Though I can distantly feel that it's his fingertips very gently touching the side of my head, in the second sight it's like his hands have wrapped around the entire scene, moving in closer and closer and threatening to suffocate me. My mind screams at me to return to the physical world, but I hold on, focusing my thoughts on the stone—until I'm wholly in my second sight again.

"Okay," the reverberating voice says. "I should be at your curtain. This is the trickiest part. I need you to let me in."

I sense him standing just outside of my vision. My *whole world* when I'm in my second sight. But I'm realizing now that this space is really very small. I don't think there's room for both of us. And . . . and it's mine. He shouldn't be here. He shouldn't—

"Charlotte! Don't push me away!" His voice is getting further and further away. It's panicked now and it snaps me back into focus. "I can't do this part; you have to *let* me come in."

I look down at Jesse. My time in my second sight has now lasted longer than my original vision and the snow is starting to obscure his features. "Jesse," I whisper, remembering why I'm here. I have to do this. I *have* to trust Smith.

I sense Smith standing at the black drape, waiting. I'm not sure what to do. I don't see a curtain. And it's not like I actually walked through one when I came; I just pulled it to the side and then I was *here*.

Maybe I'm making this too difficult. "Let him in," I whisper into the night air.

Nothing.

My chest is tight and my muscles are clenched so tightly I know I'll be sore tomorrow. I can't stay in this weird limbo for much longer. "Let him in!" I yell now, lifting my face up to the sky. "Let him—"

"I'm here."

THIRTEEN

I spin, frightened.

He looks exactly like he does in the physical world, right down to the clothes he's wearing. His hands are in his pockets and snow dots his hair as he strolls toward me. It feels wrong, like something is invading my space and stealing my air. *I did this,* I remind myself. *I let him in; it was my choice.*

But that doesn't mean I don't want it over so I can get him *out*.

"Where's the stone?" Smith asks before I can speak.

I don't understand what he means. The necklace isn't here; my physical body is holding it. But even as I have the thought, I realize there's a weight in my fingertips. I gasp as I open my hand and see the necklace, glowing red.

"Put it on," Smith says, clearly not surprised at all.

"But it's not here."

"And neither are you. Technically."

"But—"

"It's the embodiment of the necklace, just like you're the embodiment of yourself. Touching it or wearing it while you're here is essentially just like holding it in the physical world. And you're going to need it."

I lift the chain over my head and drop the gem down the front of my shirt where it sits warmly against my skin.

"Why don't you have one?"

"Just like in the physical world, there's only one. And you're the one using it now. I hitched a ride with it essentially, but I know how to stay here on my own. You're still a novice."

I don't completely comprehend his answer, but then, I don't understand half of what he's said. Or what I've done. "What now?" I ask, pushing my other questions away for now.

Smith is silent for a few seconds. He walks past me and crouches beside the dead body, staring at Jesse's open, lifeless eyes. "We have to stop this."

"How?" I ask, insistent. I want this *done*.

He stands. "Back up the scene. For starters, let's see if we can figure out who this bastard is."

"How do I . . . do that?" I ask.

His brow furrows. "You should be able to simply tell the scene to back up. Going forward, backward, stopping things, that's easy. It's learning to affect the actual scene that's hard. Just . . . tell the whole vision to rewind."

I lift my chin and concentrate. *Rewind,* I command in my head.

Nothing happens.

"You want this to be easy," Smith says, "but—"

"*You* said I just tell the scene to back up."

"You're mistaking 'simple' for 'easy,'" Smith says, and I have to bite down my impatience. "I'm not sure what technique is going to work best for you; maybe picture the scene going backward in your head and then force your mind to let it."

I'm so tired already. Smith is right—I vastly underestimated how difficult this would be. Feeling more than a little self-conscious, I decide to use my hands as a kind of focal point. Palms out in front of me, I move my arms from left to right as though I were paging backward through a book.

"Back," I whisper as I will the scene to move in reverse, wishing it with all my soul.

At first I don't see anything, but after a while Jesse isn't covered with snow anymore. Terror churns in my belly and I realize I should have considered what event will inevitably come next.

I lose my focus for a second and the snowflakes pause all around me.

"I know you don't want to see this, Charlotte, but the only way we can save him is to go back before the murder. You can do it," Smith prompts from behind my right shoulder.

I shove the fear away—attempt to anyway—and think of saving him.

Saving him.

Saving him.

The flakes are flying upward again. Maybe even faster than before.

A figure in black walks backward to Jesse's prone form. In seconds, he's on top of Jesse's chest, his hands iron vises around Jesse's neck as Jesse kicks and struggles, trying to throw his killer off.

"Stop!" I scream, and try to run forward.

But just like in my usual visions, my feet are stuck. Jesse is frozen with his eyes wide, his face purple, his mouth open in a silent scream. It's worse than blood and death. So much worse and my whole body trembles in disgust and desperation.

"Stop him!" I yell at Smith when I still can't move. "You said you could stop this!"

"You have to go further," Smith says, his calm demeanor breaking through to my rational self and giving me a sliver of sanity. "We can't fight him off— we're not in the real world. We're inside your mind. Go back more and we'll keep Jesse from being here at all. That's what I meant when I said I could stop him."

"But," I stare frantically at the frozen attacker, "the killer! He's right there. Can't we rip his mask off and find out who he is?"

"It doesn't work that way," Smith says, and while I can tell he's trying to calm me down, the frenzy inside me refuses to abate. "We're not *physically* here; we exist only in your mind. Through your powers as an Oracle, you can *affect* this world, but not in the way you assume. You need to trust me. Please, keep rewinding."

I draw a deep, steady breath and force myself to look down at Jesse. Jesse frozen in his struggle for life, only seconds away from death. I hate that I stopped everything here—a macabre photograph of almost-death.

I put my hands out in front of me again, and it's easier to move the scene this time. Probably because I want so desperately to leave this moment. The story in reverse continues to tell itself. Jesse wanders in—barely visible from where I stand—and scarcely out of sight of the place he's meant to die. His headphones are on and there's a joint in his hand.

"Sneaking out to get high," I mutter to myself. "Of course."

"I imagine he's been stressed, don't you?" Smith says, and I hate the twinge of empathy I feel toward Jesse's careless mistake.

"Okay," Smith says when Jesse's walking backward, almost at the edge of the development. "We should be far enough. You can let the scene stop again."

Stopping it feels more like letting go than forcing the scene to my will. I've been given a brief reprieve to catch my breath and rub the trembling muscles in my arms, and I take full advantage of it.

"Are you ready?" Smith asks softly, and I realize he's been giving me time.

I nod my head yes, even though I'm not sure I am.

"You're going to go up to him. Command him to go home, the same way you've been doing with the scene, and then you'll use your physical self—although technically it's a form of energy—to *push* him all the way home. When the killer comes around, Jesse simply won't be there."

"Wait, wait, wait," I say, waving my hands in front of me. "Pretty much none of that is even possible. I can't *move* in my visions. I mean, I can move my body, but I can't walk. I tried two minutes ago."

"You tried to move on your own. You need to use the power of the focus stone to move."

"I'm wearing it—it's not helping." A desperate weariness is creeping over me.

Smith purses his lips and pushes his short hair off his forehead. "Shelby said she would filter all of her energies through the stone, and the stone would multiply them, and that's how she would have enough power to break free."

I grit my teeth and think it over. It does make a strange kind of sense, but the idea that I have an entirely new dimension of abilities that I've never had any clue of is hard to wrap my head around. I think about the little section I read about the focus stone from *Repairing the Fractured Future* and remind myself that—somewhere, somehow—Oracles have been using focus stones for a long time. "Okay," I say, and I wish my voice were stronger. "I'm ready to try."

"Have you ever had one of those dreams where you're trying to run but you're moving in slow motion?"

"Yeah. I hate those."

"This will feel like that. It will take every ounce of mental energy you have, filtered through that focus stone."

"Okay," I say, ready to make the attempt. I let go of the last bit of control over the vision that I was still hanging on to. The scene starts to play and I lift my foot, determined to get this over with.

But my foot rises a mere inch. Then freezes.

"You can do it," Smith whispers when I pause. "Think of the stone making you more powerful."

I focus on the warm feeling of the stone against my skin. Distantly I can almost feel the real one pulsing against my fingertips in my physical hand. And a surge of . . . of something rushes through my body. An entirely new kind of energy fills me. This time my foot moves.

I step.

One single step and I'm already tired. I look at Jesse. He's coming my way. I lift a foot again. Two steps, three. Smith's explanation was right on and I have the surreal feeling of being in a dream instead of a vision. I continue slogging through air that feels like Jell-O until I'm only a few feet from Jesse.

"Tell him to go home," Smith whispers.

"Jesse, go home!" I shout with every ounce of force and volume I can muster.

"In your head," Smith corrects. "It's a mental thing."

I close my eyes for two seconds, concentrating on the stone again. *Go!* I scream in my head. *Go home!*

Jesse stops. He reaches into his pocket and pulls out the thin joint. He considers it for a moment and then looks up at the light pole that's dark on one side.

"Now push," Smith says.

My hands won't quite make contact with Jesse and, for a second, I don't think it's going to work. Then Jesse's turning, shoving the joint back in his pocket, and starting to trudge home.

I keep walking and pushing at the same time and I know with absolute certainty I could never have done this without the stone. My arms and legs are shaking and I'm afraid to look beyond Jesse's back to see how far I have left. I don't want to know.

After what seems like hours, we reach his doorstep.

"That should be enough," Smith says. "Rest."

At his words, I let go of everything—Jesse, the energy from the stone—and lean over with my hands on my knees, gasping for air. My whole body feels rubbery. This had better be enough because I'm not sure I could go on for one more second.

At the sound of a door closing, I look up. "He's in," I say, breathing hard. "Did we do it?"

"Probably," Smith says. "But you know how fickle the future can be. We hope that when he decides to go out on his own, he'll change his mind."

"Now what?"

"Pull the curtain back over your second sight—the one you use when you fight visions. It'll kick us both out."

I concentrate on blackening my visionary world and almost instantly I'm back at the library, sitting across from Smith, peering at the focus stone, his fingers on my temples. "Holy crap!" I say, pulling away from him and letting the necklace clatter to the table. "Did that seriously just happen?"

Smith looks at me with one eyebrow raised.

I move my arms and legs, straighten my back. I was absolutely exhausted a few seconds ago. But now I don't feel tired. The bone-crushing weariness I can recall so clearly is nothing but a memory.

Because it wasn't physically me—just like Smith said.

"Did it work?" I ask.

"Did you really change what's going to happen? Yes," Smith says with certainty as he picks up the necklace and slips it into the little velvet case. "You've worn yourself out though; you won't be able to fight visions off for a couple of days."

"I haven't been anyway," I say, too mentally tired to realize I shouldn't admit that.

Lie to someone who was just inside my head? I shake the thought away; it feels wrong on too many levels.

"That's probably good," he says. "If the universe sends you more visions that have anything to do with the murders, you're going to want to see them."

"Why aren't you tired?"

"I didn't do anything. You have to understand, Charlotte, I'm like a . . . an instruction manual. I know what to do, but I don't actually have any power on my own. I'm useless without you."

"So, is that it?" I ask as he rises.

"For now. You saved his life, don't ever disregard that. But the murderer is still out there."

"Do you think it's all the same person?"

His brows furrow. "I've been over it a million times. Different methods, differences in the victims, and no . . . 'signature,' I guess you would call it." He turns to me now. "But doesn't it seem like it *must* be the same guy?"

I nod as he voices the same suspicion I've been harboring. That I suspect everyone in Coldwater has been.

"Maybe he's a first-timer and hasn't settled on a method yet. Maybe Bethany was an accident, even. Maybe he didn't plan to kill her right then and there." He shrugs and scuffs at a stained path on the carpet with one shoe. "But *if* it's the same guy, there's a good chance he's going to kill again."

"More after Jesse?" I say, and my gut clenches with a hundred fears at once. Another death. Another gruesome vision. Another strange session in my head like the one I just went through.

"If you get a foretelling of it, you have my number," Smith says.

I nod and he starts to walk away. Then he stops— one hand on the study-room doorknob—turns back and asks me quietly, "Does he know?"

I startle. "Who?"

"The boy who helped you all those years ago?"

Linden. The story he doesn't remember. The day I fell for him.

The day I caught Smith's attention.

A burning wistfulness curls into my stomach and I whisper, "No."

"That's probably for the better. For everyone." And then he's through the door and walking away, blending in seamlessly with the sparse crowd of library patrons.

FOURTEEN

The next day, I wake up and rush to the television, but there's nothing. For two more days, still nothing. By the morning of Christmas Eve, I'm starting to feel cautiously optimistic. I think we did it. We saved him. *I* saved him.

I don't hear my mom up and moving around yet, so I lean against my pillows and pull up my comforter and let myself feel like everything's okay for a few more minutes. I try to remember the dream I had last night. About Linden. It was a good dream; I can recall that much. Lights, music, dancing. But not much else. Unfortunately the harder I try to remember, the faster it slips away.

When I finally put on some thick socks and make my way to the kitchen, Mom greets me with a hug and the smell of dough baking. Each year we spend much of Christmas Eve day making dozens and dozens of cinnamon rolls. Dough and sugar from one end of the kitchen to the other. Then we pack the rolls into foil trays and take them around to the same list of neighbors and friends we've been delivering to since before my dad died. It was the first tradition we picked back up after the accident.

Seeing my mom up to her elbows in dough at our low kitchen counter brings back a hundred memories of doing exactly the same thing in previous years. I've been so caught up with murders and visions and Smith, I'm ready for some normalcy.

"Give me just a sec," I say, and run back to my room to get dressed.

Several hours later—both of us covered in flour, dough, and sticky smears of frosting—my cell phone rings. We giggle as I try to wash my hands fast enough to answer the phone *and* not get it too messy.

I see the name LINDEN flash across the screen and my mirth melts away, replaced by something exponentially better.

"Hello," I manage to choke out.

"Charlotte?" I want to jump and shout and sing all at the same time.

"Hey," I say, hoping he can't hear the pounding of my heart that fills my own ears.

"How's your break been?"

"Good," I say, delighting in how fun small talk can be. Even if my nerves are crackling over every inch of my body.

"No more migraine problems?"

"Oh no, no problems with any of that." And there haven't been. Two little visions since Saturday with Smith. No big deal at all.

"Good. I'm glad. Well, anyway, this is kind of a weird request, but . . . are you busy tonight? I know it's Christmas Eve and I should have called you sooner, but things weren't for sure yet and—" I hear him take a breath and I'm oddly relieved that he's not always cool and collected. "I'm sorry about the late notice, but do you think your mom might let you go out?"

I glance at my mom and think about how hard it was to get her to let me go to the library on Saturday. In daylight.

But this is Linden. She'll understand.

Won't she?

"What time?" I ask, stalling.

"Eight?"

Eight. Maybe we can deliver the cinnamon rolls a little early. I mean, it's only two o'clock and they're done except for one batch still in the oven. And we're generally home around then anyway. "Lemme check."

I cover the mouthpiece of the phone and look at my mom, eyes wide. "Mom, it's *Linden*!" I say his name in a whisper. Just in case.

Mom raises her eyebrows at me. "Oh really?" she says playfully.

"He wants to know if I'm busy tonight at eight." I look at her, pleading with my eyes. "Will we be done by then?"

"What does he want to do?"

I sigh. "Does it matter?"

Her face becomes a little more serious. "Yes," she says. "I don't want you outdoors, or alone, with no adults around. Not because I don't trust *you*, because I do, but because two teenagers have *died* in the last three weeks."

Oh yeah. Real life. The cocoon of safety that has enveloped my mom and me for the last several hours is instantly gone. "Um, Linden, what did you want to do? My mom's worried about safety," I tack on, lest he think I have any reservations.

"Oh, mine too!" he shoots back. "That's why I waited so long to call. It's my family's annual Christmas Eve party. I was going to ask you last Friday, but they were still going back and forth on whether or not to hold it. Anyway, that's why I got your number."

Everything inside of me warms. It's not some last-minute, oh-crap-I-need-a-date thing. He's been thinking about it—about *me*—for almost a week. Maybe it *is* a real date. I don't know that for sure—he might just want a friend—but even if that's the case, he still picked *me*.

"It's kind of fancy, I guess," Linden rattles on, probably just filling the silence I rather awkwardly left for him, "and it's super traditional and they still want to hold it despite—" His voice cuts off and I lift a hand to my heart, aching for him. "You know," he continues after a long pause. "My parents decided that this year—more than ever—they need to help raise people's spirits. But they're being careful. Tell your mom we're doing valet service so no one has to walk to a parked car alone, and that my dad hired a security guard to patrol the house."

"Wow, they're really taking this seriously," I say, genuinely impressed.

"It'll be subtle," Linden replies. "But they want everyone to feel safe. To *be* safe." He hesitates, then says, "Listen, Charlotte, I hope this doesn't sound too weird—and I don't want you to take it wrong—but Bethany and I were . . . we were good friends, and she was friends with pretty much everyone I hang out with and we're all really having a hard time and—" His voice cuts off and I hear him take a deep breath. "I need a date who isn't going to make me think about Bethany all night. And I remembered what you said right after . . . right after she died and I know this probably isn't what you meant, but—I just . . ." His voice cracks and I have to blink back tears at the sound. "I need one night to not think about all this."

"Of course," I say as soon as I'm sure he's done speaking. "I meant it when I said you could call me for whatever." My mom has wheeled herself in front of me and is making faces, begging for hints, but I lift a "just a second" finger. "I'll talk to my mom and text you in a few minutes, okay?"

"Perfect."

"So?" my mom asks as I hit END.

"He needs me," I say, the wonder of it spreading through my veins like warm maple syrup.

Mom tries to insist on dropping me off at the party, but when I tell her about the whole valet and security-guard thing, she relents and lets me borrow the car.

"On one condition," she says sternly, and I brace myself. But she can't hold a straight face straight for very long and she breaks into a grin and says, "Take a couple of pictures with your phone. I've always wanted to see the Christiansens' house and I hear they deck it out to the nines for this party."

Sierra comes out of her room to help me get ready too. It's almost a shock to see her. I've been avoiding her since I snuck into her room, and especially after breaking every rule I know—and several I clearly *don't*—with Smith. "It's about time you had a good night," she whispers in my ear as she hugs me. I hug her back fiercely, wishing I could tell her everything that has been happening, and promising myself that I'll at least consider telling her someday.

Just not today.

With all the fuss my mom and Sierra are making,

you'd think I was headed to prom or something. It's sad proof of how sparse my social life is that an invitation to a Christmas party—and in the end, simply doing a favor—justifies this much excitement.

"Just remember, it's not a real date," I tell my mom when she sprays her best perfume on my neck.

"Says who?" she says with a smirk.

"Says *Linden*," I reply. "I told him a couple weeks ago that he could call me for anything, and he did. That's all."

My mom takes both of my hands. "That could be all it is now. But you said so yourself; he's talking to you more these days. Maybe he's starting to see what I've always seen. How special you are."

I smile and blink back tears of such mixed emotions, I can hardly begin to sort them out: guilt, pride, love, regret.

And I can't help but wish that my dad was here.

As I get in the car, a melancholy envelops me and I have to consciously push thoughts of my dad away. Instead I think about Linden. Think about him the entire snowy drive. When I come into sight of his house, I can't hold back a little noise of delight. Mom was right—this place is freaking gorgeous. It's one of those homes with ridiculously tall front doors and a huge overhang that covers an enormous circular drive.

And every inch of its perfectly manicured landscaping is covered with twinkling lights, which look especially magical in the snow. I try to picture myself coming here casually to hang out with Linden and I can't even imagine it. I don't fit. But I'm eternally grateful that for *one* night, this is where I belong.

Linden wasn't kidding about the valet service. There's a bit of a wait to pull up to the ornate front doors that are thrown wide open to allow guests in but, when I get there, a guy in a black jacket opens my car door, takes my keys, and hands me a small claim ticket.

Fan. Cy.

I walk through the front doors and wonder if I'm going to be expected to show an invitation. Surely someone is checking to make sure complete strangers aren't pulling up and crashing the party. But everyone in the crowd seems to know one another—to know who ought to be here.

As I attempt to look around me without staring— or worse, ogling—I'm 100 percent sure I'm the sole guest under fifty. And not only do I *not* belong, it's becoming slowly apparent that the people around me are starting to notice. Just as I'm ready to back out the front door, Linden appears to rescue me.

"Thank you so much for coming," he says, taking my hand and tucking it into the crook of his arm in a smooth movement that looks—and feels!—like it could have come out of a movie. I'm a little unsteady as I peer up at him and smile. "You look very pretty," he says, and though his smile is a little sad, at least it's there.

"You too. I mean, not p-pretty, obviously," I stutter, feeling my face flush. "Nice," I amend. "You look nice." If *nice* is a synonym for blow-my-mind, extraordinarily gorgeous. He's wearing charcoal-gray pants that fit him perfectly in all the right places, and a dusty purple button-up shirt crisply ironed but with the sleeves rolled up and his collar undone. The whole thing is topped with a formal vest that matches the pants. It's like a stylist dressed him.

I'm wearing a black dress with wide straps and a chiffon overlay. It's a bit formal—from a wedding two years ago—but it only comes to the knee, so it has a hint of casual too. I went back and forth between this and something more simple for about half an hour after Mom and I got back from delivering cinnamon rolls. But I'm glad I took Mom's nudge to risk being a little overdressed rather than under. I let a smile cross my face when I decide that Linden's and my outfits look good together.

He escorts me to a table full of sparkling champagne flutes and grins before asking me, "Real or fake?"

"Fake," I reply. "Driving." Which isn't exactly the reason but "I cross-my-heart-and-hope-to-die-promised my mom no alcohol" doesn't have quite the same ring.

He walks me through the crowds of people,

introducing me here and there, for the first hour. I don't say much and realize he was very honest with me on the phone this afternoon; I'm not there for him and me to get to know each other, or even because he's interested in being "just friends." For the moment, I'm a person to fill up the space beside him so no one has to ask him where his date is. So he doesn't have to suffer through badly timed jokes and ribbings about getting a girlfriend.

I'm a buffer.

But it's okay. I offered him whatever kind of help he needed, and I can see how much easier I'm making this for him.

Besides, he continues to keep my hand resting on his arm and sometimes covers it with his own, especially when he's introducing me to someone. It makes every inch of my body feel warm and beautiful as he presents me to people.

And Mom's right. This *could* be a jumping-off point. Every relationship has to start with a little step somewhere. Maybe this is *our* first step.

Finally when my smile muscles are getting a little tired, Linden walks me over to an elaborate table full of fancy appetizers and hands me a shiny, gold-rimmed plate. "Why don't we grab some food and escape onto the back porch for a little while?"

I look down the table and hardly know where to begin: small crackers with a rainbow of creamy toppings piped onto them, pastry shells full of berries and chocolate, meat rolls that look like seashells, tiny chocolate-drizzled cream puffs, and an entire section dedicated to a checkerboard of truffles and cheeses. I want to try one of everything, but I think that would take about three plates. I choose carefully and when I have a full dish in one hand and a sparkling cider refill in the other, Linden inclines his head toward the back of the house.

I expect it to be cold outside and judging by the sparse sprinkling of guests, so does everyone else. Instead, I'm greeted by warmth radiating from above. I look up in awe and Linden laughs.

"Infrared heaters," he explains. "My mom and dad had them installed last year, but no one sees them, so no one ever comes out here. All the better for me. For us," he amends to my delight, then leads the way to the far end of the porch.

I set my dishes down on the table, and Linden pulls out my chair for me. Again, something I've only seen in movies. I definitely could get used to this, and as I look out at the cloudy sky and spot one star struggling to show through, I make a quick wish on it that maybe I'll get the chance.

"I'm starving," Linden says with a sigh, and I notice that while my plate is full, his is *piled*. The formality of the party melts away and I grin as he digs in. For a few minutes neither of us speak.

"Thank you again for coming. And on such short notice," Linden says once he slows down.

"Of course," I almost choke to reply. I take a second to actually swallow, then gesture at his house. "It's really beautiful."

"Mom and Dad love Christmas," he says softly. "They always go all out. I just . . . can't get into the spirit this year."

I nod somberly and a movement catches my attention from the corner of my eye. Linden notices and we both watch as a uniformed security guy ambles down a well-worn path in the snow that follows the perimeter of the porch and then disappears around the corner.

"That's a new addition though," Linden says, and I hear that catch in his voice I heard on the phone earlier today. "I just, I can't believe she's gone. *They're* gone. Both of them. And that they haven't found a single thing to help catch the killer. Maybe even killer*s*." He laughs mockingly. "Killers." He turns and looks at me. "It feels surreal, doesn't it? Talking about murder in Coldwater?"

I nod, but let him talk.

"Every morning, I wake up and run to the internet to look up the news. I keep waiting for *something* to happen. Either they find evidence or . . . or another kid dies." His voice is a whisper as he finishes and he throws back what's left of his drink. "This isn't what I meant to talk about," he says, and changes the subject

129

by gesturing to a miniature wedge of cheese on my plate. "You should try that one; it's my favorite."

I ask him about the other foods I haven't gotten to yet and he tells me what they are. When he points at a crème-topped cracker and dares me to pop the whole thing in my mouth I do—and gag before spitting it back out.

"Sea urchin pâté," he says after he recovers from laughing. "One of my dad's favorites. As far as he's concerned, the fishier, the better. I hate it. Worse than caviar. He drags it out for *everything.*"

I clear the taste from my mouth with a truffle or two . . . or three, before Linden stands and stretches his long arms over his head and says, "Back into the fray."

He holds out his hand to me and when I slip my fingers into his, they're warm and soft. He pulls me up very gently. I reach for my plate but he assures me I'm supposed to leave it there for the serving staff.

"We'll get you another one to carry around if you'll share," he whispers close to my ear. His breath meets the edge of my cheek and curls around it like a caress. He smiles down at me before again tucking my hand into the crook of his arm. When he leads me from the dimly lit porch into the glittering world of candlelight and crystal that waits for us inside the house, I feel like Cinderella.

FIFTEEN

I wake up with the last vestiges of my perfect dream still flitting at the edges of my consciousness. It's starting to fade, but I lay still and hold it close like a well-worn teddy bear. In my dream it was Christmas Day, just like now, but I was at Linden's house.

And there was kissing. A *lot* of kissing.

What a perfect Christmas *that* would be. I close my eyes and start to imagine the scene all over again when I hear a knock on my door.

"Seriously, Char, you'd think *I* was the little girl and *you* were the mother. Get out here!"

My mom is such a kid on the inside. Especially when it comes to Christmas presents. "Coming," I say, and flip my comforter back, grabbing for my bathrobe, my toes inching toward my slippers.

That's when the darkness starts to close in. The pressure that builds in my head is almost instantaneous, threatening to explode within seconds. I sprawl back down on my bed and close my eyes. I'm learning to recognize the violent force of the truly horrendous foretellings even as they build, and this one absolutely has it. I try to relax and let the vision overtake me despite my jabbing certainty that whatever I'm about to see, it's going to be awful.

I'm not outside this time; I'm not sure where I am. The vision seems to be having trouble stabilizing and I wait for the scene to come fully into focus. When it does, a scream rises in my throat as I take in walls splattered with the deep maroon of fresh, wet blood. Even the ceiling has gruesome stripes crisscrossing it.

My breathing is unsteady as I let my focus fall back to the ground. My vision self begins to retch uncontrollably when I see someone lying in several bloody heaps on the concrete floor.

I think it's a girl. But it's hard to tell. Not without picking through the pieces. I take two agonizingly slow steps. My shoulder blades hit a wall and my hands spread out on the surface behind me to catch myself.

Only to brush something wet and sticky.

A ragged breath that sounds like a sob wrenches out of my throat and I jerk my hands away and look at the stripe of blood across my fingertips. I force my eyes closed. Surely I've seen what I need to see. Now I want out. *Out!* "Please let me out!" I scream.

Two seconds later, my room hazes into view. I'm

soaked with perspiration, though a glance at my clock tells me it didn't even last a full minute. I hear noises outside my door. Happy noises. For a moment, I can't figure out how in the world anyone could be cheerful in a world where someone committed the violence I just saw.

Then I remember.

"This hasn't happened yet," I whisper. "Smith." I almost fall off my bed reaching for my cell phone and start to scroll through my contacts.

Wait. I can't call. Someone—let's be honest, *Sierra*— might hear me. I jab at the screen and type a quick text message.

Again. It's worse. I need your help.

I pause, then add:

Text, don't call.

I peel my damp T-shirt over my head and pull another one on so I can get out of my room and pretend to be excited about Christmas morning with my family. The sooner it's over with, the sooner I can connect with Smith and stop this terrible vision from coming true.

During the next hour, I decide I've missed my calling as an actress. Neither my mom nor Sierra seems to suspect anything. Even when I pull out my phone to find the simple message:

Where? When? Tell me—I'll be there.

I just smile and say it's a friend from choir wishing me a merry Christmas. As quickly as I can, I send back some cross streets and a time I dearly hope I can actually get away with.

As soon as the last present is open—and I'm pretty sure I've delivered enough gushing to avoid suspicion—my phone buzzes again, and I look down, expecting another text from Smith.

Did you have fun last night?

I'm totally confused until I realize it's from Linden. Despite everything, a little bubble of happiness grows in my chest.

I text back:

A blast.

He quickly replies.

Me too. Any chance your mom will let you come back later today?

Breathing is out the window. I'm glad he texted instead of calling. I would be sounding like a moron right now.

"You okay?" Mom asks, and I nod so hard I probably look like a total spaz.

But I don't care.

"It's Linden," I say. "He wants to know if I can come over later."

Mom lifts one side of her mouth in an I-told-you-so smile. "He must have enjoyed your company last night."

"I guess," I murmur, a little apprehensive now. "Is that okay?"

She glances over at Sierra for advice.

Sierra turns to me and I try to look as innocent as possible. Unfortunately it just occurred to me that if they say yes, I could use this as an opportunity to meet Smith. I force my face to stay neutral as Sierra continues to study me.

"Linden's parents seem very big on safety, judging by their party last night," Sierra says, the words sounding like someone's dragging them out of her. But I could kiss her anyway.

"I'd want you back by dark, for sure," Mom says, and my heart leaps as I realize she just said yes.

"Of course," I say calmly, my thumbs itching to text Linden back.

And then to text Smith.

Linden and I have a brief text-versation and agree on noon. But I tell my mom we said eleven. An hour should be long enough for Smith. I think. I'm hardly an expert here.

"Mom, are there any extra cinnamon rolls?" I ask.

"Do we ever *not* have scads of leftovers?" she replies. "Why?"

I shrug and smile. "I thought maybe I'd bring some to Linden."

"Oh," Mom says. "That would be very . . . thought-ful." She pulls herself up from the floor and gets into her wheelchair to go into the kitchen and prepare a dozen of them herself. "Do you think he'll want a container of extra frosting?" my mom yells from the kitchen.

"He's a guy, isn't he?"

I take a long shower and stare at my closet for a good five minutes, trying to decide what to wear. Nice? Super casual? What does this invitation mean, really?

I have no idea.

After sifting through my entire wardrobe—twice— I settle on my favorite jeans and a pretty shirt I haven't worn to school in a while. When I check the mirror, I decide I look nice, but the truth is I'm having trouble mustering up enthusiasm.

I'll feel better after Smith and I have changed things. I'll get excited again.

In an odd parallel to last night, both my mom and aunt send me off, admonishing me very strictly to go only to Linden's house, and to drive right up to the door, and for goodness' sake look around the car before I get out, and lock the doors, and about a million other precautions I've been following since I was, like, four.

I get a little exasperated as I keep chanting, "I know, I know, I know," but I catch a glimpse of the worry Mom's been trying to hide, and I sober when I realize that some of this morning's gaiety was false for her too.

Once I'm in the car, I have to head south, even though the spot I asked Smith to meet me is north, because I know both my mom and Sierra will stay on the porch watching me until the car is out of sight.

Three blocks later, I make two quick right turns and head toward the corner where I'm supposed to pick up Smith. It's funny how he looks exactly the same as the last two times. Same dark jeans, same coat, although he's wearing a black ski hat today. I feel a little pang of guilt as I pull over and unlock the door for him. It's clear and crisp today—which is a nice way of saying it's freezing.

Smith doesn't waste any time. "Tell me what you saw," he says, pulling his hands out of his pockets and blowing on them for warmth.

"It was . . . it was awful. There were *pieces*, Smith. It was the most terrifying thing I've ever seen in my life." And I'm not embarrassed when my voice cracks.

"Take this next right," he says, pointing. He leads me down a road I'm unfamiliar with to a very small park that's hardly more than a three-car parking lot and a teeny clearing. "Can you work in the car?"

"Um, shouldn't I be able to?" I ask, completely lost.

"I think so. I guess I'm asking if you're warm enough and if you can relax in here. You need to be at ease."

"As at ease as I'll ever be with that picture in my head."

"That's the best we're going to get, I guess. Here." He pulls the necklace out of his pocket and drops it into my fingertips. I feel its unnatural warmth and a tiny part of me sighs in relief. I realize I've *missed* it.

I don't have time to analyze that.

"Just like last time?" I ask, the stone nestled in my hands.

"Except that it should be easier. You'll be amazed how quickly you'll get better at this."

"I hope so," I say doubtfully. But I remember the two minuscule steps I was able to take during the vision this morning. It took every ounce of strength I had, but I *did it*. Even without the stone.

I focus on the stone with my eyes wide open and remember the sensation of entering my second sight from last time. When I find myself standing in the bloody room again only a few seconds later, I'm shocked by how effortless it was. *That* part, anyway.

"Are you ready for me?" the voice of Smith asks.

"I'm ready," I say aloud, quickly looping the focus stone around my neck. "Let him in." I don't have to yell this time. I simply murmur the words and then

Smith is beside me.

I start to comment on how easy it was this time, but Smith isn't looking at me. He's staring at the carnage. He steps closer to one of the mounds of hacked flesh that looks like it might be her head, and hunkers down.

"Do you know who it is?" he asks.

I shake my head. "I think it's a girl. The—" I gag for a second then push it back and point. "The shirt is purple." Although, I realize with a start, Linden was wearing a purple shirt last night.

It's not the same shade of purple, I tell myself, trying to calm my raspy breathing. *And he's too big. Too tall. This is a small person.* "What do I do?" I say aloud when I find my voice.

Smith leans on his heels and pushes his coat back to slip his hands into his pockets. His forehead is filled with wrinkles. "A third death. I guess technically it could have been the fourth if we hadn't diverted Jesse. This has got to be the same guy." He looks down at the gory mess and shakes his head. "Let's avert this one again," he says after a long pause. "But we can't keep doing this forever."

"You want to quit?" I say but Smith cuts me off.

"You're misunderstanding me. We can't just keep avoiding the killer. Next time, we'll have to take steps to *catch* him."

"Oh," I say, feeling dumb. He showed me how to save Jesse's life and he's about to help me save this girl too. Of course he's not going to just walk away. "So what do we do now?"

"First let's figure out where we are." Smith begins to walk around the scene with an ease that I envy. It feels like I'm carrying ten-pound weights around my ankles. I touch the stone and remind myself that his freedom is only because he's powerless here. I have to funnel all of my energy and concentration because what *I* do changes things.

I take in the room, noting the cement floor and the walls made of Sheetrock. The roof slopes on both sides and is made of some kind of metal. "It's a shed or a workshop, I think."

I slowly start walking toward a set of doors on one end, and Smith nods approvingly. "You're getting better already," he says as I reach for the sliding metal doors. But even though I can feel the doors under my hands, I can't make them open.

"We're not physically here, Charlotte," Smith says, startling me away from my task. "Remember that. We're an impulse, a compulsion, nothing more."

"I'm going to have to rewind in order to see anything else then," I say. Mentally, I tell the scene to rewind. Though it starts slowly, soon it picks up speed, going faster than I ever managed with Jesse. I watch, my stomach clenching, as the same black-clad, masked figure enters the scene and demolishes the girl in reverse with a two-foot-long blade.

I'll never be able to sleep again.

SIXTEEN

I grit my teeth, grateful that at least in reverse, the girl's body is coming back together. It's only when we reach the initial strike of the machete that I'm able to figure out who it is—because the very first thing the monster does is slice his blade across her face.

My throat convulses, but I stare hard as her skin is made whole. "Nicole," I whisper. "Nicole Simmons." She's part of the student council leadership and she reads the announcements on the school TV channel every day. I've seen her each morning my entire junior year. Every student in the school would recognize her.

I wonder briefly if the killer knows this. If he slashed her face first because it was so identifiable. Or was it just happenstance?

But my personal connection with her goes back well beyond that. Nicole used to live two houses down from me. Our moms were friends. We played together all the time. My Oracle stuff wasn't even the reason we stopped being friends. Our parents used to do things as a couple and then suddenly one of them was gone and the other was in a wheelchair. Stuff like that is too much for casual friendships. And when the parents move on, the kid generally does too.

Even so, now that I know who she is, this feels even more personal. More important. Maybe she's not really my friend anymore, but she *was*.

Still, in reverse, the killer drags Nicole out of the shed by her hair and finally the doors open, and Smith and I are able to exit the workshop turned slaughter-house: him, quickly; me, with my slow, grueling steps.

"No way," I breathe as the killer takes Nicole right to her door. A few seconds later, she's safely in her own house and the killer is ringing the doorbell.

I halt the scene and, after a few panting breaths, turn to Smith. "He's going to take her from her own house!" I say in shock. "This whole time we all figured that if we were at home we'd be safe. This is going to start a panic. People are going to be afraid no matter where they are. They'll—"

"Unless you stop it," Smith interrupts, pulling me back into the moment. "Go back a little more. I bet her parents aren't home."

I swallow and nod and focus my energy on pushing the scene back even further. Sure enough, in a surpris-ingly short time, we see two adults leave in a black sedan.

"Okay, stop now," Smith says.

I do and we're standing in front of a half-raised garage door, watching Nicole's parents depart.

"Is there another car in there?" Smith asks.

I duck down and look under the edge of the garage door. "Yeah, one more."

Smith blows on his hands and then rubs them hard together. "I think the simplest thing is to get her to go to a friend's house as soon as her parents leave."

"Wouldn't it be easier to have her leave with her parents?"

"Possibly, but we don't know where they're going. Maybe it's somewhere she can't go. On a date? To a bar? You only get one shot at this and you want to pick the path that's most likely to succeed." He grimaces. "'Least likely to fail' is probably more accurate."

He has a point. "Okay. She's on student council. She's probably friends with the other girl on there. Sara Finnegan."

"That should work." He stands with his arms crossed over his chest, observing the scene. "Because you can't physically affect anything, you're going to need to go under the garage door, reverse the scene again, and slip through the door and into the house while the parents are leaving."

"Aren't you coming with me?"

"I'm going to stay here and keep an eye on *him*," Smith says, pointing at a nondescript gray SUV parked about half a block down beside a snowbank. Fear clenches at my stomach.

"Is that the killer?"

"That's him. If he gets here before you can finish your job, I'll yell for you."

"Can you do that?"

"Yell?" Smith asks, looking confused.

"No, stay here. I mean, you're in *my* second sight—shouldn't you have to stay with me?"

His forehead wrinkles. "I'm not sure. But if I stay right here—if *you* leave me right here, it seems like I could."

"What if I need your help?"

Smith shakes his head. "It's been over two weeks, Charlotte. Assuming this has *all* been the same guy—and I really think it is—then he's more than ready to kill again. We know he *would* have killed Jesse. He's probably planning this murder right now. He's got to be getting frustrated. And people who are frustrated are unpredictable. What if he suddenly changes his mind? Or comes in early? Then your vision's no longer accurate. I think one of us needs to watch his car. And since I can't actually do anything . . ." He lets his words trail off.

I look down the road where I can barely make out a dark form through the windshield. The killer, just yards away.

Except that he's not real; he's just in my head.

But this is his future.

Smith is right; *someone* needs to keep an eye on him. "You have the stone," he reminds me softly.

"I'll make it happen," I vow, and without letting myself have a second thought, I duck under the garage door.

It's eerie walking past the frozen car, feeling like as soon as I start the scene, they'll be able to see me. "I'm not really here," I whisper. "Not here."

I position myself right beside the back door and focus on moving the scene backward again. Mr. and Mrs. Simmons almost brush me as they walk backward into the house and as the door closes—opens, technically—I slip through. I pause the scene, and before I let it start up again, I take several fortifying breaths. Smith believes I can do this by myself and he appears to be right; I'm just going to have to feed off of his confidence.

As ready as I'm ever going to be, I go ahead and start the scene again. As soon as the garage door closes, Nicole peeks through a barely cracked door and then runs to the front window to watch them drive away. I get right up next to her and shout in her ear, "Go to Sara Finnegan's house!" There's an insane amount of thought and will behind my shouting, but I'm already so worn out, it's easier to vocalize as well.

I don't know what kind of mischief Nicole *intended* to get into, but when I yell at her, she straightens and gets a funny look on her face. "Go to Sara's house *now*!" I scream the word *now* as loud as I can.

Then I start to push with that same flow of energy that I used with Jesse. And Nicole moves. It's slow. Like she's fighting me almost, but she's going. I focus on the stone—on all of my energy going through it and getting bigger, stronger, and together, we walk. We're halfway across the kitchen when she suddenly veers off and I almost cry in disappointment, knowing I'll have to catch her and *then* get her back on track.

"No! Sara's house!" I yell after her, my slow steps not equal to her near run down the hall.

But a few seconds later, she appears with a jingling set of keys in her hands, and relief courses through me. *I'm okay; it's working.* I start pushing again. I push, I shove, and for the second time today I break into a sweat and feel my clothes dampen, but I don't give up. I'm so close.

Nicole pauses for a second at the garage door, looks at the small white Suzuki, and then dubiously down at the keys in her hands.

She's going to change her mind. She has no reason whatsoever to go to Sara's house. But I picture her mutilated body in my mind—especially that first strike that destroys her face—and put every ounce of will into my command as I shout Sara's name once more and shove with all my might.

Ten seconds later, Nicole is in the car and the garage

door is rising. I'm on my knees, too exhausted to even stand. I know we're not out of the woods yet, but there's nothing else I can do except keep shouting in my head for her to go to Sara's.

It's only as her car starts to move that I realize I've got to get out of the garage or I'll be stuck on the other side of the door from Smith. I don't want to leave the vision without finding out what he saw. I crawl across the cement. One hand, one knee, the other, the other. Slowly I make my way out of the garage as Nicole backs out. The door closes just inches from hitting me, and her little car makes its way down the snowy roads in the direction of the town center.

I kneel in the snow in front of the house and let the scene continue to play. For a second, I don't see Smith anywhere. Then I catch sight of his form jogging up the road, just ahead of the gray SUV.

"Charlotte," Smith says, gasping, when he reaches me. "He just saw Nicole leave. He's *furious*."

The SUV pulls right over the edge of the yard, plowing through the snowbank. A masked man jumps out and I hear an unearthly scream emanate from his mouth that makes every drop of blood in my veins turn to jagged ice.

The shriek of a monster.

I leap to my feet as he draws near. Something whistles by my head and I hear a loud thud and turn my head sharply toward the workshop.

The machete. He's thrown it into the side of the shed where it digs in just enough to stick, and wobbles crazily back and forth. He gets back into his car and—after a couple of tries—backs out of the pile of snow, driving slowly down the road in the opposite direction from Nicole.

"He was waiting," I whisper, my eyes still glued to the machete. "He had this all planned."

"Looks that way," Smith says tightly. "She's safe now. Let's get out of this scene."

It takes hardly a thought for me to cast us both from my second sight. Then we're back in my mom's Corolla, the heat blowing hard on both of us and the touch of Smith's fingertips very light on my temple before he lets his hands fall and leans heavily against his seat. "Doing this right—catching this guy—is going to take work, Charlotte."

"Thank you, Mr. Killjoy. Can't we take two seconds to celebrate the victory we've had?" I ask with my teeth chattering despite the hot, stifling air in the car.

"One, two," Smith counts mechanically. "I went over to this guy's car and he was already masked with the machete on the seat beside him." He turns to me. "He was ready. We don't know how much he planned before, but he's definitely planning now. And he looked like he was hungry for a kill."

"So what are we supposed to do?"

"Like I said before, we have to get him *caught*. Leaving

behind the machete—not to mention tire marks—was a stupid move at best. Next time . . ." He pauses, then holds both hands out in a calming motion. "Now just think about this, okay? Next time I was thinking we could let the victim get attacked, but not killed. I know that sounds harsh"— he rushes on when I gasp—"but not only will that allow the killer to let off a little of the pressure building up inside him, whoever it is might get close enough to see something. To get a fingernail full of DNA, you know, that kind of thing." He pauses. "Maybe the cops could even catch him in the act if we draw it out enough. I think it's worth a shot."

I hate that it makes sense. "I'll think about it," I finally say.

The car is silent as I drive about a mile back to where I picked Smith up. He starts to grab his door handle, then stops and turns back to me. "You did well in there. And if we had a year to do this, I think you would be enough just by yourself. But we don't, so I think you should take this."

He holds out the ancient velvet case and, despite everything, I suck in an excited breath when it touches my hand.

"Wear the pendant while you sleep," Smith says. "There's a whole plane of existence that contains all of the possible visions of every possible future. I don't know if it's in your head or somewhere else entirely, but Shelby used to talk about going there in her dreams when she wore the necklace. She always described it as an endless dome full of visions of the future."

The domed room. From the book. The supernatural plane. *Holy shit! It's real.* My blood races with excitement, but I try to appear calm.

"She said she could practice altering reality and everything all night and never be tired in the morning. It wasn't somewhere I could go, so I can't help you with it, but try it and if you're dedicated, I know you'll get stronger." He clenches his jaw. "And you're going to need to be strong to beat this guy."

"I just wear it and go to sleep?" It sounds too easy.

"Think about going there *before* you go to sleep. It'll feel a lot like a dream, but one where you're completely in control and can move about at will."

"Won't I . . . change things?" I ask, nervous about doing something to make everything even worse than it already is. Not to mention getting caught by Sierra. This is so beyond rule-breaking that I have no idea what she would do.

"Not while you're sleeping," Smith says, pulling my attention back. "You won't be entering a specific vision—it'll be the supernatural plane in general. Shelby said it was like seeing every possible future all at once. And because she knew she couldn't actually change the future in her sleep, that's where she would practice."

I can hardly even comprehend such a place, but

then, Shelby probably couldn't either before she went. "Okay," I say, slipping the necklace case into my deepest pocket. "And thank you."

"Whatever you do, don't let your aunt see it. Promise?" Smith asks.

I chuckle bitterly. "Believe me, Smith, that is one thing you do *not* have to worry about."

"Okay." He opens the door and steps out, tucking his scarf back into the front of his coat. He starts to swing the door shut, then stops and leans down so I can see his face again. "And be careful, just like the other teens are supposed to be. I know all you Oracles supposedly find out ahead of time when your deaths are and everything, but if anything should happen to you—" He closes his eyes and shudders. "No one here knows it except me," he says soberly, "but we're all depending on you. You are the *only* person standing between that monster and your friends. And if you die . . ."

His voice trails off, but instead of finishing his sentence after a few seconds, he stands and pushes the door closed.

"Message received," I whisper to his back as he walks away.

SEVENTEEN

I'm not feeling especially cheery as I walk up to Linden's door—*thanks, Smith*—but at least Nicole is safe. She'll live. The sickening display of carnage in the workshop will never happen.

And her parents will never have to find it.

I give one last little shiver at that thought and ring the doorbell. It opens scarcely two seconds later. "I saw you coming," Linden says with a grin, "but I wasn't quite fast enough."

I'm staring; I'm sure of it. His smile practically radiates sunlight as he stands in the foyer, backlit by floor-to-ceiling windows behind him, loose jeans balanced on his hips and a long-sleeved black T-shirt hugging his perfect ribs. For years, I've watched with envy as he flirted with other girls—but this, this is something else entirely. Linden at home. Casual and at ease.

"You want to come in?" he asks, holding the door wide.

"S-sure," I stutter, but he doesn't even crack a smile. "I brought these for you," I say, proffering the tray of cinnamon rolls once the door has closed the chill out of the room.

Linden's eyes widen. "Dude, are these cinnamon rolls?"

"My mom and I make them every year."

"Wait, wait, you *made* these? Like, from flour and sugar and stuff?"

I eye him strangely, and he bursts out laughing. "Sorry, that sounded weird." He leans in closer and whispers, "My mom doesn't make anything except French toast. And I mean, she uses store-bought bread and dips it in Egg Beaters she put some cinnamon in. It makes her feel domestic."

I smile back and follow Linden into the kitchen— one of the rooms I didn't get to see last night. I guess I'm not really surprised that everything is sparkling clean less than twenty-four hours later, but I do wonder how many people it took.

Linden puts the tray on the counter and stares at it for a few seconds before looking up at me with a guilty expression. "Is it really six-year-old of me to ask if I can eat one of these now? They look amazing."

"No, please do!" I say, grinning from ear to ear. "You have to do it right though."

He peers at me dubiously. "There's a *right* way to eat a cinnamon roll?"

"Yes! Hot roll, cold frosting, eat with your fingers," I say with a laugh. In the end, I cave and let him use a fork, even though I inform him that he is missing the *best* part of the experience.

He puts a big bite in his mouth and then closes his eyes and groans. "Oh, man, this is so good. I'm not just saying that because you're here. These are amazing." His eyes fly open and he swallows. "I'm such an ass, let me get you one." And he's turning to grab a plate before I can stop him.

"No, no, no," I say, putting my hand in his way as he tries to fork me a cinnamon roll. My stomach is still clenching from the horrific experience I've just had. At this rate, I won't be able to eat for the rest of the day. "I swear I've eaten a whole dozen in the last two days. I honestly don't want one." That sounds convincing, right?

"Suit yourself," he says, taking another bite. "But I'm going to be so very rude and eat this in front of you because I literally cannot stop."

I laugh as he continues to munch and we chat a bit about our Christmas presents. I feel the tension from the last hour start to loosen. He shrugs off his new snowmobile when my jaw drops at the thought of getting something so expensive and he smiles at just the right moment when I tell him about the tunic top my mom made for me. I'm not sure how real-life Linden manages to be even more perfect than in-my-head Linden. But somehow, he does.

By the time he sets his fork down on the empty plate, I've managed to clear my chest of the fear and tension my session with Smith worked up.

"Thanks again for coming last night," Linden says, and his voice is quiet now. "I had a really good time. A—a better time than I thought I would. Not that I didn't think I'd have a good time with you," he corrects, sounding almost nervous. "But I . . . I had a good time."

He scoots the plate out of the way and leans across the bar with his elbows on the counter. His nose is less than six inches away from mine, and my stomach feels like worms are trying to wriggle out of it.

"Me too," I reply, too wimpy to lean closer. What if this kind of close proximity is normal for him? What if it doesn't mean anything?

"And I'm glad you came today," he says. This time I'm *sure* it's not my imagination that he leans forward another inch or two.

"Because I brought you cinnamon rolls?" I ask teasingly. *Did I just flirt with him? Go me!*

"A bonus," he says, and this time I can feel his breath on my face. I nod. There is *no* speaking left inside me. My hands feel useless sitting on the counter until his fingers slide up and cover them. "When we go back to school, I hope we can hang out more."

"I'll think about it," I say, though it's like every nerve in my body is connected to my hands. I hope they don't start to sweat.

"I think it's dumb that people avoid you because you have health issues. It's not like it's your fault."

Hello, reality. My stomach twists and I wish he had said anything other than that.

"Hey, hey, don't look like that," Linden says, and he lifts my face with two fingers beneath my chin. "We don't have to talk about it. I'm sorry."

He's sorry? Because I'm a liar? I force myself to smile. "It's okay. I'm used to it." I pause for a few seconds and then, feeling emboldened by the touch of his hand on mine, I ask, "Do you ever feel out of control of your life?" He laughs, and I protest. "I'm serious!"

"Me too," Linden says, still smiling. "But isn't that what being a teenager is? I swear my parents monitor every step I take."

"Really?" I ask, a little surprised. That's not a problem I have. I never considered my mom to be overly trusting, but maybe she is.

"Sure. And they want to plan my life. I'm not even a senior yet and my dad already has my college picked out for me. And grad school. Wants me to be a big-shot lawyer like him."

"Is that what you want?"

He snorts. "Work his hours? Defend the scum he

defends? No way." The laughter has disappeared from his voice and I can tell this is something he seriously resents. "I don't know what I *do* want, but his life isn't it."

"Me too," I say, thinking of Sierra. The plans she has for me with a secret group she won't tell me much about. The future I'm not sure I want.

"Your mom? Really?"

"My aunt. She lives with us."

"We should make a pact," Linden says, and his grin is back. "That we'll both do what we want after high school. And that we'll help each other." His tone is light, but he sounds mostly serious, like he's really looking for a coconspirator.

He doesn't know how serious that kind of a promise is for me.

Or how appealing.

My heart races as I stick out my hand. "Deal," I say, hoping I sound flirty, not nervous.

He slides his hand into mine and grips it tightly. "That's a promise," he says softly.

"Promise," I echo, and something about saying it out loud makes me feel like I *could* take control of my future. Grab it with two hands and do it my way.

"We should seal it, somehow," Linden says, studying my face.

I raise an eyebrow. "You're not going to make me spit on my hand, are you? Or poke my finger with a needle?"

"That wasn't really what I had in mind," he says, and as he leans forward, he pulls on our joined hands, bringing me closer to him. "Just to make it official," he whispers.

Then his lips gently brush mine.

It's not long. Or passionate. It's just the barest hint of lips against lips.

And it's perfect.

His mouth is warm and he tastes like sugar and cinnamon and something else entirely his own. I know it's not Linden's first kiss, but it *is* mine.

And it is everything—*everything*—I dreamed it could be.

EIGHTEEN

When I get home from Linden's house—sadly, there was no more kissing, not even when he said good-bye—I go right to my room and start studying the photos of *Repairing the Fractured Future* from the beginning.

As the sky outside my window darkens, I'm starting to get at least a small part of what the book is saying. Apparently the supernatural plane is a place that actually physically exists, but on a slightly altered dimension of reality. But you don't, like, disappear from this world to go there. You project a physical version of yourself with your mind. I guess it's like what I've been doing in my second sight when I revisit my visions. I think. Or, that's what the author of the book thinks. It all sounds a little sci-fi to me. But what seems to be clear is that it's a different place from my second sight, where I see my visions. My second sight definitely exists *inside* my head.

According to this, to get to the supernatural plane you "jump" into the alternate dimension with your projected physical self. Whatever the hell that means.

It's hard to get much more decent information out of the text. Maybe because I haven't been there. Haven't seen it. Yet.

That night when I go to bed, I lock my bedroom door. It's becoming a habit and not one that I like. But my life is full of secrets now. Well, it was always full of secrets, but now I'm even keeping them from Sierra.

I lie in bed with my fingers clasped over the necklace, waiting for sleep to take me.

And waiting.

And waiting.

Sleep never comes easy when you really want it to. But somewhere in the midst of my tossing and turning, the blankets begin to envelop me in a distinctly nonrealistic way. I'm not completely conscious—more the sensation of being in a dream that you somehow suspect is, in fact, a dream.

I'm floating, no, more like *swimming* through thick water. And I'm reaching, reaching for something I can't see. I want to get there so badly. I'm almost there and then . . .

Sunlight pierces through my eyelids.

I wake up feeling like I didn't actually sleep. *Rest*, I guess. And there's a sense of disappointment that almost overwhelms me. I'm not sure why. I didn't get to the supernatural plane . . . at least I don't think I did. But maybe I was heading there?

I'm pulling a shirt over my head when my mom calls my name excitedly. Which makes me nervous. I hate that this is my life now.

It's Nicole. She's all over the news.

But it's because she's *alive*.

"I just had this feeling," Nicole repeats again and again to every reporter who asks. "My parents had just left and I had this feeling I should go to my friend Sara's house. I *knew* I had to leave," she says very seriously as her hands reach up to grasp her cross necklace. The implication is lost on no one. Her bright blue eyes are wide in both the horror of what might have happened and the excitement of her fifteen minutes of fame.

There would be no excitement if she actually knew what was *supposed* to happen. The mental picture still chases my appetite away.

The cameras continually go back to the machete, still stuck in the shed wall as police circle it and take photo after photo. The tracks where the killer rolled over the snowdrift are also taped off, though the police have said that they don't expect to be able to retrieve any useful evidence from them.

My mom is so excited that someone evaded the killer, but I feel like there's a countdown clicking in my head. Despite the fact that we headed this one off, Smith is right; we've got to do more. There was less than twelve hours between me having the vision and the actual event taking place. The few visions I've had and been able to track in my life were always days early at the very least. I remember when I was six, waiting almost two weeks for all of the signs to happen that I saw in the vision of Sierra dying.

I'd never had a vision come to pass in less than a day before this guy started murdering kids. He's so *angry*. I shiver. I've got to get better at this changing-the-future thing. I have to stop him.

Back in my room, I pick up my phone to start studying the Oracle text again when it starts vibrating in my hand and I freak out and drop it on the floor.

Perhaps my reflexes are not quite catlike.

Linden's name flashes on the screen, and my heart-beat jumps right back up to racing—albeit for a completely different reason this time.

I'm bored. What are you doing today?

I groan and flop back on my bed. For six years, I've wished that Linden would show some kind of interest in me. Why does all of this other crap have to be going on at the same time? I stare at the phone screen for a long time trying to decide the likelihood that my mom will let me out of the house at all today.

Not sure my mom will let me do anything.

My mom still has her security guy.;)

I raise an eyebrow and text back:

Can't hurt my case.

My phone buzzes again with his reply:

Want to go snowmobiling?

It sounds like heaven. But seriously? I push the button to call Linden so we can actually talk in full sentences. "Good morning," I say when he answers, and it feels somehow intimate to greet him like that while I'm lying in bed.

"So what do you think?" he asks. "My new machine is *dying* for a test run."

"Is that safe?" I ask in half a whisper, just in case my mom is within hearing distance. I shouldn't have to worry. I *should* get a vision before the killer strikes again. But I don't know that for sure. Still, I would know if my own death were coming, right? It's what I've been depending on these last few weeks.

"Do you doubt my abilities as a driver?"

"That's not what I mean," I say. "Should we be out alone with the . . . the murderer still out there? I mean, after the thing with Nicole?"

Linden is silent for several long seconds and I feel

guilty. I know he likes that I help him *forget* about the killings, even if only temporarily. But we have to be reasonable. "I think my rig is fast enough that I could get away from anyone who might approach us. And I'll keep us out in the open. Would that make you feel better?" I expect him to sound annoyed, but he doesn't. He sounds like he really wants me to feel okay.

I chuckle dryly. If only. "It's not me you have to convince; it's my mom." I stand and poke my head out of my door and look both ways down the halls before asking quietly, "What if I told her I was just going to your house?"

He laughs and the bright sound chases away my melancholy. "You do what you gotta do. Just . . . just come, okay?"

I've never gone snowmobiling before. It feels like flying! I hang on tight to Linden and squeal when he hits a snowdrift that launches us a few feet in the air only to land softly in a mound of powder, and then we're gliding again.

I'm dressed in a full-body snowsuit that Linden grew out of ages ago. And I'm grateful for the warmth as the frigid air whistles past us. We last for a full two hours of crisscrossing acres upon acres of perfect, untouched powder and by the time we pull back into his parents' six-car garage, I'm bursting with delight and excitement even though my cheeks are so cold I can't feel them.

"That was awesome," I say when Linden unfastens my helmet for me and I pull it off, the world stunningly bright without the visor in front of my eyes.

"It's a good machine," Linden says, looking down at the shiny snowmobile and then running a hand along the side of it.

Getting out of our snowsuits is almost as funny as when we got into them—with Linden again having to assist me with half of my fastenings.

"I feel like I'm four," I say, giggling. "I need so much help."

"You'll get used to it," Linden says so casually it makes my heart skip a beat. His simple, easy assumption that we'll do this again. Soon, and often enough that I'll grow accustomed to the silly snowsuit.

"You look cold," Linden says, and lifts his hand to push a damp strand of hair off my face. He meets my eyes and his hand freezes. For a moment, I think he might kiss me again. A real kiss, not a deal-sealing kiss. But after a few seconds of tension he smiles, drops his hand, and inclines his head. "Let's go inside."

We stop in the kitchen and Linden pushes a button on a very high-tech-looking shiny thing and a few minutes later, we're both holding steamy cups of frothy cappuccino. "This is so cool," I say, my hands warming around my mug. "It's like Starbucks in your house."

He leads me into a rec room where a huge TV stretches across one wall and a sectional big enough

165

to seat at least ten people lines the wall. Linden drops onto the built-in chaise and pats the space beside him.

Not the seat beside him, but the space on the same cushion *right* beside him.

With a quick *you can do it* inner pep talk, I carefully lower myself down next to him so I don't spill my drink. Our thighs touch and our shoulders rub as I tentatively put my feet up on the chaise close to his.

As I sip my foamy coffee, I subtly take in the space around me. The décor is fairly sparse and almost entirely black and white. Multicolored pillows line the couch, deep jewel tones that are the only bright spots in the entire room. It's so elegant and beautiful.

But it does make me worry about getting coffee on *anything*.

I'm not sure I'd like living in such formality. I study Linden's profile and wonder if he finds it stifling.

Before he catches me staring, I turn away and as I do my gaze finds a long, wide mirror mounted above the couch on the adjacent wall. I gasp and put a hand to my hair. Helmet hair is the *least* of what I have. It's like helmet and bed and teased hair all rolled into one almost-beehived mess.

Linden looks up at my sound of dismay. When he realizes why I'm upset, he snickers.

"You knew!" I accuse, pointing a finger at him.

"Aw, come on. It's cute," Linden says.

I set my coffee down on the end table and jump up

to try and bring some sort of order to the mess on top of my head. Something smacks me in the back and I turn to see one of the pillows on the ground. I grab the pillow nearest to me and lob it at him. He puts his hands up to block what would have been a perfect shot to the face, then launches it at me again, following it immediately with another one.

I shriek and we both laugh and toss pillows until all of the formerly perfectly situated decorations are on the ground. Linden grabs me around the waist and flops back onto the couch, pulling me against him.

He runs his fingers over my messy hair, fixing some of the strands. "You look adorable like this." And then, with almost no warning, his lips are on mine and he's pulling my hips tight against his and I can barely breathe.

This one is a *real* kiss. It's warm and soft and purposeful in a way the sort-of kiss yesterday wasn't. One hand runs down the side of my ribs, down my hips, my thighs, then he hooks his fingers under my knee and pulls my leg up and across him, our bodies so close that he warms me even better than the creamy cappuccino.

After a long, soft, lingering kiss, he pulls away and leans his head on one elbow to look me in the face— though he keeps ahold of my leg so our hips are pressed deliciously close.

"Why didn't I notice you before?" he whispers, and runs one finger down my cheek. I pause at the funny sense of déjà vu his words provoke. Is it because I've imagined this conversation happening about a thousand times? Or did I actually dream about a scene just like this?

I smile up at him as he lowers his face to mine again. It's so exhilarating and surreal and I don't know what to do. Honestly, it feels a little fast. But not for me, for him. I've been dreaming about this for years. Maybe Linden just moves kind of quickly.

I can't say that I mind.

His fingertips find bare skin on my back, between my waistline and shirt. He hesitates, as though he's unsure what to do. Then his fingers slide across my spine and pull me even tighter against him.

I let all my worries go. It doesn't matter. Today, right now, everything feels wonderful.

Everything feels *right*.

NINETEEN

"You didn't see this coming?" Smith's words shock me most of the way awake.

"What? Smith?" I say groggily.

"Please tell me you didn't see this—not that you decided not to tell me."

"See what?" The fuzziness is starting to clear, but it's not gone yet.

There's a long silence at the other end. "Go watch the news," he says with a despairing edge in his voice that wakes me up the rest of the way. "Call me later." He hangs up without saying good-bye.

The sinking feeling in my stomach is a better premonition than my Oracle abilities at the moment. I shove my slippers on my feet, don't bother with my robe, and almost run out of my room and into the kitchen.

No one's up yet. It's the butt-crack of dawn, two

days after Christmas. *I should be sleeping.*

I turn on the television and keep the sound low, standing with my face close to the screen as everything inside me turns to jelly.

Someone else is dead and I got no warning whatsoever. Why wouldn't I get a vision? I should have gotten one.

Shouldn't I?

I study the crime scene—what I can see of it—and I'm not sure what to think. It looks like an empty lot, and I don't see any blood. There's a body draped in the middle of a patch of snow with straggly brown grass poking through, but the form appears—thank goodness—to be in one piece. There are footprints all around, but I can't begin to tell which ones were already there and which ones belong to the cops.

The news reporter talks about how the police have been working the scene all night and how long they think the victim has been dead. I count back hours and realize with the acid of shame burning in my throat that the killer probably committed this murder while I was busy making out with Linden yesterday.

Completely drained of strength, I sink down onto a chair and fight back tears. Rationally, I know there's *nothing* I could have done without a vision. And I remind myself that I've saved two other teens from terrible deaths.

But none of that seems to matter right now. I didn't save *this* one.

I have to do better. I have to do *more*.

I'm so lost in my self-pity that Mom catches me unawares and I jump when she touches my arm. She sees the tears I didn't have time to swipe away and her grip on my arm tightens. "What's the matter?"

I gesture wordlessly at the volume-less television.

"Oh no," my mom says, more of a scratchy sound on her breath than actual speaking. "Not again." Even in her chair, she visibly slumps and the two of us lean against each other and stare at the screen. I'm sure there are details we're missing because we can't hear it, but they don't seem to matter very much at the moment. What could possibly be more important than the simple fact that another kid—one so much like me—is dead?

I tilt my head when the camera pans to a taped-off scene behind the reporter. "They've brought in the FBI," I say, seeing the stark letters on the back of a handful of black jackets. Mom hesitates, and then turns up the volume.

". . . used different methods to kill each victim, police are now saying that there are other signs that point to the same person being responsible for all three murders. Agent Johnson, can you tell us a bit more about that?"

The camera swings to a man in a suit who looks tired and rumpled. "There are a few things that we've noted in all three cases. The first is a complete lack of DNA evidence, fingerprints, et cetera. The second is that the size of the killer is about the same in all three cases, and thirdly, the methods of killing have no hesitation. They have a marked precision and lack of faltering. We are officially declaring this to be a serial killer, and our profilers are suggesting that it's a first-time murderer, but that this individual has been planning these attacks, possibly for years."

"Thank you, Agent Johnson." She turns back to the camera. "We'll have continued coverage of the Coldwater Killer as details emerge."

Coldwater Killer? They've given him a name. I don't know why that makes me so angry. Maybe because it sounds like someone who plays a killer on television, not a real-life psychopath who would chop a seventeen-year-old girl into pieces.

"Serial killer for real now," Mom says weakly. "And no one can argue that our cops don't need help. This isn't exactly their area of expertise."

Mom and I sit together as the sun begins to rise, saying nothing as the same footage runs over and over again. When my eyes are too tired to look anymore, I rub them and stand up, thinking I'll go try to drown my feelings in a scalding-hot bath.

As I do, I catch Sierra leaning against the doorway like she doesn't have the strength to hold herself up. I'm shocked to see tears glistening in her eyes. Sierra's spent her whole life fighting to keep her emotions even and at arm's length, because it's easier to fight visions when you're calm. She's always seemed so strong, so in control.

And tired. I've spent thirteen years bracing myself against visions and it makes me tired every single day. Sierra's been doing it for over thirty years. I wonder if she wakes up tired. I try not to see my future in her. It's too depressing. But on days like today, I can't help it.

Sierra meets my eyes and her eyelids lower immediately, like she's ashamed to have been caught in such a vulnerable moment.

But she doesn't know—nor can I think of any way to express—how much I'm grateful for this sign that she still *feels*.

The steaming water that generally helps to clarify my thoughts is *so* not doing its job today. It all seems to be getting worse. I was half convinced that I was meant to help catch this killer—convinced that that was why the visions were so strong.

But if that were true, shouldn't I have seen this one? Or maybe this murder was just a fluke? An impulse kill?

Still, shouldn't I be able to see an impulse kill? I've seen lots of unplanned things in my visions. This one shouldn't be any different!

None of it makes sense.

And it makes me doubt, which is worse.

On top of that, I didn't make any progress on getting to the supernatural plane last night. But I did have that feeling of swimming through thick water again. I don't know if I should expect more after only two nights of sleeping with the pendant—it just feels so pointless. It was a little clearer and the need to get wherever I was going was more urgent. I don't know if that means I was closer or not.

Maybe I just need more focus.

Not that I'm sure exactly *how* I'm supposed to focus when I'm sleeping.

Smith said to think about the supernatural plane before I go to sleep. I'll do that.

But I did that the last two nights too.

Maybe I let myself get too carried away with Linden yesterday. I certainly forgot about the murders for an hour or two. Maybe I've got to focus on nothing but reaching the supernatural plane—even when I'm awake—in order to get there. I'm not sure how to picture a place I've never been.

It's been several hours since Smith called; I have to call him back. But I have no idea what to say. Where do we go from here? I think about his idea of getting a victim close—almost certainly close enough to get injured—but not killed. Every time I've considered it, I've pushed the idea away. This is all supposed to be about saving people, not hurting them.

But the killer is so careful. Always masked, always

gloved. The FBI guy said it himself: *no* DNA evidence. And they think he's been planning this for a long time.

I've got to get better at manipulating my visions. It's the only answer. I've *got* to get to that supernatural plane.

As the water is draining away and I'm toweling off my hair, I have an idea. The text from *Repairing the Fractured Future* talks about the importance of sleeping lightly. Wouldn't a nap in broad daylight be a lighter sleep than at night? Maybe? It kind of makes sense. At the very least, it's worth a try. And having gotten up so early this morning, I have a good excuse.

Assuming I can calm down, because as soon as I think of this, I get all nervous and excited. Not exactly the best way to prepare to *sleep*.

I wish I could get my hands on the rest of that book! If Sierra leaves, I might be able to go in and look at it again. Hell, I'm about at the point where I'd just *take* the book and risk her noticing.

If only I could talk to her.

But I've gotten so far into my lies that I can't tell her without confessing everything I've done. Everything I still *plan* to do. And I don't think I have the guts to do that.

Besides, it's not like she'd help me. I'm breaking every rule I've ever heard of. She'd stop me—I'm sure of it. I'm going to have to do this on my own.

"I can't meet you," I whisper into the phone when

I'm finally brave enough to call Smith back. "My mom is so paranoid she's barely letting me go to the bathroom without supervision." I peer at my closed door. "I even tried to get her to let me drive straight to my—" I hesitate. "My boyfriend's house who has, like, tons of security and it was an absolute no."

Did I just call Linden 'my boyfriend'? Well, when you spend an hour doing . . . what we did yesterday, isn't that what he is?

"Besides," I continue, shaking that thought away for the moment, "what would we do?" The urge to cry starts to form in my throat again, but I shove it back. "I don't have a vision to go into. I didn't get *anything* this time."

"Then I guess we wait until you do," Smith says, and I can hear the frustration in his voice. I can empathize; I hate feeling so helpless too.

But I've felt that way for my whole life; he's still getting used to it.

"Smith?" I say, even more quietly than before. Because what I'm about to say I wish I could hide from *myself* as well as my mom. "Your suggestion that we have a victim get attacked but not killed? I think you're right. That we're going to have to do something like that to get anything useful on this guy."

"Are you sure you're ready?" Smith asks, like it wasn't *his* idea. "It's a big step. And a difficult decision."

"You think I don't know that?" It's ripping my heart in two just to say it—but I don't see another way.

"I'm just saying you need to be fully committed. It's going to require a lot of skill and not a small amount of risk. Have you been sleeping with the stone?"

"Yes," I say quickly. "I'm not sure it's helping though. I don't think I'm getting there. I'm close—I'm know I'm close."

"Well, keep trying. Hopefully you'll be able to manage it soon."

"I'm going to try to take a nap," I say, feeling like I have to defend myself. "Maybe I'll sleep lighter that way and be able to focus better."

"Listen," Smith says, "call me as soon as you get another vision and we'll try to make a plan, okay?"

"Sure," I agree listlessly, then hang up. I lie back against my headboard and rub at my aching sinuses. I haven't cried this much in one day in a long time and it makes everything hurt. I glance down in surprise when my phone buzzes, and I find a text from Linden.

Are you okay??!!!!!

He probably just woke up and found out about the third murder. A warm feeling slides through me. This time, someone is checking up on *me*. But then I sigh, and feel guilty all over again. I text back:

I'm okay.

I don't have the energy to send anything else. And apparently neither does Linden. It's over an hour later before my phone buzzes again, and I haven't moved an inch.

No one knows who yet. Have you heard anything?

I text back a no and then, despite feeling bad about it, turn my phone off. He knows I'm alive; beyond that, he'll live for a few hours. I have to focus—I have to work. I drag myself out of my room and to my mom's office to set my plan in motion.

"I don't feel good," I say, only half a lie.

"Coming down with something on top of all of this?" she asks sympathetically, though her eyes are red rimmed too.

"Maybe," I say with a misery I don't have to fake. "Or maybe it just *is* this," I add. "I'm going to lie down and try to take a nap, and just wanted to let you know so you don't come knocking and wake me up. I got up too early."

I go back to my room and discover just how hard it is to sleep when you really try. I've filled my room with all sorts of distractions to help me not sleep too deeply—music playing softly in my earbuds, curtains pulled wide to let the light in—but they're keeping me from going to sleep. I start to concentrate on my breathing instead, closing my eyes and blocking out the noise as I breathe in for ten counts, and out for five. All the while I concentrate on the drawing of the domed world in Sierra's book that seems too strange to be true.

Suddenly I'm swimming. My arms move slowly, but this time when I stroke, I move. I can sense a surface far above me and I kick with my legs and pull with my arms. I blink and see a light with the same all-colors-and-yet-none quality that the focus stone has and somehow I know—I just *know*—that's where I'm trying to get.

I burst free of the strange air/water, and my knees hit a hard, flat surface. I stay there on my hands and knees, panting.

And when I look up, I know I've done it.

TWENTY

I push myself to my feet and take a tentative step forward. It seems like I was right about the napping and the concentration thing, because I'm *definitely* here. The floor is like a mirror, and it's surrounded by a huge dome filled with rows upon rows of images—all playing at a low volume that sounds like a buzz when they blend together.

Squinting, I focus on one for a few seconds and the dome moves and spins, bringing that image closer.

Which completely disorients me and makes me fall to my knees, my hands spreading on the smooth surface of the floor to remind myself which direction is up, and which is down. I feel lost and dizzy.

I don't like this.

But I'm here now. What do I do?

I start by grounding myself. I sit, push my feet out in front of me, and splay my fingers wide on the glassy floor. "Down," I say to myself. "This is down, and now I won't lose it."

I remember the focus stone and when I tip my head, there it is, hanging around my neck. Probably because that's where it was when I fell asleep. I grip it in my fist, holding on to the only familiar thing in this weird world. Then I look back up into the endless sphere of images above me and pick one at random. I focus as the dome rotates and brings it to a stop in front of me.

It's a girl from school, at home fighting with her parents. I watch for about a minute, but unless this girl is the person who ended up dead yesterday, I'm not interested.

Smith told me I should be able to manipulate things in my dreaming more easily than in visions. Since I've finally managed to retain some kind of focus, I decide to try that. Can I get the answers I need here? Smith said this is every possible future, but what about the past? Can I see the past too?

I think about the news report I watched earlier today. I picture the scene in my mind and try to grasp on to every detail I can remember. The tufty grass sticking up through the snow, the reporter standing in a field of slush filled with dozens of footprints. When I open my eyes the dome is rolling and the crime scene is coming toward me.

I tamp down a feeling of success and focus on the square. It's not quite the same as watching it on the news—it's unedited. The reporter is blotting her eyes with a tissue as an assistant stands by with a powder brush. The reporter nods after a moment and the assistant covers up her slightly reddened nose with makeup. Then she takes a steadying breath and turns back to the camera.

Is this the past? The scene looks different.

It hits me like a punch in the gut.

The body is gone.

This isn't the past. It *might* be the present.

So where is the body? As though answering my question, the dome rolls and I have to brace myself on my arms to keep from losing perspective again. A brightly lit room appears before me and I realize it's the morgue.

I search around the room for a clock and it reads 6:20. Probably p.m.

I get it. Only the future. Near future, sure, but *only* the future. Not the past. *Damn it!* I can't follow this victim's trail backward to the killer. Not unless I have a vision. I want to howl at the unfairness of it all.

But maybe I can find out who the victim is. The scene is bustling with so many people in lab coats, everyone bending over the body; I can't get a close enough look and even when I rise up onto my knees and crane my neck, I can't see past them.

Smith said Shelby went *into* scenes. Maybe I can do that too.

But what if I get stuck? Smith talks about this place like it's a playground for practicing, but it must be more than that for it to feature so heavily in Sierra's book.

For her to keep it a secret.

I know so little about it—what if I screw everything up?

But then I remember talking with my mom. "No risk, no reward," I whisper to myself.

I push my nerves away and rise from the glass floor slowly, pressing my fingertips on the ground until the last second to make sure I can keep my balance when I straighten. I stare at the scene in front of me, using it to help me stay upright.

One step, two. I wobble, but remain standing. The noise gets louder as I draw closer and when I actually step over the short frame and into the scene it feels like a warm, tingling rush of water cascades over me.

And then I'm simply there, in the morgue. When I look back I can still see the odd, rainbow brightness of wherever it is I started, but it's a small circle that I'm too big to fit through. I wrinkle my brows at it in worry and take a step backward, but as I do, the circle grows and I realize I'm not trapped. It's waiting there for me.

Confident I can get back, I turn around and take a few more steps into the morgue. I like the feeling of being in one of the scenes. The ground here is solid and opaque and feels so much more real than the plane behind me.

I focus on the table a mere eight feet away. On the person lying there. I figure I'm not really here since nothing I do can affect anything in the physical world. But it's a little creepy when the men and women take oddly veering steps to avoid me. Like I *am* there. Like they can see me.

Still no one speaks to me or tries to stop me from approaching the body, so I'm pretty sure I'm not actually visible. When I reach the table, I'm disappointed to see the face is draped. But this isn't a vision. Maybe . . .

I reach out and touch the edge of the thick, white cloth with my finger.

My fingertips caress the rough threads, sliding along until I reach the edge. I lift it away from the lifeless face and look down.

Eddie Franklin.

My heart sinks. He's a senior. He was in science with me. He was really quiet and one day at the beginning of the semester we were assigned to exchange quizzes.

He got every single answer wrong.

I got every single one right.

I caught him after class and told him we could work together if he wanted. He called me a nosy bitch and told me to mind my own business. But two weeks later, after a big exam, he came to me and apologized.

And asked if the offer still stood.

We studied during lunch, hidden in his car with the heater on. He told me a bit about his home life with an alcoholic dad, how much he wanted to move out. But if he failed this class, he wouldn't graduate.

I wouldn't say we were friends, exactly—he never talked to me other than at lunch, and our study sessions stopped after Bethany was killed—but we had this tentative respect.

I wonder if he passed his final. Then realize it doesn't matter.

He was kind of a loner without very many friends. Maybe that's why no one knows it was him who got killed.

I clamp my trembling jaw and look down at his pale body. The left side of his face is a mass of bruises, as is his throat. It looks like Eddie was strangled.

Like Jesse was supposed to be.

But with Jesse, the bruises were centralized around the throat and the body was tossed aside once the life was gone.

The killer wasn't satisfied with just *killing* Eddie. His head is oddly shaped on one side, making my stomach churn. I bet his skull is broken underneath. Both arms and legs are bent at sickening angles and one side of his chest is caved in. I have to look away before I throw up.

If only, *if only* I could have done something.

I turn away, anxious to be anywhere—even the nausea-inducing dome—other than here. I trip over my own feet as I stagger out of the circle that leads me back to the mirror floor, but I don't care. I just lay there, wishing everything around me would fade away.

Because even though that scene at the morgue is somewhere in the near future, Eddie's death isn't. He's gone, and the abilities of an Oracle are powerless against the past.

I have to think of something good before I drown in despair. I close my eyes and picture Linden to center myself. For several long minutes, I let myself focus on nothing but him until I'm ready to open my eyes. When I do, I am surrounded by visions of Linden. Him with me, him alone, him with someone else, his parents, teachers, friends, other girls.

"Every possible future," I whisper. I catch a glimpse of myself far above my head on my right, and focus on it. I know what to do this time, and as the scene comes closer, I rise quickly and step into it, needing something comforting after the morgue.

There we are, sitting together on his couch, laughing. I walk forward and as I approach, he says something I don't hear and the scene blurs, then splits and offers me two new scenarios.

A choice? I didn't get a choice in the morgue.

Maybe there was no choice to make. There is no future for Eddie.

I stare at the two scenes in front of me. In one, we're obviously fighting, so I step into the other. For the next several minutes, I walk forward, a smile on my lips as I veer into one framed scene, then another, creating a pretend future for Linden and me. Sometimes when the two frames appear, just for fun, I don't always choose the best one. But if I see kissing ahead, I'm generally swayed.

I see numberless scenes of kisses and caresses or long talks on the phone. Of introducing him to my mom, of getting to see his college apartment for the first time. I want to cry at how much better this is than following a murderer through his victims.

But that thought worms its way through my blissful state and I think about how my entire dome filled with Linden when I concentrated hard enough.

Could I do the same thing with the killer?

I look wistfully at the next choice I have with Linden. If I handle things right, though, I won't need stolen moments on the supernatural plane—I'll have Linden for real. I turn and focus on the domed room and the circle that will lead me there appears instantly.

When I reach the glassy floor, I ground myself again and think of the killer. I don't have anything specifically to focus on, but I concentrate on what I do have. The terrible faces and mangled bodies of his victims, the figure Smith and I saw in my vision of Nicole.

And that scream. That terrible, terrible scream.

Somehow I can *feel* when I've succeeded. There's a nearly tangible evil surrounding me. A raw sickness. Cringing, I open my eyes.

Everything is dark. The dome is covered with an

array of shadowy faces. Sometimes running, some-times rubbing a cloth up and down a knife, sometimes just standing and watching. But every scene is dark.

Too dark for me to see.

I focus on a slightly brighter scene and move it close, then step into it before I can lose my nerve.

I'm safe here, I remind myself, but it's doesn't stop my whole body from shaking. He's sitting in a cor-ner, watching a television screen. But his face is in full shadow and no matter how I move around his chair, I can't make out his features. After a few minutes, I give up and go back out the bright circle and try another scene. He's walking this time, and regardless of how fast I run, how hard I push myself, I can't catch up. And even if I could . . . he's wearing the mask.

I turn back to the bright circle and try again. And again. But each time he's too fast, or the shadows won't move from his face, or he's masked, or the vision sim-ply blacks out and ends. None of the scenes offer me a choice the way they did with Linden. It's like someone, some*thing* is blocking me.

Is this an Oracle rule I don't know about? Or is it simply that knowing who he is would change the future so vastly that I can't do it in a dream? I stare up at all the images of the monster, wishing I could do *something*. But even here, on the supernatural plane, his identity remains a mystery.

I feel an almost imperceptible ripple go through the

dome world and distantly I realize I'm starting to wake up. I'm ready, I suppose. I found out about Eddie. And I guess I "practiced" in the Linden scenes; Smith said everything helps. But I can't help but feel like I'm missing something. Some way I could help if I only knew better. I focus back on the Linden moments—so that at least I don't wake directly from the dark presence of the killer—when a flash of color catches my eye. It glints and disappears for a moment, but then it's back. It's a door. A door in the wall of the dome.

The longer I stare at it, the more solid it grows until it almost appears that the entire dome is sloping toward it. It looks far away, but I start walking in that direction. As I do, the door seems to retreat. I'm catching up, but not as quickly as I *should* be. I'm twenty feet away, and after speed-walking about fifty feet, I've gained another ten. I'm almost there when the weird ripple happens again. A few seconds later, my physical eyes flutter open and I'm back in my bedroom.

The clock tells me I was asleep for a mere hour—but it felt like much longer. Smith was right though: I don't feel tired.

I think about the door I couldn't reach and a strange sense of foreboding wells within me. Maybe I'll be able to get to it tonight, now that I know it's there.

But first, I have to send a message. I turn on my phone and press Linden's number. I send him a single line of text.

It's Eddie Franklin.

I shove the phone into my pocket and wonder how long my mom will let me hole up inside my room. I should probably at least unlock my door, let it sit open a crack so she doesn't worry about me. More.

I'm just starting to stand up when the tingling in my temples erupts. As the pressure in my head grows, turning into a tornado inside my skull, I know it's got to be another murder vision. Gritting my teeth, I sit back down on the bed and let it come, hating it already.

As the vision clarifies and I find myself standing in a shadowy tunnel, I'm taken off guard by just how badly I wish I wasn't here. How much I wish I wasn't me—wasn't an Oracle. That someone else had been chosen for this job.

Because whoever the victim is in this vision, I'm not going to save them. I'm going to put them right in the path of danger in order to get closer to the killer. The vision pulls me forward, forcing me to take step after step toward a mound lying on the ground at the mouth of the rounded tunnel entrance.

I'm about to find out whose life I'm going to risk to catch a monster.

TWENTY-ONE

"You're sure?" Smith asks when I call him from my bedroom with my music on to cover up the sound of my frantic whispers. "How can it be tonight? He just killed yesterday!"

"I don't know, okay?" I hiss. "But it's going to happen tonight and we have to do something."

"What do you suggest? I have a feeling your mom isn't going to suddenly let you out."

"I don't know," I say, almost too loud. "I was kinda hoping *you* had a plan. It was your idea."

There's a long pause and I can hear him muttering under his breath, but I can't make out the words. "Listen," Smith says—audible finally. "You have the stone. Do you think you can get into the vision on your own?"

"You said it was going to be really hard."

"It will. Are you going to let that scare you off?"

"No," I protest, feeling weirdly guilty that he would even ask. "I just want this to work."

"Then focus. Harder than you've ever focused in a vision before."

"I can do that," I say shakily.

"When you get in there, take her back as far as you can and try to figure out why the hell she's walking *alone* by a train tunnel, okay?"

"Got it."

"And you didn't see any signs of a weapon around her?"

"Clara," I emphasize, needing to give her a name—to keep all of this real and personal—"had no knife marks or gunshot wounds. But that doesn't necessarily mean he won't have *something*. Maybe, like, a baseball bat? You know, something that damages but doesn't cut."

"Okay. I guess you're going to have to make her fight him off, or run. Get her to take her phone out right before he comes. Maybe she can get a call off to the cops. Or someone else and have them hear her get attacked so *they* can call the cops."

I breathe a small sigh. "That's a great idea. And the cops will be out in force after this morning anyway, I'm sure."

"Pray hard that they are," Smith says. "Call me if you need anything else, okay? Do you want me to go to the tunnel in real life? Just to watch over her? Clara," he adds.

"Maybe, but . . . won't that change things?"

"It might. What if I got there early?"

"I don't know, Smith. I don't want to screw this up."

"All right. I'll stay home. Text me when it's done."

I've got three hours before it actually happens. We got lucky with the location. The train station has clocks posted all over the place along with routes and updates and such—that's how I knew it would be tonight.

I think Smith's got a good idea about the phone thing. But if the killer hears her talking on the phone, will he still attack? I feel like everything's balanced on a knife's edge. One imperfect move and it'll all go wrong; she'll die, or we'll miss the opportunity entirely. I'm not sure which would be worse. Who knows how many more people will die if I don't do this?

When I come out of my bedroom, Mom's banging pans around the kitchen in her classic tell that she's angry. Hopefully not at me.

"You okay, Mom?" I ask from the doorway of the kitchen. I draw in a quick breath as I see her standing; standing on her own two feet and bending over to pick up a canister she would have had to reach *up* for in her wheelchair. My mouth is dry and I can hardly believe my eyes.

I blink.

And she's back in her chair. Too fast to have moved there. *What just happened?*

Mom looks over at me and then sets down the frying pan she was banging around. "I guess." She gestures vaguely down the hall. "Sierra went out."

"Tonight?" I ask.

"What is she thinking?" my mom mutters, and I'm dismayed to see angry tears running down her cheeks. I want to tell her that no one's after Sierra—that it's going to be another teenager—but I can't.

"It'll be okay, Mom," I instantly assure her, though there's no way for me to tell her why. "She's smart," I add, like that means anything. "And . . . the wrong age," I tack on.

"So far," my mom mutters. "But who knows what this psycho will do next?"

I step tentatively to where she's gathering ingredients for something I don't yet recognize; she's an angry cooker. "Can I help with anything?" I offer, my mind screaming at her to say no.

She pauses midreach and really looks at me for the first time since I walked in. For a moment, I'm afraid she's going to say yes—that this is about to turn into a mother-daughter night. And that Clara's going to die because of it.

But she turns away and grabs the canister she was reaching for. The same one she was bending *down* to get a few minutes ago. *No, no that can't be right. It wasn't real. It* couldn't *have been.*

"I'm okay," Mom says. "I just need to beat some

dough for a while. If it's still fit to eat when I'm done, we'll have pizza tonight."

"Sounds great," I say, then I back out of the room and try not to make a sound as I head down the hall.

To Sierra's door.

I look both ways before holding my breath and turning the knob.

Locked.

Frustrated tears work their way to the surface and I have to take a few deep breaths before I manage to stop them. This is the first time I've seen her leave the house since I got the pictures of *Repairing the Fractured Future*. I wonder briefly if I could get a screwdriver and take the whole knob off. If Sierra took the time to tell Mom she was leaving, it's probably more than a coffee run. Surely she'll be gone for at least an hour.

Clara or the book? I slowly withdraw my hand.

I believe in omens; it goes hand in hand with being an Oracle. Sierra being out of the house is the perfect scenario to either break into her office *or* change the vision. But I have to choose.

What is the universe trying to tell me? Do I *need* that book? If I let Clara die tonight but I get the resources I need to save the next person, is that worth it?

But what if there isn't anything useful in the rest of the text? What if I'm wrong? Then an innocent girl is dead and I'm back at square one.

I walk back to my bedroom. Tonight I go with the sure path.

After giving the hallway a quick listen, I sprawl down on my stomach and grab the pendant from its hiding place inside the box spring of my bed. Then I sit cross-legged on the floor and brace myself with pillows. I hold the necklace in my hands and fix my eyes on it. It sparkles with glints of red, blue, and purple and, as I continue to stare, yellow and orange make appearances too.

Then I'm in the tunnel. So easily it's almost jolting. I'm convinced that somehow, we Oracles are *supposed* to do this kind of thing. It's too easy for it not to be our natural path. It's like a part of me awakened the first time Smith showed me how to enter my visions, and now I'm ready to fulfill its potential.

But Clara first.

I walk forward and it's like climbing uphill, but not nearly as difficult as it was before. As I approach the murder site, I begin reversing the scene in my head. The first thing I have to do is find out what the hell Clara Daniels is doing out alone, at night, the very same day a murder was discovered.

I watch as emotionlessly as I can while the brutal murder plays out in reverse. I was right about the weapon; the masked killer wields what looks like a short bat with sickening efficiency and soon we reach the point where they're both alive.

I'm both relieved and surprised when Clara walks backward through the night by herself a few seconds later. He really did just see her and swoop in. Or he will in a few hours. But what could possibly make her walk away on her own? In the dark. With a murderer on the loose.

I trail her, growing more and more puzzled as she walks in reverse through the train station, right down the middle of the seediest neighborhood in Coldwater, and then up around some designer condo development. From there, we continue on to a nice middle-class neighborhood. I don't know much about Clara outside of school but after the vision, I figured she lived near the train yard and maybe her parents didn't have a car. Because then it would make sense for her to be walking there.

But as I follow she walks up the steps of a nice two-story home a good half mile from the murder site, and when I slip through the door behind her, she sheds her coat and walks backward to settle herself on a couch.

Now I'll see something, I tell myself. *A fight with her parents, a weird text or phone call.*

But I see nothing.

She just reads. Panicked about time—who knows how long it'll be before my mom calls me for dinner— I go ahead and let the scene play forward. But watching it in real time doesn't give me any more answers than fast in reverse. If anything, it gives me more questions.

She's reading a book—a novel, not even schoolwork or anything—and then, very abruptly, she looks up, tilts her head to one side, and rises from the couch.

It's the weirdest thing I've ever seen. She says nothing. Just slips into her coat and goes out the front door. Again, we walk side by side, as though we're friends on a stroll, all the way back down toward the tunnel. Twice Clara stops and looks back the way we came, but each time she turns forward, and starts walking again.

We're nearly to the train yard when I realize I've been watching her so carefully that I've almost missed my cue. I don't know who her friends are, so as I walk alongside her I say, "Call your mom. Right now. Get your phone out and call your mom."

Her steps slow and she looks confused, but she doesn't reach for her phone.

"Call your dad then," I shout. "Call someone, right now!"

She pauses this time, and I nearly die of relief when she reaches into her pocket and pulls out her phone.

And then just looks at it.

Why is this so hard? I can walk, I could probably push her over if I really tried, but she's not following my commands. I shout step-by-step instructions at her— willing her with every fiber of my being to follow them—until finally she hits SEND and raises the phone to her ear. As soon as she does, she continues walking, as though pulled by an invisible string. She says nothing and I measure the remaining steps with my eyes, hoping *someone* will answer before it's too late.

Her head clicks up in an unnatural motion and she says, "Hi, Dad, I . . . I'm . . ." She pauses and her whole face crumples in confusion. "I don't know what I—"

And then he's there. I manage to shove Clara very slightly out of the way so the first blow that was supposed to be straight to the head wings her shoulder instead. She lets out a piercing scream of agony, and guilt shatters me from the inside out. It would have been so easy to divert her. To *save* her.

But I can't think about that now. I've got to keep her alive until the cops come. That scream was so loud surely her dad is calling 911 right now. I shove her around as fast as I can, though even colossal effort on my part leads only to tiny changes in Clara's movements. Her screams continue as she gets hit over and over—her arms, her legs—but I'm managing to protect her head.

Until the killer gets smart and takes out both legs with one low swoop I can't block.

He stands over her and while I can't see his face, I know from the sick, low chuckle that emanates from his throat that he must be grinning.

No! I agonize as I watch him raise his bat to deliver what will surely be the deadly blow. *I can't have done all of this for nothing.*

But I can't do anything. Smith said I can't affect the world physically.

Even so, as the bat comes down, I throw myself over Clara's crumpled, sobbing body, and raise my hand to block the blow.

It slams into my arm with a force that jars my shoulder and radiates all the way to my spine, the pain exploding within me.

He was wrong, I realize in wonder as the killer pauses to look down at his bat in confusion. *Smith was wrong! I can save her!* I cover Clara's body and absorb the next hard blow as well, a scream tearing itself from my throat as pain like nothing I've ever felt before spreads across my back from the savage strike.

Two more blows across my back, and then the scene is wavering. It's too much. I'm losing the mental strength to stay in it. Once more the bat strikes me, at the back of the head this time, and in the last moments before I lose consciousness I look up and see a dark figure in a familiar peacoat running toward me.

Smith, I realize. *He's coming to save me. No, to save* her.

And as the vision fades, I hear the most beautiful sound in the entire world.

Sirens.

TWENTY-TWO

I come to with a whimper in my own bedroom. Everything hurts.

Wait. That's not quite right. It's a weird kind of pain that's slowly receding like the waves on a shoreline. I'm lying on my floor and my face is wet with tears, but I'm here. I'm out of the vision.

Was I kicked out because I lost consciousness or because I couldn't hold on any longer? I'm not actually sure which one came first.

A deep ache throbs in the arm that took the brunt of that first hard blow and I move it gingerly. In my vision, I was sure the unforgiving bat had shattered the bone, but it's whole and straight and doesn't hurt as I move it this way and that.

The rest of my aches are slowly fading too. Like phantom pain. "It was all in my head," I whisper in wonder. I've never, ever felt anything like that and I was sure I was going to die with Clara.

But I didn't. I may have saved her. I'm not sure how much good it did though. I was right there with her and I didn't see a single distinguishing characteristic in the killer.

But the sirens. The sirens were coming.

I curl up and pull my knees to my chest, trying to process everything that happened. I blocked his bat. And the killer knew it! I remember so clearly the way he paused, everything in his posture indicating surprise, when the blow he aimed at her head connected with *something*, but it wasn't her.

I affected the physical world. That means that next time I can rip his mask off. It's possible I could even hold him until the police arrive. Maybe call in an anonymous tip to make sure they come.

This changes *everything*.

The fact is they might catch the bastard tonight. But if they don't—if he slips away—then I can end it *next time*. I glance up at the clock. There's probably an hour before Clara leaves her house. Part of me wants to go hide and see the vision play out—but I didn't see myself there. I can't risk changing even the tiniest detail. Better stay here.

Wait, I think, searching my fuzzy memory. *I did see someone else.*

"I saw Smith," I whisper aloud.

I chuckle and shake my head. He *said* he trusted me

to do it on my own, but of course he wouldn't be able to just let it happen. He's too much of a control freak. I should have known he'd go check on me.

Even if he doesn't know it yet.

Amused at knowing something he doesn't, I grab my phone and call his number. "It's done," I whisper when he answers.

"Tell me *exactly* what happens," Smith says. "From the beginning."

"It was weird," I say, still whispering. "I followed Clara back all the way to her house and there was seriously *no* reason for her to have left. She was sitting on the couch reading and then she got up and walked out the door. It was like . . ." I pause, hating the comparison. "It was kind of like what *we've* been doing. Like someone was talking to her in her head and telling her to go, and then she did. A couple of times she even stopped and looked back and seemed really confused, but she kept going."

"Charlotte? Are you *sure* there are no other Oracles in Coldwater? Or anywhere *near* Coldwater?"

"There aren't. I asked my aunt a couple weeks ago. The Sisters of Delphi follow the bloodlines so closely, it's almost impossible for someone to be missed."

"What about your aunt?"

I snort. "Oh, please."

"It's not uncommon for Oracles to snap and go crazy after fighting their entire lives. Shelby's great-grandmother went totally insane when she was seventy, and eventually the Sisters . . . they put her down, for lack of a friendlier term. Because she was hurting people."

"That's not funny, Smith."

"No, it's not," he replies. "But what you described sounds like another Oracle steering someone from their second sight."

"I'm not saying there can't be another Oracle involved. I'm just saying it's not my aunt. Maybe there's someone off Delphi's radar. Or they're not from here. Did you ever think of that?"

"Where is your aunt?" Smith says softly.

I refuse to admit to him that she's not here. After all, if she *were* doing something with her own second sight—which is completely and utterly ludicrous—she could do it from her bedroom.

"I have more to tell you. Clara walked to the tunnel at the train yard and I got her to call her dad and he answered *right* before the killer attacked. It was perfect!"

"Excellent," Smith says. "Then what?"

"He hit her with a bat and I kept shoving her around, trying to avoid, like, death hits, I guess you could call them. But he was too strong and he got her feet out from under her and he lifted his bat to finish her off and I stopped him!"

"What do you mean, you 'stopped him'?"

"I put out my hand and the bat hit me instead. I affected him physically, Smith!"

"Did you save her?"

"Are you listening?" I press. "I did what you said I couldn't do. This changes everything!"

"Did you *save* her?"

"I . . . I don't know for sure. I think so," I say softly. "I took a lot of hits for her and then I heard sirens."

"You heard them?"

"Just before I blacked out. I'm pretty sure that's what pushed me out of the vision. I was lying on top of her and I'm hoping I helped block maybe another hit or two after I lost consciousness, but I—" Guilt floods through me. "I don't actually know."

"Did you see anything else?" Smith presses. "Anything else that could be helpful?"

I think about seeing him running into the scene. Should I tell him? Maybe I shouldn't. I don't want to make him change the future by deciding *not* to go and then ruining everything I worked for. "No, nothing else." I can practically hear his thoughts right now. *She's not sure she saved her—I'd better go watch just to be safe.* Truth is, there's a chance that Smith running in at the last moment *will* save her.

So I don't tell him. This one thing I will simply let play out.

"I know her," I say when the silence gets heavy. "She was in four of my classes last semester."

"Are you guys friends?" Smith asks, sounding confused as to why I'm telling him this.

"No, not really. But if I . . . if I weren't, you know, *me*, I think we would be. It's something I've thought a lot the last year or so, actually, since we keep having classes together. We like the same things, we're both advanced juniors, I think we'd get along really well."

"Was there a point to this?"

I hesitate, not sure I'm ready to voice something that's been bothering me since I first saw Clara's face in the vision. "I know *all* of these victims. Well, Bethany I barely knew, but other than that, all of them—even the ones we saved—have played a part in my life. And that's saying something since I don't have much of a life."

"Charlotte," Smith says, and his patronizing tone makes me clench my fists. "You attend a tiny high school. Of course you know everyone."

"It's not *that* small," I say defensively.

"I don't have time for crazy theories," Smith says, and I can hear the nerves in his voice. My role is finished; he's still deciding if he should play his. "We just have to wait and see," he finally says.

"Yep." I glance back up at my clock and see that it's only been three minutes. "It's going to be a long night of clock-watching," I say as much to myself as him.

"I guess we'll talk tomorrow."

"Okay," I say, pushing to my feet in the jumble of

bedding I totally messed up while revisiting my vision. "And Smith," I add just before hanging up. "It's cold out there tonight."

I pass the next few hours fighting the urge to go to the train station and watch, but even if I could get out of the house without anyone noticing, I'm terrified that any little change could erase what I did.

I briefly consider trying to break into Sierra's room, but she's already been gone for over an hour—I can't risk it. It's killing me to have the book ten feet away and completely inaccessible. But it can't help Clara now.

Besides, there's a decent chance they'll catch the murderer tonight and then I won't be so rushed for time. I'll be able to wait until she leaves her door unlocked again.

Finally I go sit in my mom's office. She's behind on work because of all of the drama, so she just gives me a smile and keeps on working.

I have a half-hour-long text-versation with Linden, but it feels shallow compared to spending time with him in person, and when I finally say good night to him, I'm no calmer than I was before.

I think about Clara. And Eddie and Jesse and Matthew and Nicole. I don't care what Smith says; I think it's weird that they're all people from my life. Bethany breaks the pattern . . . but ever since? It's weird. Who would know me well enough to know the people that mean something to me—or used to mean something to me? I had practically forgotten about half of them. But *someone* remembered. How crazy of a theory is it really?

At eight thirty I know the attack is over and I keep glancing at my mom as she watches a TV show, waiting for the news to break in and report *something*. I mean, if I did save Clara, it would be because the police came. And they would report that, right? When the front door opens, I'm so on edge I almost shriek, but it's just Sierra.

I look up at her and hate that I note the time and realize Sierra could easily have been at the train station. "Where were you?" I ask before I can stop myself. I just want to hear her answer. That's all. I'm not actually suspicious.

I'm *not*.

"Out," she says without elaborating. "I tell you," she says as she slips out of her coat, "it's cold out there tonight."

The exact same words I told Smith.

Coincidence? How could it be anything but? Unless I really think she's . . . what? *Spying* on me?

And yet I wonder.

I hate that Smith has planted this seed of doubt, but he's right about one thing: there does seem to be another Oracle involved who's compelling the victims to go meet the killer.

And didn't I just ask myself who might know me well enough to be aware of who was involved in my past?

The news finally hits about an hour later. I watch with a strange mixture of disappointment and anticipation as I hear that the killer got away—but only after a long chase during which he dropped his bat. The Feds are all over that and their spokesperson is talking about trace evidence from the scene and testing for DNA and stuff.

Where was Smith? Maybe he ended up not going after all. Maybe I sounded overly confident during our phone conversation and he changed his mind.

But that's not the part I'm most focused on. Clara's condition is critical. Judging by the doctor-speak I only partially understand, I suspect the killer got in one more good hit to the head after I "left." She's in surgery right now and I don't like the tone the spokes-person at the hospital uses when questioned about her chances of survival. He says only that it's "still too early to speculate."

Her parents aren't at the scene of course—they're with Clara at the hospital—but things went exactly like I figured they would. Her dad received a call, heard screaming, and called the cops. They were able to trace Clara's phone because it was still connected, and they arrived just after I lost consciousness.

Ten seconds too late.

They play a clip of her dad repeating over and over again that he has no idea why his daughter would leave the house. That he was there, just upstairs, and didn't hear her go out the door.

One more picture flashes on the screen of Clara's parents sobbing and holding each other for support, and my stomach is sick with guilt.

I could have saved her. Even if I couldn't have stopped her from leaving the house, I could have slowed her down enough that she wouldn't have made it to the tunnel.

Did I do the right thing? Or did I make it worse?

If the killer *had* been caught, I would have comforted myself with the old "the ends justify the means" thing. But in this case, did they? Will the evidence the killer left behind be enough?

And what if she dies?

I tremble a little as I remember the feel of those blows falling on me. Clara took more of them than I did. How long would it take me to recover if that had been my *physical* body? Even if she wakes up, she'll have the memory of that nightmarish experience to haunt her for the rest of her life.

I stare unseeingly at the television as the reporter rehashes everything all over again. It seemed much simpler when Smith and I came up with the plan. I figured Clara would get injured—like a broken bone or two. That she would be lauded as a hero even more than Nicole was. That would be worth it.

But now? I thought the worst-case scenario was death. Maybe it's not; maybe it's this.

For the first time since all of this started, I doubt everything Smith and I have done. I wonder how much we've screwed things up. I thought this was my purpose—my destiny.

Maybe it's just my downfall.

TWENTY-THREE

I'm a prisoner in my own house.

Even when my mom lets me go to the store with her—in broad daylight of course; minors have a town-wide curfew now—I'm not allowed to leave her sight. Everywhere I look I see cops. They've brought some kind of backup in from other towns in the vicinity and I'm sure every single officer hopes they're the one who catches the killer. Not simply for accolades, but because everyone truly wants to end this nightmare.

And that's what it is: a living nightmare.

Without Linden.

We text a lot, but I haven't done a ton of texting before and I'm just not good at it. I don't understand the shorthand, and Linden spends half our conversations explaining them. We talk. Generally once a day, and that's *better* . . . but it's not the same. I want to be able to feel his hands, his skin. To see his easy smile that makes all of my worries wash away. It's weird to miss someone who lives just a couple of miles away, who wants to come see you as much as you want to go see him.

It's been days since I had a vision. Even before all of this started, that was kind of a long time. Smith says it's because the killer has to be careful. Not only with the extra cops around, but because now the Feds have evidence on him.

I'm not sure why that should stop me from having visions of ordinary things. The lack of visions is a little disconcerting in the face of everything else.

"Maybe he'll just leave town," I suggest when Smith calls to check on me.

"I doubt it," Smith says. "He'll see this as a challenge."

Based on DNA from the bat that matches two tiny strands of hair from Clara's coat, the cops have confirmed that the killer is a man. I breathed a tiny sigh of relief when that happened and wanted to throw Smith's ridiculous insinuations about Sierra back in his face.

But the vacant look on Clara's face when she got up and left the house still haunts me. Because it looked like Jesse's face when I pushed him back to his house, and Nicole's face when she left to go to her friend's house. Just because a woman isn't the one wielding the weapon doesn't mean she can't be an accomplice.

I hate that I have to even consider it, but it's true.

It doesn't have to be Sierra. I refuse to believe it *is* Sierra, but somehow, there's got to be an Oracle involved.

Sierra hasn't left the house since that night. No opportunity to try to get another look at the book. For the last three nights, I've managed to get into the supernatural plane, but it's harder to focus when I'm sleeping deeply so I just chased images of Linden and sometimes got sidetracked watching other people. It's more like a combination of soap operas and Choose Your Own Adventure than a supernatural realm. I always try to catch a glimpse of the killer, but just like that first time, his face eludes me as though it has a mind of its own.

The door is still there. I haven't tried to reach it again. When I'm sleeping soundly, I don't seem to have the concentration to pursue one task for very long. But at least I can always get to the plane now—sleeping heavy or light. It's some kind of improvement.

Maybe I'll chase the door tonight. It bugs me. It feels like it doesn't belong there. But then, what the hell do I know? I've scoured the little bit of text I have for mention of a door, but there's nothing.

I'm lost in my thoughts, plodding beside my mom down the baking aisle and pushing the cart when I hear my name.

"Charlotte, hold up!"

I'm nearly bowled over by Linden pulling me into

a violent hug. I throw my arms around him. I'm so happy to see him. Face-to-face. Holding him chest to chest. Hearing his life-declaring heartbeat.

"I've missed you so much," he whispers in my ear, squeezing me until it hurts and I don't care. It feels so good to escape from everything into Linden's arms for a few seconds.

I hear my mom clear her throat, but I can't let go of Linden just yet. He represents more than soft kisses and skin-tingling touches. He's the embodiment of everything our lives simply *aren't* anymore. And the hope that someday they can be normal again.

I finally manage to allow Linden to let go of me. I give him a beaming smile. "I am so, *so* happy to see you."

"Me too," he whispers, and squeezes my hand.

"Linden, this is my mom," I say, turning to gesture to her. "She's mostly responsible for the cinnamon rolls the other day." *The other lifetime.*

"Mrs. Westing," Linden says with a touch of formality, and I'm relieved that he doesn't either speak loudly to her or do something schmaltzy like lean down and get on her level like you might do to a small child. Mom hates that. He just holds out a hand. Yet more reasons to adore him.

"It's nice to finally meet you, Linden," she says, and the smile that hovers around her mouth tells me that she approves of the person Linden has grown into.

Much more dreamy than the twelve-year-old I used to point out during school music programs when we were in junior high.

"I know this is kind of sudden," Linden says, still addressing my mom, "but my parents hired me a personal security guard." He pauses to scratch the back of his neck like he's embarrassed and then gestures to a guy in a plain blue uniform. I force myself to stifle a laugh because, truly, it *isn't* funny, but I understand why he's embarrassed. "And I wondered if you would mind if I . . . well, invited myself over. I was going to text later today anyway," he continues, "but running into you two is . . ." His face breaks out in a big, wide grin and he throws an arm around my shoulders. "It's more than lucky."

"That would be great," my mom says. "I hope you understand why I can't let Charlotte go to your house."

He nods. "I do. And it's okay." Then he gives me such a smoldering look that if it were possible to literally melt into a puddle, I would, right there in the middle of the grocery store. "On top of that," he says, breaking our eye contact to look at my mom again, "my guard guy will drive me to your house and then stay out front the whole time, so both you and Charlotte will be safer too."

"Win-win," my mom says cheerfully, but with a touch of melancholy that I know comes from having to even consider such a thing.

"Maybe tomorrow?" he says. "I know a great Italian place and I can bring takeout." He looks over at me again, one eyebrow raised. "And then a movie?"

"Sounds perfect," I say, feeling better than I have since Clara's attack. We hash out some times, and Linden says he'll leave us to our shopping. He hesitates for a second and his eyes dart to my mom, but before he pulls away he gives me a quick kiss right on the lips in front of everyone.

Awe. Some.

I'm completely unashamed as I turn and watch him walk all the way down the aisle until he disappears out of sight, seeming to take some of the daylight with him.

"Well, Charlotte," my mom says, and I turn back to her, having almost forgotten in the moment that she was there. She gives me a light punch on the arm. "You done good," she says with a sappy grin.

That's the night I reach the door.

I see it as soon as I step out onto the reflective floor. I start to sprint, but it seems to fall away from me even faster when I run.

So I stop and walk instead, keeping a steady pace. It's *changed*, I realize, as I draw near at that same odd two-steps-forward-one-step-back kind of thing. When I first saw it, it was a rough-hewn but solid door made from long, thick beams of heavy wood. Lately there've been windows. First one small window, then two. Now the door is filled with four long, thin panes of glass that cover nearly the entire surface.

I'm three feet away when I lean forward and make a grab for the doorknob.

Only to have the door retreat and widen the distance.

So I wait and walk, and soon I'm so close I almost can't *not* touch it. I don't stop walking, but I raise my hand and slowly bring it toward the doorknob. Only when my fingers are wrapped all the way around the knob do I finally let them close into a fist.

And the door stops, as though anchored to reality by contact with my hand.

One thing I know for sure; I am *not* letting go.

I turn the knob and it's locked. Should have figured.

But those windows. I step closer to the door and peer through the beveled-glass panes.

On the other side is a similarly domed room, but infinitely smaller than mine. Not to mention darker. There are a handful of scenes cast onto the ceiling, but I can't make out any details from here. A strange energy pulses right at the door—almost like vibrations from loud music—and I have no clue what it means.

I see a stirring of movement behind the slightly wavy glass.

Is someone in there? Somebody else on *my* supernatural plane? That doesn't make sense. But *someone* locked the door. I pound on the door's rough surface

218

and the movement retreats until I can't see it anymore.

"Hey!" I shout. This is *my* world; at the very least I should be able to boss the people in it around.

In an effort to get whoever's in there to come back, I raise both hands to pound even louder but as soon as my skin loses contact with the doorknob, the door slips away.

"Damn it!" I yell. I stand staring at the door, wondering if I can catch it in a shorter time if I start walking right now.

But before I can make a decision, the dome around me darkens. Not darkens—dims. Just enough to notice. There's one glowing square high above, and with no focus or effort on my part, it rolls down the spherical wall and comes nearer until it stands right in front of me, inviting me to enter.

"Linden," I breathe, and step into the scene, forgetting the door.

It's tomorrow, I think. Linden is walking into my house, a grin on his face, steaming take-out cartons in his arms, and lacy bits of snow in his hair. As my mom wheels up and offers to take something, I see myself slip my hand into his, twining our fingers. I look at those fingers, wishing I were living the scene, not just watching it. Wishing and wanting so hard that I start to feel warmth against my palm.

And then I look up into Linden's eyes as he squeezes my hand.

He leads the way into the kitchen, leaving me standing there with the chilly air blowing snowflakes into the foyer.

I'm *in* the scene. Living my own role. I lift a hesitant hand to push the door closed and am a little surprised when it moves. A smile curls across my face. The only thing better than a perfect date is getting to experience it *twice*. Without another thought, I throw myself fully into the scene, desperate to enjoy myself for once.

I can hardly believe this isn't real as I fork a buttery mouthful of Alfredo sauce into my mouth, bite into a crispy crust of bread, taste the bitter tinge of espresso in the tiramisu. There's nothing that *doesn't* feel real as the meal ends and the movie begins. Not that Linden or I see much of the movie. That's the beauty of a dream world. I feel the scene subtly shift to my whims.

Of course I pick the choice with the most kissing. What can it hurt? I know that tomorrow when we're actually at my house, on my couch, with my mother only a room away, I won't be bold enough to do all of the things my dream self did, but tonight I revel in it.

"It's my parents," Linden says when his phone chimes out a text message. "Time for Mr. Bodyguard to bring me home." He pulls me close and lays his lips against my neck. "I'd rather stay here." He kisses me again, long and lingering, before standing and pulling me to my feet.

"I'll walk you out to the car," I say, stretching.

"No," Linden says so quickly it startles me. "The guy will come to the door," he says.

I turn very solemn. "Are you afraid?" I ask, knowing I would never have the guts to ask something so personal in real life.

He's quiet for a second and I see the muscles on his face flex. It makes him look younger. "For you? Yes."

"For yourself?" I press.

"Sometimes," he says. He turns and runs his fingertips down the side of my face. "But I would risk a lot of danger to see you." He straightens and opens the door, leaving without a kiss. But his confession feels somehow even more intimate and a small hollow part of me mourns that it wasn't real.

As the door swings closed behind him, my eyes flutter and open to the sunlight filtering into my bedroom through my half-open blinds and I sigh in sheer content.

TWENTY-FOUR

Real life smacks me in the face as soon as I leave my bedroom. Sierra's door is closed but Mom's working in the office with her small television on. More about Clara. It's been days and the doctors still can't give a solid answer on whether or not she'll live to tomorrow, much less the next fifty years.

Her parents have managed to come out of her room and make brief statements and every station just plays the clips over and over. Thanking people for their support, a call to find the monster that did this to their daughter.

Am I that monster, at least partly?

I tried to protect her from as much of her attack as possible, but I know I could have done more.

But then, what would the cost have been? Another kill I wouldn't have gotten a vision of, like Eddie? And what if I had ignored the vision entirely? Clara would be *dead*. But I hate that I made that decision for her.

I'm not sure I can survive another day cooped up in this house with the television constantly reminding me of what I've done. What good is it to have power over the future when the tragedy is in the past? I wish I could just go back to bed and sleep the day away, but even I can only sleep so much.

I manage to pass the hours by playing my new *Harvest Moon* game, attempting to reread my favorite book, and taking one short nap. It's the first time in my life I *wish* I had homework. I'm considering working ahead in my trig book just to numb my brain.

Finally it's about time for Linden to arrive and I get nervous, hoping I haven't ruined things by already living a version of what tonight could have been. I chide myself for being silly—real life is always better than dreams; it's like books and movies. But even so, I pick different clothes from what I was wearing on the supernatural plane last night.

Just to prove that I can.

The weird sense of déjà vu doesn't bother me when Linden walks in with the exact food he had last night, and especially not when it's just as good in real life. My aunt joins us and I make those introductions.

That's a change too. It was just the three of us in my dream last night. I try not to read any meaning into that, but I can't help but wonder if she's watching me.

If somehow she was watching me last night.

I don't know how that would even be possible. But I'm starting to question every tiny thing.

Sierra sits silently at one end of the table while Linden keeps us all cheerful with new jokes and stories we haven't all heard multiple times. I'd never before considered that the life of three single people all trapped living together might be a little, well, boring, but after the light and energy that Linden has brought to our table tonight, I wonder what it will take to make the house not feel empty.

As soon as the food is gone, Sierra excuses herself with a murmur and a quick grin, and Mom pleads a backup of work. With a significant glance in my direction, she declares that she will retire to her office instead of joining us for the movie. With zero adult supervision, there's a chance that tonight's reality might come close to the excitement of last night's dream sequence.

Close. Surely I'm not *quite* as brave as I was last night in my own head.

We debate the merits of this movie or that, but the looks we exchange make me pretty sure neither of us is going to actually watch much of whatever show we pick. We settle on *The Princess Bride*—nothing like a classic—and proceed to get rather busy *not* watching the movie.

"I've missed you so much," Linden says, the tip of his nose running along the edge of my earlobe and sending a massive shiver of pleasure down my spine.

"You must be going crazy cooped up here all day, every day."

"Pretty much," I whisper back as steadily as I can. For probably the hundredth time, I marvel at how odd it is that the best and worst things that have ever happened in my life are happening simultaneously.

But tonight I push everything else aside and just let myself be with Linden. To love the feel of his hands as they explore my body and the whisper of his lips on my skin, in my hair, and of course, on my lips. Despite the supernatural life I live, and the isolation that I know lies in wait for me in the future, this experience is so fresh and new I feel like a little kid.

The movie is almost over and my nerves are thoroughly, though pleasantly, exhausted when a tinny chime peals through the den. Linden pulls out his phone and the screen illuminates his face in the darkness.

"It's my parents," Linden says. "Time for Mr. Bodyguard to bring me home." The alarm bells start to sound very softly in the back of my head as he nestles his lips against my neck. "I'd rather stay here." His lips find mine, but I can hardly respond as he kisses me. I mean, I knew the scene I was in last night was a *possible* future, and it's followed fairly closely tonight. But the word-for-word dialogue is a little disconcerting.

I laugh inwardly at my paranoia. It doesn't *have* to be that way. It was just a dream vision, and I don't have to play my part. So I try not to speak, to hold my mouth shut, but the words tumble out anyway. "I'll walk you out to the car."

Wait. No. This isn't right. I should still have a *choice.*

"No." Linden says, just like last night. "The guy will come to the door. I don't want you exposed to danger for even a second."

I look up into his face and again, I fight to hold my mouth closed. I don't *need* to ask him this. I don't *have* to. "Are you afraid?"

What's wrong with me?

The hesitation—the flexing of his facial muscles. They make me want to cry. "For you? Yes." Where do these words come from? Are they his and I simply heard them ahead of time last night, or did I *make* this happen?

"For yourself?"

"Sometimes," he says. And before his fingers make contact with my face, I'm already familiar with the feeling. "But I would risk a lot of danger to see you."

I stand in the doorway and watch his guard escort him out to the car. He pauses before he slips into his seat and I know he's waiting for me to close the front door. He won't leave until I do.

I made all of those choices last night. *I* decided which paths to follow. So is it my choice when I step back and close the door, or did I dictate my own future in my dreams last night?

The scenario *was* different. I wasn't a third party like I have been all the other times. I was playing myself in the dome. Does that change things?

And the way I got into the scene in the first place— the way it rolled down without me willing it to. Did I do that? Did someone else do that?

And if it was just me, was everything Linden said and did tonight a lie?

I trudge down the hallway, almost forgetting that my mom is still awake. She turns her chair around with a smile. "So?" she asks.

I have to smile for her. I have to make the edges of my mouth go up even though I feel like my world is crumbling to pieces in my hands. "I think I love him," I say, shocked at myself when the words come out. I wish I could take them back. What the hell will Mom think of that? Even though she's known about my "crush," she doesn't really understand the years of pining, of wanting, of knowing I would never have him. Only to get him after all.

And not know if it's real.

The Christmas party, I tell myself. That was before I'd figured out anything about my second sight. I couldn't have possibly made *that* happen.

Mom simply smiles at my declaration and says, "Are you kidding? I'm half in love with him myself."

I laugh, but inside I want to cry, especially when she takes my hand and squeezes it. "It's about time you had someone in your life. And lord knows we could all use a little happiness right now."

That may be true, but some of us deserve it more than others.

I'm turning to leave when my mom adds, "The doctors are saying that Clara's condition has moved to stable, but that if she doesn't wake up soon, she probably won't."

I back out of her office, slowly and silently, in case she hears me and decides to say something else. I can't handle any more tonight.

In my bedroom, I pull on stretchy yoga pants and an old, faded T-shirt and climb under my comforter. When I woke up this morning, I didn't think much about the fact that I had put myself actually into the scene with Linden while on the supernatural plane. Did that make a difference? Did I dictate my own future because I put myself in the scene? Or did I simply live out the one that was going to happen anyway?

But it was so exact! Sure, I was able to wear a different outfit, and Linden did tell us ahead of time that he would be bringing Italian food. And there were other differences. Most notably, Sierra joined us.

But that conversation. Not only was it word for word, I felt like I couldn't *not* say the words. It was like a strange compulsion. That was how Smith always described what we do in my visions.

There was an Oracle using her powers on me, somehow.

But was it someone else, or was it just me?

A tiny spark of an idea begins to shine inside my mind. If I can put myself in a dream scenario and make it come true, shouldn't I be able to put myself in a *real* vision? One I know is going to happen?

I don't think I can just *create* a scenario in my supernatural plane that has me revealing the murderer—even the dome only holds *possible* futures as of that moment. I don't think I can invent a future from nothing. But if I get a vision of the next murder and take the victim's place in it, I can bend the future to my will. Can't I?

I dig the pendant out from under my bed and loop it around my neck with the stone clutched in my fist. I have to practice putting myself into my dream scenarios tonight. Because if I can put myself into a *dream* vision, surely I can put myself into a foretelling vision. And *that* is central to my plan.

A plan that will only work if I can do the two things I think I can—the two things that Smith told me I *couldn't*: affect the physical world while in a foretelling, and change the future while dreaming on my supernatural plane.

Which raises the question—did Smith actually not know, or has he been lying the whole time?

TWENTY-FIVE

I awake the next morning from a dreamless sleep.

No, this is wrong, I think groggily as I try to shake the cobwebs from my thoughts. I should have gone to my second sight last night; I was wearing the necklace. *I needed to practice!*

My hands fly to the pendant—maybe it fell off. But no, it's still there. Around my neck. Why is it wet? I look down and a scream rips out of my throat.

I'm covered with blood. So much blood it's not a bright, garish red, but a deep maroon. It puddles in my lap, soaking onto my bed and spreading across the sheets. I struggle for air as my hand brushes something cold and my hands curl around the handle of a knife.

The blade is caked with blood that has already dried in crooked rivulets. Flinging the knife from me, I tumble off the bed and onto the floor where my right hand makes a perfect red handprint in the beige carpet.

"Charlotte! Are you okay?" I hear my mom's voice from down the hallway and Sierra's running footsteps.

I jump to my feet and lunge for the door, hoping to lock it before they can reach me, but my legs are tangled in my bedding and even as I stand, it trips me and I sprawl across the floor, spreading the blood even more. The door flies open, barely missing my head, and Mom and Sierra look down at me with wide eyes.

"I can explain!" I blurt, even though I know I can't.

They just stare at me. At the room. Until Mom finally asks, "Did you fall off your bed?" with a hint of laughter in her tone.

I'm rigidly still, wide-eyed in confusion, and then I chance a look down at myself.

The blood is gone.

I glance behind me at the bedding strewn all over the floor. Clean. *What just happened? I know I saw it. I felt the knife. It wasn't a dream—it wasn't a vision. What the hell is going on?*

"Yeah, I kinda did," I finally choke. The emotional roller coaster finally gets the better of me and tears of relief are streaming down my face. A maniacal giggle wants to escape my throat, but I know better than *that*. "Bad dream," I settle on.

"Oh, Charlotte," my mom says softly. "Of course you're having bad dreams." She leans down and pulls me to my knees and wraps her arms around me. She holds me for a long time as I try to stop hiccup-crying and pretend I'm upset for the reason she thinks I am.

I glance up and Sierra is still there. I squirm a little under her intense gaze.

"Charlotte?" my mom says in a hesitant voice, and my whole body feels instantly chilled. "I know you're already upset, but I should tell you before you see it; there's been another murder. A boy. They said he's a teen, but his name hasn't been released. I just . . . I think after a nightmare like this it's probably best you hear it from me rather than the news. Or even Linden."

"Linden!" I shriek.

"I took the liberty of calling his mother. It wasn't him."

I can't move. Can't breathe. "When?" I gasp.

"They think in the middle of the night. No one knows why he was out."

"How did he die?" The question terrifies me more than anything that has happened to me so far, but I have to ask.

"What do you mean, how?"

"What . . . what did the killer use? What kind of weapon?"

My mom strokes my hair. "Sweetie, I don't want you to be so upset. Maybe we should just turn off the news for the day and—"

"A knife," my aunt interrupts.

"Sierra!" my mother scolds.

"She asked the question; she deserves the answer,"

my aunt says evenly.

My mom's silence as well as the firm press of her fingers on my back tells me she doesn't agree, but it's too late to take the words back.

I'm numb. *A knife*. What's happening? Is this a different kind of vision? Or are my reality and my second sight blending? Maybe I've gone too far. Maybe I've messed with my abilities so much they're . . . malfunctioning?

I look back up at my aunt and my mom, the two women who make up most of my world, and feel so very alone. The filtered morning light illuminates them with murky brightness and I realize how early it is.

"I'm okay," I say. "Honestly, now that I've calmed down, I think I'd like to just go back to bed." I make myself smile, though I know it must look forced at best. "It's New Year's Eve. I don't want to fall asleep before midnight." *I don't want to fall asleep again ever.*

My mom looks at me funny, but nods, and turns her wheelchair down the hallway toward the kitchen. My aunt doesn't leave. After a glance at my mom—her *sister*, I often forget; the person she's been hiding her secrets from her entire life—she says, "A vision?"

I don't know what to say, so I nod. It *was* a vision, technically. It just wasn't the kind of vision she's referring to.

"You knew about the knife," she says, and it's not a

question. "Did the vision overwhelm you?"

"It was a different kind of vision," I burst out, needing to tell someone. Needing to tell *her*—the woman who has been my confidante for as long as I can remember. "There was no warning, no blacking out, just—seeing it!" I know she thinks I mean seeing the murder—not myself covered in blood—but I can't confess more than that.

I'm afraid to.

She stands looking at me with her lips pursed. Then her face softens and she says, "Everything, *everything*, gets harder in times of crisis." She lays her hand on my shoulder and squeezes. "You're not always going to win, but keep fighting."

"It's so hard," I whisper.

"I know—they've been battering me too."

"Really?" I don't know why I'm surprised; of course Sierra would be getting visions similar to mine. Oracles always get visions about the most relevant happenings of their community. And this is her home too.

But she's strong enough. Even if I were trying to fight the visions, I'm not. They beat me.

"It's so important to close your mind, Charlotte. Even though we don't use it, your second sight is vulnerable and more powerful than you could ever imagine."

My tears cease at her words and for a second I wonder if she'll continue.

But she just runs a hand across my forehead, tucking my hair behind my ear. "Be vigilant, Charlotte. Fight."

Then she leaves and I remain kneeling in the middle of my floor feeling like the world's biggest failure. I feel the tears build again, and for once, I do exactly what I said I was going to. I push my door shut, grab my bedding from the floor, pull it over my head, and slip back into a dreamless sleep.

I stare at Smith's name glowing on my phone's screen for a long time while I decide whether or not to answer his call. I don't like the niggling suspicions I have about him. That he lied to me about what I can and can't do on the supernatural plane and in my visions. He seems to know so much. How could he not have known what I can do there?

Either he lied, or he's not as knowledgeable as he pretends. Regardless, it makes me question him.

And I don't like the doubts he planted in my mind about my aunt.

I wish that I would have a vision about *him*.

Taking a deep breath, I decide to go with both bravery and honesty. I slide the bar to answer the phone and say, "I'm not actually convinced I want to talk to you."

Silence. I've shocked him.

"What is it that you think I've done?" he asks quietly.

"I'm not sure," I say in a whisper.

"I am so tired of justifying myself to you when I've only tried to help. Don't let this monster make you paranoid. You need to be able to think clearly."

"To do what?" I hiss. "Not only did I *not* have a vision of this latest murder, when I woke up, I had no memory of being on the supernatural plane at all. Even though I slept with the stone on. And then—" I cut off before I can say anything else. I don't want to tell him about the blood. About the knife. I don't want to tell anyone, but at that moment I especially don't want to tell *him*. "Smith," I say instead. "He's better than us. We can't do this anymore. We're hurting people."

"We're *saving* people!" he snaps. "Maybe you've forgotten about Jesse and Nicole, but I haven't. Can you really sit back and let people die?"

"They're dying anyway. Or worse—look at Clara. We did that!"

"What happened to Clara is awful; I'm not going to lie to you about that. But it's never going to stop if you don't help."

I don't know what to think. What to do. The hopes and plans I had last night seem a million miles past impossible right now. How am I supposed to catch a brilliant serial killer who might, somehow, have an Oracle on his side? I don't think I should even *dream* myself into my second sight anymore. I can't risk it. Someone is controlling me there. I'll have to find another way.

That reminds me. "Smith?" I say tentatively. I'm not sure I want to trust him, but I have no one else to ask. "Did you ever go to the supernatural plane with Shelby while she was sleeping?"

"No. She could only invite me into her visions when she was awake."

"But did she tell you about it?"

"Often."

"What did hers look like?"

He hesitates, then seems to realize this is a test—he gives, I give. "An eternal room with a glass floor," he says. "And an infinite dome overhead. A vast horizon holding every future in the world. I always wanted to go there."

"There . . . there's a door in mine."

"What do you mean?"

"At the very edge of my dome—of my floor, maybe—there's a door."

"One you can go through, like the scenarios you can step into?"

"No. I can't get through it. It's locked." I don't know why I'm so focused on this door, but both the text from *Repairing the Fractured Future* and Smith describe the supernatural plane the same way.

And neither of them mention a door.

It doesn't fit, and anything that doesn't fit is suspect in my mind.

He's silent for several long seconds. "Then it's probably a place you're not supposed to go and your mind is telling you that."

"Did Shelby have a door?"

"Shelby never saw a door."

I wait, letting a full minute go by as I try to sort through my thoughts. "What am I supposed to do?" I ask, desperation winning over my stubbornness.

"We wait for another vision and try again. It's all we've got."

"But what about the murder last night?"

"It's in the past, Charlotte, and you are a master of the future." Frustrated, I hang up without saying good-bye.

Master of the future, I think cynically as I stare at my phone. *Some master.*

I realize I'm still wearing the pendant and thank the universe that Sierra didn't notice. When I crouch down to put it back in its hiding place, my hand brushes something cold. I grab for it and pull back with a hiss when it bites into my skin. Putting my sliced finger in my mouth, I kneel beside the bed and reach more carefully this time.

It's the knife.

It's clean now, but it is definitely the same knife I flung away from me when I woke up covered in blood this morning.

What the hell was I doing last night?

TWENTY-SIX

I'm sitting at the kitchen table when the next vision overtakes me. Home has always been one of the most dangerous places for me to have a vision because my mom might see me. But since I've stopped fighting the foretellings, it's doubly risky because *Sierra* could catch me. And if Sierra knew I was just letting them come—especially now—there would be hell to pay.

At the very least. I briefly wonder what she might be able to do before I lay my head down like I'm exhausted and let the vision take me.

I'm so tired of standing in the snow first thing in my visions; it's ruined for me forever. It used to make me think of sledding and children playing and the holidays. Now I only remember how bright-red blood looks on its sparkling-white surface.

It's daytime. That confuses me. Maybe this will be a normal vision. But I shake that hope away. This one has the same nearly unbearable pressure inside my skull that I've almost gotten used to. It'll be violent—that's all I know for sure.

But in the middle of the day? I glance up at the sky and guesstimate that it can't be later than one or two in the afternoon. Who murders someone in broad daylight? In a town that's already on high alert?

Maybe I'm too late. Maybe for some cruel, sadistic reason, the universe only wants me to see the bodies *after* they're already dead. To show me how helpless I really am. I look to my right when I see a flutter of something black in my peripheral vision. A figure turning a corner on the newly shoveled sidewalk.

"Smith?" I whisper. But all I saw was a black coat. There are thousands of black coats in Coldwater. Still, I swear . . .

I take off running after him and am a little surprised when my vision lets me, with no added effort. Apparently that's where I'm supposed to go. My feet don't slide on the slick cement and I make good time, but when I fling myself around the corner, the sidewalk in front of me is empty.

I walk slowly and nothing moves. No one is out; no voices to be heard. It's like a modern, frozen ghost town.

But then, isn't that what Coldwater has become with four teenagers dead? What else could we be?

I keep trudging forward simply because that's what

my vision is telling me to do. I see movement again—brown this time. Not the same person. I hurry toward it anyway.

My footsteps echo on the bare sidewalk, and the girl in the brown coat turns as I draw near. And smiles at me.

My feet slow. *That's weird*. No one in my visions has ever been able to see me.

Except when I put myself in the scene with Linden.

But this isn't the supernatural plane. This is something else entirely.

"Hi, Charlotte. You couldn't take being pent up anymore either?"

Charisse, from choir. We sit next to each other even though I sing alto and she sings second soprano, because Mrs. Simkins said we're both strong enough singers to handle it. A compliment to each of us—we've been friendly ever since.

"I know I shouldn't be here," Charisse confides, "but aren't you going crazy?"

I nod. "Totally," I whisper, meaning it more than her question intends.

"I snuck out. My dad is away on business and my mom got called in to work last minute. She made me swear about a billion times on everything from my grandpa's dead soul to the baby Jesus that I would stay in the house and not answer the door to anyone." She turns and points to a house across the street. "I live over there and after she left, I couldn't help it," she finishes with a shrug.

She takes in a deep breath and spreads her arms wide. "It was worth it. Besides," she says after she pushes her hands into her pockets and starts walking again, "who's going to try to kill someone out in the open in the middle of the day?"

"Me," I say from just over her shoulder. I grab her hair and twist it back, exposing her throat. She's so shocked she doesn't make a sound until I've pulled the knife across her neck and then it's too late.

She's alive for another second or two when I drop her into the snow with blood pouring over her chest, and she stares up at me with eyes that ask so plainly, "Why?"

I jerk myself from my vision and I'm breathing so hard I feel like I've run miles and miles since I laid my head down on the table just a couple minutes ago. My sight is still black, but my feet are so cold it feels like I *actually* went walking in the snow. I shiver; my whole body is freezing.

My hand seems to have a memory all its own as it recalls the sensation of the knife so vividly it feels like I'm actually holding it. I blink and the sunlight finally invades my sight.

I shriek and jump back.

I'm outside. In my socks and a light hoodie.

And the knife is *in my hand*.

I instantly shove it under my sweatshirt and out of sight. My head whips around, searching for anyone who might be looking at me; anyone who witnessed . . . whatever just happened. "No," I whisper. "It's not possible. That's *not* what happens!"

But nearly every vision I've ever had has come true.

And why the hell am I outside? Worse, how am I going to get back in without Mom or Sierra noticing?

The back door. That's the one closest to the kitchen and farthest from Mom's office. It's my best shot as long as Mom hasn't decided to angry-cook again. I duck and jog to the back gate and let myself through. I slip in and pull the door closed behind me, but I hear Mom's humming making its way down the hall. My bowl of chili is still on the table and I slide across the linoleum to the table and slip into the chair just as she comes around the corner.

"Aren't you done yet?" she asks as I shove a huge— cold—spoonful into my mouth so I won't have to speak. But she doesn't actually seem all that interested as she reads an email printout while unwrapping a bagel. After toasting it for what feels like an eternity, she slowly wheels out of the kitchen and back to her office without giving me a second glance.

As soon as she's out of sight, I dump my chili in the garbage and hurry to my room. I turn on my heating pad and wrap my feet in it before pulling the knife out from under my hoodie.

"Nobody's dead yet," I whisper, staring at the sharp, shiny blade. But as an Oracle, it's hard to even consider that the future I just saw won't come true. I mean, it's not for sure, but that's where the future is headed. I'm already on the path to murder.

So which side of me is stronger? The Oracle, or the human? And how long until I find out?

Somehow, someone is taking control of my abilities and until I figure out who, and how, I can't use them.

What else am I supposed to do? There was no indication in my vision of when I'm supposed to kill Charisse. But she talked about being cooped up, which means that the killer is still at large.

Maybe that's my answer. If I can find the killer before Charisse's destined death, I can derail fate and stop everything. *Change* everything.

Completely freaked out, I stash the knife under my bed. It occurs to me that if I was able to sneak into our house so easily—in the middle of the day, no less—how hard would it be for a killer to slip in?

Or for Sierra to slip out in the middle of the night.

But they said the killer was a man.

Everything in my life has turned inside out.

I pull out my laptop and check out the stories on the newest murder. A knife, just like Sierra said. And they've released his name: Nathan Hawkins.

My heart sinks. I know him too. We were both in an experimental advanced track in eighth grade. There are about seven hundred kids in our school; after four murders and four *additional* potential victims in my visions, you'd think at least one of them would be a stranger to me.

But the most disturbing part is the FBI officer's statement a few paragraphs down:

> **There's something different about this killing. The killer seems to have hesitated; there are a number of shallow, nonfatal cuts as though he had not quite made up his mind to take this young boy's life.**

And the worst part—the part that chills me right to my bones:

> **There's a chance we may be looking at a copycat killer.**

I shudder, the spasm racking my entire body as I close my laptop, unable to read another word. *Is it possible I killed this guy? Is that why I don't remember last night? Why I woke with visions of blood all over me? And why was I outside after the vision with Charisse?* Doing things I can't remember is terrifying considering the current circumstances. *Could another Oracle make me murder someone? Without me even realizing it?*

The tiniest spark of hope lights in my mind. If an

Oracle could do that to me, maybe I could do it to the killer. *Make* him turn himself in.

Unless *I'm* the killer. The only killer.

No. Even if I'm involved, it can't just be me. I was with Linden when Eddie Franklin was killed.

Probably. Science has been known to be wrong.

"Charlotte?"

I almost shriek at the sudden sound of my mom knocking at my door.

"Can I come in?"

"Sure," I say, willing my heart rate to slow. It's just my mom. I look up and a wordless scream gets stuck in my throat. Her head is sitting nearly on her shoulders, her eyes unseeing, blood from her severed neck pouring down her chest, dripping off her chair.

"Charlotte, are you okay?"

I blink. The blood is gone. She's back to normal— whole and healthy—her eyes focused worriedly on me.

"You startled me, that's all," I say, but I can't hide the shakiness of my voice. I wonder if she can see that my entire body is trembling.

Her hand is resting on my doorknob as she studies me. "Charlotte, do we need to go out of town? Maybe we should go see your cousin Jennifer until school starts back up. This whole thing is really starting to affect you—not that I blame you," she adds with her hands palm out toward me, as though placating a

247

young child. "It's having an effect on me too."

I contemplate this silently. If I leave, I can't help catch the killer. But if I stay, I might *be* the killer. Am I trying to run from my fate? To change things that can't be changed? For all I know, we'll leave tomorrow, get as far as Henderson Park, the car will break down, and that's how I run into Charisse.

Sierra once told me that the future is like a stubborn, old man—he'll get what he wants even if he has to go to hell and back to make it happen. Look at the murders. Yes, we saved Jesse and Nicole—and you could argue that we saved Clara too—but Eddie and Nathan? I didn't even get visions of them. Would they still be dead if I had let the killer get Jesse and Nicole? Am I simply swapping one person's death for another?

For the first time, I realize I might not be changing *anything*. Not really. I've been operating on the idea that the future is fluid, but maybe some things are set in stone. Maybe if I'm supposed to pull that blade across Charisse's throat, one way or another, I have to. No matter how impossible it seems.

"I don't know," I finally say, unable to make a decision.

Mom purses her lips for a few seconds, then nods. "I'll call Will and Saundra and see what their plans are this next week and we'll go from there."

I nod weakly, feeling like a complete wimp for

giving up. As I close the door behind her, I've almost convinced myself that I'm doing the right thing when the familiar tingling starts in my temples and another vision overtakes me.

TWENTY-SEVEN

Dinner is a painful affair. Mom tries to smile and talks about the trip we're leaving for tomorrow as though it were a normal vacation instead of a desperate attempt to protect her daughter from the nightmare our small-town life has become. I can see in her eyes that she'd rather go immediately, but fleeing on New Year's Eve seems pretty extreme.

Plus I can't go. Not yet.

Because if I do, Michelle will die.

And even though she abandoned me last year, we were friends for a long time. Anyone else and I might continue to justify leaving rather than making things worse.

But not her.

I'm pretty sure it will be tonight. In the vision I got when my mom left my room, Michelle looks up at a dazzle of fireworks in the sky. It's not city fireworks—they've been canceled. But a lot of people around town will still celebrate for the same reason Linden's parents decided to hold their Christmas party: to show the killer we're not afraid.

Even though we are.

I didn't tell Smith. I didn't try to enter my vision and change things. If there's another Oracle involved, I'm going to have to do things the old-fashioned way. The risky way, but also the *human* way.

I spent the entire day in seclusion. I didn't even text Linden—although I will need to tell him we're leaving town. Assuming we still do after tonight. At eleven o'clock, I tell my mom I've decided I'd rather sleep my way into the New Year, and retreat to my bedroom. I lock the door and reach under my bed for the overcoat, hat, and scarf I stashed there earlier. I hesitate, and then grab the pendant as well. The stone is glowing a bright blood-red tonight and I try not to take that as an omen. I don't know what I expect to do with the necklace, but it makes me feel stronger somehow.

And I take the knife. That doesn't make me feel stronger at all, but I might need it. It's simply the truth.

I don't turn my bedroom light off—Mom knows I'm weird and sleep with it on. Ideally she won't try to check on me, but if she does, I'm going to have to hope that she'll decide I just want my privacy.

If not . . . I'll have to deal with that later. I can't think about it right now. I lace on my warmest boots and once I'm bundled up, I push my window open and crawl through it. Turns out it's way harder than movies would have you believe to climb out a window. Especially in a coat. But eventually I manage.

And immediately fall over in the snow.

Cursing under my breath, I brush myself off and carefully turn around to close the window, making sure it'll still open for me.

Ducking my head against the frigid wind, I start off toward a neighborhood only about half a mile from my house. I don't know exactly what time Michelle will be passing by and it's possible I already missed her. I stand huddled under a lamppost with my face buried in my scarf for almost an hour before I see her. I don't know why she's all dressed up, but as she approaches she's the epitome of an all-American girl in a green wool coat and bouncing sable curls. I fall into step with her as she passes by. I don't know what to say. "What are you doing?" I finally settle on.

Michelle doesn't react, doesn't startle, doesn't seem to have even heard.

"What are you doing?" I ask, sharper this time, yanking her arm to turn her to face me. "You shouldn't be out here. Alone, especially."

Her eyes are vacant for a few seconds and I grip her tighter.

Then with a few slow blinks, her eyes come into focus. She yanks away and snaps, "What the hell are you doing to me?"

"It's okay, I'm here to help," I say, putting my hands up to show her I mean no harm, even though what I want to do is grab her and make sure she doesn't bolt.

"Where am I?" she asks, and I can tell she's on the verge of melting down.

"You've been—" Somehow I don't think the term *mind control* is going to help right now. "Hypnotized," I decide on, "out of your house and I'm here to send you back home." I gently lay a hand on her arm but she jerks away.

"Get away from me. Freak," she adds. Even though I know the words are fueled mostly by panic, they stab my heart just like the knife I'm trying to hide from her.

"Fine," I say with a sigh. "I'm a freak, but you're the one out in the middle of the night with a serial killer on the loose, Michelle. *Why are you here?*"

She hesitates, unable to counter the blunt truth of my words. "I don't know," she says, and I can hear the edge in her voice. "I was . . . I was at home. Someone was coming to see me."

"You should go back. You're close. You just have to turn around and go down that street."

"Why are *you* here?" she says, and it's clearly an accusation.

"To save you," I say simply.

She stares and I can see fear and suspicion warring in her eyes. "Should I call the police?"

As tempting as it is to just say yes—to let the cops

swoop in and rescue us both—I already called them with just enough information to get them to the right place at the right time. I hope. Michelle calling now would screw everything up. "No. Please don't."

"If you say so," she says dubiously, but starts to turn, clearly anxious to be indoors. And away from her crazy ex-friend.

"Oh, just a sec," I say, a hand on her shoulder. I hesitate, and for a moment I want to renege—to take my whole plan back and just run home and burrow down under my blankets. But I can't. I have to do this. "Switch coats with me." I'm already slipping my arms out of mine.

"Why?" Michelle asks, clutching at her beautiful emerald-green coat—a Christmas present, I bet.

"Because I'm going to take your place," I say softly.

She stares hard at me for a long few seconds, but something in my face—maybe that years-old connection, I'm not sure—convinces her and she begins to unfasten her buttons.

We swap quickly.

She steps away, but doesn't leave—seems to be waiting for something.

"Listen, Michelle, I know we don't get along anymore, but I need you to not tell anyone about this. About what we just did. No one. Ever." I end with my voice hard as a rock.

She's quiet. I itch to leave, but I have to know what

she's going to say first. "There's something *wrong* with you," she says icily. Then she turns and walks away for a few steps before breaking into a run. She doesn't look back.

I wait until she's out of sight before taking her place on her route. I'd better hurry if I'm going to rendez-vous with the killer on time. I speed-walk until I'm a block away from the scene I saw in my vision. Then I force my stride to slow to the almost drone-like pace Michelle was using.

I swear my heartbeat is as loud as a bass drum as I approach the basketball court in the public park where I watched Michelle get slaughtered in my vision this afternoon.

Except that now *I'm* the girl in the green coat.

I continue walking, following the path I remember her taking, ready to jump out of my skin at any sound, any movement. Even so, I'm unprepared when an arm wraps around my neck and pulls me backward against a hard chest. I see the flash of steel before I can even suck in a complete breath to scream and I wonder why the hell I thought this was a good idea.

At least this means I won't kill Charisse, I think as the killer lifts my chin the same way I did in the vision with Charisse.

"Charlotte?"

My eyes fly open as the killer thrusts me from him. "Smith?" I have to force my voice to make a loud enough sound to be heard as everything I thought I knew shatters into a million pieces.

But even though my mind is screaming that I can't have been so deeply betrayed, the rational part of me recognizes the medium build, the average height, the sheer normalness that makes Smith blend in so smoothly, your eyes slide right past him. A human chameleon.

It's too late to deny, so Smith doesn't bother with pretenses and rips his mask off. His eyes burn like red-hot coals, searing me with his fury. "What did you do?" he spits at me.

"It's over," I say, rising very slowly to my feet. "The cops are on their way—they might be watching right now."

"You're lying," Smith says, but I hear the doubt in his voice.

"I called them before I left home."

"An anonymous tip? And you think they'll believe that?" he sneers, but his bitterness is laced with desperation.

"With four teenagers dead, the Feds in town, and the killer still at large, I think they are taking *every* tip seriously," I say, trying to sound more confident than I am.

He pauses, then focuses very hard on me. "And what are they going to do when all they find is a teenage girl wielding a knife with traces of blood on it, and a fake name of someone she swears exists?" he asks with a cruel smile, and I'm horrified to realize my hand is out of my pocket and gripping the knife, pointing it at Smith.

I try to put my arm down, to conceal the knife again, but I can't move. "How are you doing that?" I ask shakily. "You're not an Oracle."

"Oh no, Charlotte. I'm what Oracles dream of in the darkest of nights."

"What are you?" I whisper.

"They call me the Feeder," he says. "I live on the energy from your visions. The ones you don't fight. Do you have any idea how much stronger you've made me in the last three weeks?" He grins, an expression that makes my heart race. "No one can stop me now. Especially not you." He turns and begins to run.

"Stop!" I scream, but not with my mouth. I scream in my head, with the same kind of command I use in my second sight. I reach for him with the same hands that pull the drape away from my second sight. In an instinct I don't understand, I picture the future that's only seconds away—but is the *future*, nonetheless—and see Smith stopping, turning. Coming back.

He wears a pained grimace, but a few endless seconds later, it works. He returns to stand in front of me, his teeth clenched so tightly the muscles are standing out painfully on his jaw. "You can't keep this up for long," he says. "You have so much less control than I do."

"You don't want either of us to get caught," I say. "You'll sacrifice me if you have to, but you know I'm innocent. And they'll find that out too."

"Are you?" he asks, and his smile deepens as blades of terror slice through my heart. "If you're so innocent, then where were you last night?"

My control splinters. Smith takes advantage of the tiny lapse and turns to run again.

"No!" I can't let him get away, I *can't*! In that moment, I have no idea what I'm doing; there's no thought, only an impulse I don't recognize. I wrap my fingers around the pendant, and pull us both out of reality and into . . . somewhere else.

I lay stunned on the mirror floor, staring up at my dome. My supernatural plane.

And Smith is here with me.

He scrambles to his feet and starts running and it takes me only a second to realize he's heading for the *door* at the edge of my reflective floor. The one he claimed to have no knowledge of.

And another second to understand: he's been here before.

He sprints and for some reason the door doesn't recede for him—and as long as I'm on his tail, it doesn't for me either.

He's faster than I am—he reaches it first and for a second I wonder what he thinks he's going to do. It's locked. But he doesn't even hesitate as he grasps the doorknob, pulls it open, and disappears through it.

"No!" I scream, and dive for the door as it's closing.

I'm too late and I slam into the hard surface, but my fingers close around the doorknob, forcing the door to stay close to me.

It's locked.

Locked to *me*.

It's *Smith's* door. It's always been his. The depth of his lies makes me feel angry and stupid all at the same time. I grip the knob like my life depends on it—and I suspect it might—and realize it's changed again. Almost the entire door is a pane of glass, with only a thin wood frame around it. I can see clearly into it now, but the knob still won't turn.

I have to get in there. I have to find Smith and keep him from getting out of my second sight or he'll be able to control his physical body again and get away.

And leave me lying there, unseeing.

I stare through the beveled glass at the shadowed room that lies behind it and fume. This is *my* world and I most certainly did *not* invite Smith to even enter, much less make his own pocket within it. I need . . . I need . . .

A hammer. Something *like* a hammer.

I'm supposed to be able to control this world—why shouldn't I be able to summon one? I try to picture a hammer appearing in my hand, but that's too easy and somehow I knew it was. I try to think like an Oracle.

To reflect back on what I've learned during my nights here.

I consider the scene with Linden the first night I reached the door. The way it just appeared. It must have been Smith, trying to distract me from the door.

Well, if he created a future for me, then I can certainly create one for myself.

I look up at the dome and picture the very near future and a lighted scene starts rolling my way. It's going to be tricky—I need to step only halfway into the scene while still holding onto the doorknob—but I pull the near-future frame very close. It's not a full scene. It's simply me, standing in the darkness, holding not a hammer, exactly, more like a bat or one of those nightsticks cops always have on TV. It'll work. I put one foot into the scene, and like the night I took my own place in the scene with Linden, I will myself to be the person I'm seeing. And to not let go of the doorknob.

It takes several seconds for the future to reach me, but in a few moments, the stick is in my hand and I swing at the door with all my might.

The glass shatters with a crash that echoes through the entire eternal dome and I plunge into Smith's domain.

TWENTY-EIGHT

Everything is dark and small. It's like my supernatural plane in faded miniature—a lesser twin of my own world. I keep the bat clenched in my hand. I don't know where Smith is or what he's doing in this little alcove in my brain. I don't know anything. Even the few things I'd figured out about the supernatural plane are uncertain because of Smith's lies.

The air darkens even further and I feel my stomach twist as I peer up at the scenes around me. It's the murders. All of them. Even the ones I *didn't* see.

Bethany running from black-clad Smith. He loops an arm around her neck and pulls her against his chest. His knife flashes. Red.

Eddie, Smith standing over him, a short bat in his hand. He swings it above his head like an ax, bringing it down on Eddie's body with all his strength. Matthew, the back of his head exploding. Nathan . . .

Nathan!

I step toward his scene. There's a dark figure holding a knife, but I can't tell if it's Smith.

Or me.

I run forward, ready to fling myself into the scene, but just as I leap, the dome rolls and a dark chuckle emanates from the space surrounding me.

I trip and fall on a gravelly surface that's cold, but not snowy. The wind blows my bangs across my forehead as I get to my feet. I'm on the hill beside a freeway bridge overlooking a section of the road near my house. A sinking feeling engulfs my heart as I realize where I am.

I'm standing beside a truck—a light gray Chevy—and I know without looking that its license plate number is AYT 247. My breath comes in gasps as I peer into the driver's seat at the man I've never known and always hated.

He's not alone. There are two people.

Him.

And Smith.

I watch Smith point up the road and then slip quickly out of the passenger seat. As soon as the heavy truck door slams shut the truck takes off, spraying pebbles that sting against my skin.

I can't look.

I can't *not* look.

My breathing is ragged, as I watch the gray Chevy

slam into the white car, which holds my parents, Sierra, and six-year-old me, with a deafening crunch.

I saw this once before in a vision. When I was six. But that time the truck hit the hood of our car, swinging it around to where another vehicle rammed the door closest to Sierra. I watch now, my throat choking, as the gray truck plows into the passenger door, pushing the car around just enough for the passing vehicle to hit the driver's side door, pinning my parents in a veritable death trap and leaving Sierra and me almost unharmed.

Six-year-old me made the change—I delayed us over ten minutes by spilling juice all over my shirt. It *should* have been more than enough and I've always wondered why it wasn't.

It did matter. Couldn't have mattered. It was no accident—he was waiting for us.

I whirl back around to vision-Smith. "You did this!" I shriek, even though I know he can't hear me. He's not really here; he's just a phantom. A memory. I stand there, barely managing to remain upright. Everything I always thought I knew was wrong.

I didn't kill my father.

Smith did.

And my entire world tilts off-kilter.

"How could you?" I whisper.

He stands there, silently, out of sight of the crash scene, with a tiny smile of satisfaction on his lips. I want to strike him, to punch him in his smug mouth, and my hands are clenched into achingly tight fists when he turns, looks directly at me, and grins.

My two seconds of surprise give him the upper hand and by the time I lunge at him he's already moving away. I leap, but a second later I'm sinking through the ground and settling into another scene. I turn, looking for Smith, wondering where I am, but he's gone.

I try to walk forward but something holds me back. I look down at my arms and there are thick strands of black twine tied around them. My hands, my elbows, my feet, my knees. I try to brush them away, but they only tighten painfully until I let out an agonized groan and stop trying.

"That's better." Smith's voice again. But not from all around me like before; it's definitely from *above*. I look up and see a giant Smith's face, enormous fingers holding something. All of the strings are connected to it and it takes only seconds for me to realize that he's put me in a bizarre puppet/puppeteer scenario.

"This isn't real," I whisper in confusion. These strings, this weird setup, it's not actually true. It can't be. His dome is somehow different than mine. It shows the past. It shows physically impossible scenarios. I don't understand any of it.

But my hands are moving and now that I can see past the strings, I realize I'm at my house. I'm making coffee. My hands reach into my pocket and pull out a small, dark glass bottle. I add something to the drink and then wrap my hands around the steaming mug. The heat from the coffee seeps through the ceramic and burns my palms, but I can't let go. Tears sting my eyes from the excruciating pain, but the strings just guide my feet down the hallway to my aunt's room.

"Thought you could use a fresh cup," my mouth says against my will as I set the mug on my aunt's desk and am finally able to release my burning, throbbing fingers.

"Oh, thank you, Charlotte," Sierra says with a smile, and takes a sip.

The strings yank me backward and I fall on my butt, jarring my spine. But still, backward, backward, until the lighting changes and I'm in a new scene.

A grave site. I stand by my mom as she sobs. I don't want to look but the strings turn my head and I see Sierra's name on the stone. "No," I whisper. "I won't do it."

"You'll do whatever I want you to," Smith says from above.

I try to run. But I take only two steps before the strings pull me back again. I claw at the grass, my fingernails tearing against the stony soil, but still the strings drag me. My bathroom this time. The air is steamy and I see my mom's empty wheelchair sitting beside the deep tub. She's lying in the warm water with her eyes closed, a rose candle burning on the edge of the bathtub.

My hands are rising in front of me even as I try to push them down. I'm silent, despite the screams in my mind, and she doesn't even open her eyes until I've grabbed her head with both hands. She's too shocked to resist when I slam her skull against the handicap shower bar with all my might. Blood pours from her temple, but she fights me now.

I have too much of an advantage; I'm whole and on solid ground. My arms shove her beneath the surface and hold her there as she thrashes. I scream, I beg for this to end, but I can't even close my eyes as her body stills, gives one final twitch, and then relaxes.

"You can't make me do this!" I yell to Smith, and finally the words escape my mouth, rattling my teeth.

"I can make you do anything," Smith says, not in a victorious voice but simply stating a fact: like the sky is blue, and grass is green.

"No!" I grit my teeth and reach into the water that's turning red from my mother's blood. I have to rescue her!

Before I can touch her, the strings pull me away and suddenly I'm dangling from them, swinging violently back and forth. I look up as the tiled bathroom wall rushes toward me and I brace myself for the hard impact.

There is none. Smith swings me into another scene where together, we torture someone I don't recognize. Then time is passing quickly and scenarios flash by in more of a montage than individual snapshots. Soon it becomes clear that I'm rising in power and wealth. And influence. Everywhere people pander to me. I order; they obey. I see myself clutching the necklace as I change the future to my favor, gain influence, and rid myself of enemies.

But now, in the background, so nondescript that everyone's eyes pass over him, I see Smith. Within arm's length all the time as we kill, as we curry favor, as we trample those weaker, smaller, until I'm sitting behind a huge desk in an ornate office somewhere, signing documents.

The text is blurred—of course he wouldn't reveal his true intentions to me now. But I know whatever I'm signing can't be good. It must mean destruction, agony, death. Smith is standing by my elbow, silently, but now he steps forward, addresses me directly. "This is our future, Charlotte."

"It's not *my* future," I say through gritted teeth as my hand scrawls my signature across another paper. I don't fight it. I can't beat him physically. There has to be another way.

"These," I say, gesturing to the strings on my arms, "they aren't real. Everyone would see them. That," I say caustically, pointing at the giant Smith-face above our heads, "is obviously not real. Every vision in *my* dome has the possibility of actually happening. This is some twisted version of my plane, and I can tell the difference."

His lips tighten and I know I've said something right.

"These are your desires," I continue, rambling in what I hope is the right direction. "And . . . your memories," I add, remembering the scene of my dad's accident. *Non*-accident. Then I understand. "You don't have any actual Oracle power here. You can't affect the future in your dome. Only *I* can do that."

I expect another angry look, but he smiles. "You think you're so smart. So invincible. I control *you* now. I've been wrapping tiny strings around you for weeks—ever since you let me into your second sight. Every hour you spent using the necklace to come here strengthened my hold on you. Did you really think you were just practicing?"

Shame burns through me—that's exactly what I thought.

He circles me like a vulture as I hang, unable to move. "You say these strings aren't real, but they may as well be. We're bound so tightly, you can't resist me." A low chuckle escapes his throat. "And you have no one to blame but yourself. The very first time you let me into your mind, *you* made the door. And every time you use the necklace with my spell in it, the door gets bigger. My *world* gets bigger. And it's pulling your world in without any help from me at all. It's too late to stop me—you had your chance the first night you reached the door. But what did you do? You went and had a date with Lover Boy instead. And now the balance has tipped."

"No." But the word is quiet, a no of surrender. I hang limp from my strings and want to cry. *What have I done?*

But . . . I *brought* Smith here. And his world is so much smaller than mine. How can he have the power? It doesn't make any sense.

I brought him here with the *necklace*. He talks about the stone like it only helps *him*, but it's helped me too. It gave me the power to pull him onto my supernatural plane.

Against his will.

I still have the upper hand. Or, at least, I do with the focus stone. I feel it pulsing against my chest and know I must be right.

It's my only shot. I move my hand slowly, hoping he won't notice. It's hanging just inside my coat—between my shirt and my coat. I need to touch it, grab it.

"Why me?" I ask, keeping the resignation in my voice. Anything to keep his attention away from my hand.

He chuckles and the sound frightens me so much

I almost forget about reaching for the necklace. "Because, Miss Charlotte, you are my perfect revenge. You will be everything Shelby wasn't." He draws in a deep breath like he's smelling a delicious scent and I don't understand again. "Those tiny visions you couldn't fight—I fed off of them for many years. But just barely. Now I feast like a king."

"What happened to her? What happened to Shelby?" I fling the words at him desperately. He cares about Shelby—I know he does. And the more emotional he is, the better.

His face snaps somber and I feel a little thrill of victory. "I couldn't break her," he says, his voice quiet. "I couldn't make myself go all the way. I won't have that problem with you."

Straining against the twine tied on my arms, my fingers wrap around the stone and a surge of power runs through me. I picture the strings breaking and with a leap of faith, I throw myself forward, imagining myself strong and powerful. Stronger than *him*.

For a moment, the strings strain against me and I think I'm going to fail. Then, almost as one, they snap and I'm free.

Smith's eyes are wide as I tackle him. He puts out his hands to break his fall against a rounded wall, but when my weight crashes into him, we sink through it to somewhere else.

Voices shout around me and one of them sounds like Smith's, but I can feel him struggling beneath me and the sound is coming from somewhere to my right. Smith stills when a female shouts something I don't quite understand. I look up to see a younger Smith—his hair dark with no sign of gray—his arm outstretched toward a tall, slim girl maybe a little older than me with strawberry-blond hair that falls down her back in shining waves. I can't see her face, but I can tell there's . . . there's something wrong with her.

And then I realize her limbs are bent funny and she's walking toward Smith like she's trying not to. It's a sensation I understand all too well.

Young Smith's expression is weird too—like he's fighting *himself*. When she gets close enough, a scowl curls across his face and he draws his hand back and slaps her so hard that her head snaps to the side.

And I see her face.

Sierra.

Shelby. Sierra *is* Shelby.

You don't know how bad the visions can get, she told me when this whole thing began. *Not even you.*

I stand there immobilized by shock as a younger version of my aunt sobs, her shoulders shaking. Then in a show of strength she doesn't look capable of, she somehow wrenches free of his control and jumps on top of him. For a few seconds, fists and fingernails fly, but Smith throws her off and then he's above her. His hands clench around her neck. I scream as her body begins to twitch, her face purpling.

But just as I'm sure she's about to die, Smith's hands fall away. His body collapses and writhes, and a small trickle of blood trails from his ear as Sierra gags and coughs.

The scene fades and I'm shoved violently off of Smith and barely manage to keep my fingers clenched around the necklace. Smith stands and looks down at me and I hold out my fist with the silver chain trailing from it in front of me like a talisman.

"You think that's going to save you?" Smith says, and the fury in his eyes takes my breath away. I was *not* supposed to see that scene. I wasn't supposed to know his secret.

Her secret.

"I'm more powerful than you," I say, willing it to be true despite my trembling voice.

He grins and reaches out for my legs. I try to kick away but his hands are so strong and he pulls me across the floor to him. His nose is inches from mine and I'm frozen in fear as he says, "You think you're in control? Even your powers are not your own anymore." Then he reaches out two fingers, braces them against my forehead, and shoves me.

I fly across the room, through a wall, and expect to land in another scene—another grotesque dream of

Smith's—but there's only blackness. And I'm falling. A scream tears itself from me and I pinwheel my arms, trying to find something to grab on to.

But I just fall.

Fall.

Fall.

Until I hit the ground with a bone-splintering crunch.

TWENTY-NINE

Lights flash across my eyes as I blink them open slowly.

"She's alive!"

"Miss, miss, can you tell me your name?" A flash-light is shining in my eyes and a rubber-gloved finger lifts one eyelid and then the other before I can finally focus on the bright light.

What happened?

He pushed me out. Smith pushed me out of my own supernatural plane.

Or is it *his* now? That thought makes icy terror pump through my veins.

"I'm fine," I say, pushing the hands away. I can't stay here. I have to go to Sierra.

But what will I say?

"Miss, what is your name?"

"Charlotte," I say, pressing my body up to sitting. "Charlotte Westing."

"Please lie still," the guy with the flashlight says, trying to push me back down.

"I'm not hurt."

"You may not feel hurt now, but when the shock wears off you could be seriously injured," he insists, pushing harder.

"Do you think shoving me down is going to help?" I ask loudly, flinging his hands away from me. "I'm not hurt."

Then another voice. "Miss—"

"Charlotte," the EMT offers oh so helpfully to the cop that just walked up.

"Charlotte," the cop amends, "you've just survived an attack—I think you should stay put."

I open my mouth to tell them I wasn't attacked, but realize the humongous can of worms *that* would open and close my mouth again. *No memory,* that's what I'm going to have to say.

And I do. Over and over again. To every cop who comes within earshot. I don't know how I got here, I don't remember leaving my house, the last thing I *do* remember is lying in my own bed. I hear the press start to gather and I turn my face away, hoping beyond hope that the backs of all the cops have been able to block me from the cameras.

Smith isn't nearly so lucky. I'm not sure if he beat me out of the supernatural plane or not, but he's sitting in the snow, handcuffed, with two officers

275

pointing their guns at him.

Seeing Smith here in the physical world jolts me like a blow from an enormous hammer, shaking me from head to toe. He peers up and meets my eyes and I freeze. I feel like he should be looking at me with hatred, betrayal, anger at the very least. But he looks complacent. Almost like he's won. I have to turn my face away. Even being looked at by him feels like a thrust from a knife.

The knife!

Where is it? I don't have it. I don't *think* I have it. But where did I put it?

If they find the knife—my life is essentially over.

I try to look around the scene while the EMT takes my temperature, blood pressure, pulse, and do everything but pull out the little mallet to tap my knee. But I don't see it anywhere. I shiver on the tailgate of the ambulance and since the EMT seems to be done, I shrug back into my coat. Michelle's coat.

And feel an unfamiliar weight. I carefully pat an inner pocket to be sure.

There it is. Hidden. The things my unconscious self does. I can't suppress a shudder and it catches the EMT's attention.

"You okay?"

"I just want to go home," I mutter. "I'm fine, right?" He hesitates before admitting that he can't find anything wrong with me. I toss the pastel-blue

276

blanket aside and walk over to a cop before the EMT can stop me.

"Officer," I ask, tapping the shoulder of a man I think I recognize as an actual Coldwater cop. "Can you *please* take me home before the cameras find me? I need to tell my mom I'm okay."

And tell Sierra that I *know*.

"Yeah, we should do that," the officer says kindly, and I hope and pray I've found the right person to get me the hell out of here.

The cop checks with some of the other officers and they look at me askance until I bring out the words that always work on television. "I'm a minor," I say, trying to sound confident, "so I can't say anything else until I'm with my mom."

The younger officer doesn't try to disguise rolling his eyes and I can tell several of the other cops are thinking something along the lines of "smart-ass kid," but they know I'm right.

"I'll take her," a cop who looks close to retirement offers. "My cruiser's parked near the back." He gestures to another officer who joins him and they flank me on each side. I don't escape totally unscathed— the media are taking pictures of everything that even moves—but I think my face *may* have stayed blocked by the two cops and the windows of the cruiser are tinted pretty dark. I keep my head pointed down at my chest anyway.

Once we've pulled away from the crowd, I lean my head against the headrest and try to figure out what in the world I'm going to tell my mother.

I don't have long to find out. It's all of a four-minute drive from the park to my doorstep. "You can just drop me off," I attempt, but as I suspected, they don't buy that for even a second.

My mother's face is white when she opens the door to see me standing between two cops. The moment I see that terror in her eyes is the closest I get to regretting everything I've done.

Until I see Sierra too, her bathrobe hastily tied, hanging back with her arms crossed over her chest.

Anger and empathy fight to rise up inside me. I don't know what to feel.

But the most important fact at the moment is that Smith is behind bars—or will be shortly. I caught the Coldwater Killer. My mother's very temporary fears are a small price to pay for that. "I'm fine, Mom," I say before either cop can get a word out.

"More than fine," the older officer says, his tone downright jovial. "Your daughter survived an attack by the Coldwater Killer and helped us catch him in the process!" I can practically see him jamming his thumbs through his suspenders, he's so excited.

"Thank you, Lord," my mother says with her hand over her heart, even though it's clear she doesn't really understand.

"We'll leave you alone tonight, but you'll be seeing lots of us in the next few days. We'll need to get an official statement and I'm sure the Feds will want to talk to your daughter," he says.

"Thank you," my mom repeats, mostly automatically.

I slip past my mom's chair and into the house. After the door closes, my mother turns around. "Well," she says, and even in that single syllable, her voice is trembling.

I don't know what to say. Do I go with the same story I told the cops? I guess I'd better. I'm going to have to tell that story a lot.

"Whose coat are you wearing?"

Well, shit. "I don't know." It comes as easily as all the lies about my "condition" have. I guess I've gotten good at lying after so many years. Not really something I'm proud of.

"What do you mean you don't know?" my mom asks, clearly not buying it. I chance a glance at Sierra and she is staring at me calmly, her eyes glittering in alertness.

"All I know is that I went to my room to go to bed; I went to sleep, and when I woke up I was at a park surrounded by cops. That's *all* I know," I say, some of my self-loathing slipping out and making me sound angry.

My mom sighs and rubs her face with her hands. "I didn't even realize you were gone." I can hear the guilt in her voice and I want so badly to let her know that this isn't her fault in any way, shape, or form.

But I can't. Because the truth would hurt even more.

"Are you okay?"

"I'm fine. I'm not hurt."

All three of us are still and silent for a moment before my mom bursts into tears and wheels herself forward to throw her arms around me. I crouch down beside her chair. Guilt fills me, overflows, and soon I'm crying too. From remorse, yes, but also relief, betrayal, the adrenaline wearing off—a bit of everything.

I glance up and my wet eyes meet my aunt's.

She didn't buy my story. She gives me a look that tells me she'll be seeing me soon, and turns and walks away.

"It's late," Mom says, pulling back with a sniff and reddened eyes. "We can talk about things tomorrow— I'm just glad you're okay." She squeezes my hand. "Go to bed."

I nod, but can't muster up any words. Mom sees me all the way to my room and even goes so far as to watch me walk in so she can close the door behind me. I suspect she sits outside my door for a while, just listening. But that gives me a few more minutes to prepare for Sierra.

Sure enough, about fifteen minutes later, I hear a very soft knock and the door swings open far enough to allow Sierra to slip through. It closes and we stare at each other.

"Who does the green coat belong to, Charlotte?

And don't tell me you don't remember because we both know that's a lie." Sierra's never been one to bother with subtlety.

"Michelle," I say simply, not that I expect Sierra to actually remember who that is.

"She was supposed to die tonight, wasn't she?"

I nod and my eyes fill with tears again, not because I'm sad or scared, or even because Sierra makes me feel like an awkward little kid again, although she does. It's simply that even though everything has turned out okay, I know now that I screwed up royally. I went against everything I've been taught. I let a murderer into my head and he went on a killing spree. If I had fought every single vision—and ignored the ones that got through—fewer people would have died.

Even the fact that I've discovered Sierra's secret, my anger at her for not telling me, not *warning* me, can't overpower the fact that people in this town are dead because of me.

"You switched places with her, didn't you?"

I nod again and now tears are running down my face and I feel like I'm about two inches tall.

"And what did you expect to accomplish? Getting yourself killed?"

"I called the cops before I left," I burst out.

"And if they had arrived two minutes later? You'd have been dead. And then what?"

I bury my face in my hands and hear Sierra sigh, and

then feel the dip of her weight on the end of my bed. "Charlotte, I know how hard it is to do nothing. But you need to understand that what you did tonight was *wrong*, even though the killer was caught."

"Like you wouldn't have done the same thing when you were my age," I snap back.

"Why didn't you come to me when you were having problems?" she asks softly.

"Maybe because you've been lying to me my entire life!" I explode in a sharp whisper. "You expect me to be this perfect Oracle; you tell me I can do it, that I'm strong enough. But you did all sorts of things that you won't let me do."

Her face is absolutely still now, though her eyes dance with fear. "Who have you been talking to?" she whispers.

It's time. Now that Smith is behind bars, it's time to come clean. I'm surprised by how much I *want* to tell her, consequences be damned. I open my mouth, but the words get stuck in my throat. I suddenly *don't* want to tell her. Don't want her to know anything else about Smith.

No! That's not *what I want!* But something . . . something is telling my brain that it *is* what it wants. I'm so tired and can't even think straight anymore.

"Charlotte, this isn't funny. You have no idea what's at stake here." Sierra grabs my shoulders, gripping them so hard they hurt. I don't think she's even aware that she's doing it. "Has a man been talking to you? You have to tell me!"

"No," I say, the lie bursting from me against my own will. "I . . . I . . ." The half-truth forms without thought. "I went through your room while you were gone."

Her entire body slumps in relief. "My stupid journals," she says under her breath. She shakes her head back and forth a few times, then sits up straight. "We can discuss this tomorrow," she says, her voice weak. "After we've both gotten a little sleep."

I'm silent, even though I'm desperate to say *something*. I don't know why my mouth won't form the words. But I'm suddenly so tired. So very, very tired. My eyes are closing on their own.

"I'll see you in the morning," Sierra says, then slips out the door.

The moment before she disappears from view, a dark stain blooms on her back and maroon-dark blood starts trickling down between her shoulder blades, staining her pink shirt. With a gasp I throw the covers back and run to the door and pull it open.

But all I see is my aunt's back—whole and unscathed—traversing the final few steps to her room where she closes the door behind her.

The sound of the lock sliding into place fills the entire silent hallway.

THIRTY

The Feds pound on our door at eight the next morning. It's utter hell as they ask the same questions over and over, in slightly different words, and all I can do is repeat again and again, "I don't remember anything."

They don't need me, I tell myself. *Don't need my testimony.* The forensic evidence will link Smith—whose real name I imagine I'll find out soon—to the crimes and one teenage girl's shaky testimony probably won't even be necessary. But I still hate lying.

It's noon before they leave us alone and Mom has sat in on every session, so she seems to be out of questions for me, too. Sierra hovers, but she's silent. I want to talk to her, but now she's the one avoiding me—stepping away whenever I try to approach her. Finally she just leaves the house entirely.

Tonight. I'll tell her tonight. I'll try. I must have just been too scared last night. Too tired. Too keyed up. Tonight we'll talk. For sure.

We obviously had to cancel our travel plans so I have yet another endless afternoon stretching out before me. I'm contemplating going back to bed, crying myself to sleep, and taking a long nap, when my phone pings and my heart races to see a text from Linden.

Think your mom will let you come over now?

He's my hero.

But what will I tell him? Part of me—the biggest part—doesn't care. I just want to be with him. I'll figure it out later.

It takes a bit of pleading to convince her, but finally my mom decides I deserve a few hours out . . . as long as I'm back before the sun even *thinks* about setting. Apparently it will take some time for the paranoia to wear off.

I stop in the front entryway and my stomach sinks when I realize Michelle still has my coat. And the only one I have is hers. But the need to see Linden overcomes any sense of guilt or hesitation and I dig the beautiful coat out from under my bed where I hid it last night and head out the door. It feels strange to be free again. To go somewhere, anywhere, without an adult hovering. I did this; I made it happen.

I'm not far from my house when I feel the tingling start in my temples. Instinct kicks in and I pull over to the side of the road. But in the mere ten seconds I have, I sit paralyzed by indecision. Do I go back to how my life used to be? Fight the vision? Follow my aunt's counsel? The Sisters' rules?

When the pressure rises in my head and makes me want to scream in sudden pain, I know I don't have a choice. Every murder vision I've had has seemed stronger than the last, but this one is so intense I can scarcely breathe; it's exponentially stronger and all I can do is let it overwhelm me. Shatter through my body. The last sensation I have of the physical world is feeling myself slump forward over the steering wheel. Then blackness.

I hear laughter before I see anything, but once the world finally brightens, I'm surprised to discover it's coming from *me*. Like the vision with Charisse, I'm not seeing the vision, I *am* the vision. I feel everything to a degree that's one step beyond real life; the snow is ultra white, the crisp air extra cold, and the hand in mine soft and warm beyond anything I've ever actually felt.

Linden. I'm walking with Linden through the snow and we're laughing. I look down at our twined fingers and realize I'm wearing the green coat. Weird. Maybe Michelle won't want it back.

I turn my attention back to Linden and the

conversation fades in like someone turning the volume up on a television. It's nothing exciting; we discuss school, which is starting back up soon. We both grow somber as we talk about the classmates who'll be missing. But there's nothing out of the ordinary and I can't figure out why a vision of a casual conversation like this would create such a fever-pitch pressure in my head. And then Linden turns to me and takes both of my hands in his.

"I can face it with you," he says, and his eyes are so serious, so intent, I squeeze his hands as hard as I can. "It *is* hard. I think it's going to be hard for a long time." He leans down slightly, and rests his forehead against mine. "But you make me feel strong and I don't know what I would be doing right now without you." He laughs, the sound colored with self-deprecation. "I'd probably be scared and holed up in my room, to be honest. Instead, I'm here, in the beautiful snow, with a beautiful girl, and despite everything, I'm okay. And I'm so grateful."

Then he lifts his hand to my face where he tips my chin up toward him and kisses me. I lean into the kiss and pull him closer.

Closer.

There.

I jam the knife into his stomach and Linden chokes in pain and pulls away just in time for me to raise the already bloody blade and slash it across his throat.

Blood pours down his chest and his wide, blue eyes meet mine as he staggers backward and falls into the snow.

It's mere seconds before his pulse stops and his eyes grow sightless.

I open my mouth to scream but the vision is fading, pulling me back into the physical world where the guttural sound I'm making fills the car. This is worse than the vision with Charisse—so much worse. I can't kill Linden—*why the hell would I kill Linden?!*

I don't understand why this is happening. I know that Smith had some kind of hold on his victims, but there's no way he could do anything like *this*. Not to me. Not without access to my supernatural plane. Right?

But he got in last night. I start to shiver at the possibility that he could access my plane on his own. From a cell.

Dear God.

I sit parked on the side of the road for ten minutes with the heater blasting warm air at me before my body stops shaking. I can't go to Linden's house. I'm not sure I can ever speak to Linden again, even though the thought makes me want to sob. I just can't risk that horrific vision coming true.

Sierra can talk about right and wrong all she wants, but I will *fight* this vision with every shred of will I have for the rest of my life. I would rather turn the knife on myself than kill someone I love. I remember the feeling of poisoning Sierra, of bashing Mom's head against the bar. *Never again. Never. Again.*

I reach into my pocket to pull out my phone to text Linden and my hand curls around something else— something cold and hard, and I know what it is even before I pull it all the way out of the deep pocket to check. The knife. The green coat. I wanted to throw the knife in a Dumpster last night, but there wasn't an opportunity—not without letting either the cops, or my mom, or Sierra see it.

I'll do it now and then go right home. I'll tell Linden I'm sick until I can figure out something else. I lay the knife on the seat beside me, shift into DRIVE, and pull out, thinking I'll go to a corner a few blocks away where there are several fast-food places that all share a parking lot. Surely there will be a couple of Dumpsters in the back.

I reach the intersection where I'm supposed to turn right and my hands start steering the wheel left. "The hell?" I whisper under my breath as I try to force my hands to correct the mistake.

But they stay steady on the wheel.

With a flash of horror I realize where I'm going. I'm going to Linden's house.

"No!" I yell at my hands. "No, no, no!" But they don't stop, don't release their hold on the wheel. My mind keeps repeating back the words that Smith spoke to me last night.

· You think you're in control? Even your powers are not your own anymore.

I beat him last night by getting him arrested—or at least I thought I did. But now I understand that smile he gave me. I won the fight, but Smith has every intention of winning this war.

I think about the way I couldn't confront my aunt last night, even though I wanted to. Even then, he was controlling me; I was too tired to consider it. He *made* me too tired to consider it.

I'm nearly hyperventilating as my hands steer me up to Linden's house and into his half–circle driveway. Now that I'm here, I stop trying to pull my hands off the wheel and start gripping them instead. Maybe I can stay here in the car. And never leave. Ever.

But my fingers are already loosening and my right hand is grabbing for the knife on the seat beside me. I can't stop myself as I tuck the blade into my pocket. Then I'm pushing the car door open and rising to my feet.

I don't even have to ring the doorbell; Linden is in the doorway waiting for me. I look up at him and stop cold as he stands there with blood pouring from the gaping gash in his neck just like in the vision.

Am I too late?

But I blink and the gruesome red is gone. Exactly like the weird visions of my mom and Sierra. Just . . . gone. Instead, my heart breaks at the *reality* of Linden. Tall and lanky, those perfect eyes, perfect hair, that smile that makes sparks ignite in my chest every time I see it. All of it seems so devastating today.

My puppet strings feel all too real as I'm dragged up the steps, and Linden—who doesn't notice anything's wrong—wraps me in his arms. I try to walk in the house but Linden stops me and I see his coat draped over his arm. "I know it's a little cold, but can we walk? I am so sick of being cooped up indoors."

"Of course," my lips say as my head screams, *No!* "I've been sick of it too."

In one fluid movement, he slips into his black coat and wraps my hand in his and we start walking down the newly snow-blown sidewalk.

"Pretty coat," he says, his eyes taking me in with an appreciation I would have adored in any other circumstances. Now it just makes me want to cry. "Did you get it for Christmas?"

Something like that. "Yes," I say brightly and flash him a winning smile, a cruel contrast with the way I feel inside. I know if I can't fight Smith in this scenario, I will *never* win against him again. It will be over for me.

But nothing, *nothing* is working. I don't even have the necklace with me—I didn't think I would have any use for it. I remember what Smith said when I asked if he was an Oracle: *I'm what Oracles dream of in the darkest of nights.*

We walk silently for several minutes. "I can't believe it's over," Linden says after a while, his words a puff that hangs in the air for a second.

It's never going to be over for me. I begin to weep on the inside.

"The news is saying he attacked a girl and she fought him off long enough for the cops to come," Linden says almost casually.

Well, that was *kind of* the way it happened.

"She totally fought him off. I wish . . . I wish . . . it doesn't matter." I hear the grief in his voice and it tears everything inside me in two. "You can't change the past. I'm just glad someone stopped him. She must have been very brave."

I can hear the faint echo of Smith chuckling in my head.

Don't do this, I plead.

It's what I do, an echoing voice replies.

I'll do anything.

Yes, you will.

Please.

Silence.

"School starts soon," Linden says. The conversation from my vision is beginning.

My mouth forms the responses I heard in my vision even as I try to clamp my teeth shut against them. I'm dismayed at how light and joyful my laugh sounds. How carefree.

Then comes the moment I've been dreading. My

muscles are aching from fighting the movements I'm forced to make, but still I throw everything I have into resisting Linden as he pulls me close. It's not working.

"I can face it with you," he says, and my eyes start to tear as I squeeze his hand tightly, trying to keep myself from grabbing the knife. "It *is* hard. I think it's going to be hard for a long time." Just like in my vision, he leans down and our foreheads touch. "But you make me feel strong and, I don't know what I would be doing right now without you."

He laughs, and my tears are coming in earnest now as I feel my right hand move to my pocket, grip the cold handle of the knife.

"I'd probably be scared and holed up in my room, to be honest. Instead, I'm here, in the beautiful snow, with a beautiful girl, and despite everything, I'm okay. And I'm so grateful."

I'm choking on my sobs now, but Linden doesn't seem to notice as I pull him closer, closer.

"No!" I manage to scream, but my hand still shoots out, stabbing the knife into his abdomen.

The thrust is off. I fought it enough that I can already see the cut is deep, but maybe not fatal. The vision isn't done with me though, and neither is Smith. My arm swings out in a wide arc, but between me fighting it, and Linden just lucid enough to duck, the blade misses him entirely. He's on his knees clutching at his side, staring at me in horror and confusion.

"Linden!" I cry, but my body is not my own. I circle around behind him, the blade of my knife already bloody, and I grab his hair and force his face to the sky. I reach my arm across his body and begin to pull back like a violinist on a bow, the knife sliding toward his bare throat.

"Charlotte, stop!"

THIRTY-ONE

My arm hesitates and it's the moment I need to grab a tiny sliver of control. I can't release Linden; I can't even move the knife from where it rests against his throat, but I can hold it still, though every muscle in my body is screaming in protest.

"Charlotte, you don't have to do this."

I almost lose my grip on that control when I see Sierra moving quickly toward me. She stops when she sees the knife against Linden's throat. I want to speak, but it's like trying to force your voice to work after having the wind knocked out of you. When the sound finally escapes, it's at a scream: "Sierra, help me!"

"Charlotte, listen. I know you think he's stronger than you, but it's a lie. It's his *best* lie. *He's* the parasite—he's feeding off of you. He'll never be as strong as you are. You have to cut him off and you have the power to do that."

"I can't," I say in that same yelling voice that seems to be the only tone I can speak in right now. "Look what he's made me do already."

Sierra's eyes dart to Linden. To his bloody shirt. "I suggest you don't move," she tells him. "This will be over soon."

Over soon. Over for him or for me? Or both?

My fingers press on the knife and I can't fight it as my arm starts to draw it across Linden's throat again. I hear him gasp—in fear or pain, I'm not sure—but it's a distant awareness.

Then I hear the *click.*

"I will kill her. You do this and I will *kill* her before I let you use her!"

I look up at my aunt and am terrified to see a gun pointed at my head. "Sierra?"

"I know you can hear me, Jason. You cannot win. Not today."

Jason. His real name. Not a lie. For some reason that allows the tiniest sparkle of confidence inside of me to begin to shine.

Sierra takes another step forward and peers into my eyes. "Look at my face. Don't think for a *second* that I won't do it. If Linden dies, she dies. And if she dies?" Then she chuckles; a dark sound so reminiscent of Smith that I shiver. "I was too strong for you, and so is she. There is no revenge here for you today." Sierra takes one more step forward. "If you try anything, I will sacrifice her to stop you."

"Charlotte," she says, softly now, "I understand this is hard, but you've got to jump onto your supernatural plane. He can't fight you on two fronts and he won't kill Linden as long as I have this gun on you."

I don't have the necklace. I'm not even sure how I jumped last night. "Can't. Fight. Knife," I barely manage to get out.

"Linden," Sierra says, turning her attention to him now, "When I tell you, push Charlotte's hand away with all your strength. Charlotte, get ready to jump."

I grit my teeth and nod, trying to gather focus. *What if I fail? Will Sierra kill me to save Linden?*

I hope so. I don't want to live if my life is going to be the hell I saw in Smith's world last night.

"Charlotte, when you get there, you have to find his world," Sierra says, pulling me back to her. "It'll be in there somewhere."

"I've been in his world," I choke out between clenched teeth.

I see a flash of fear in her eyes and I can tell that wasn't what she wanted to hear. But she recovers quickly. "Go to his world and destroy it. Smash it. Whatever you have to do. No matter how he tries to stop you. You have to destroy everything. Especially him. You have to banish him."

She looks at Linden. "Are you ready?" I notice she doesn't ask me. Because I'll never be ready for this.

I feel Linden nod very slightly against my arm.

Sierra says, "Now!" and Linden's large, strong hands wrap around my arm, still holding the knife to his throat. He pushes back an inch. Two inches. That's as far as he can force my arm away, but it's enough.

"Jump, Charlotte!" Sierra orders. "And hurry. He needs a doctor."

To save Linden, I think and hold on to the image of his face as I let my whole body relax and I reach for my supernatural plane—wanting it, willing it more than anything I've ever needed in my entire life.

It takes so much will and effort to make the leap that I stumble before I even reach it and a second later, I'm sprawled on the reflective floor. But my legs are hanging off an edge.

An edge that wasn't there before.

I glance back into an abyss of the same kind of black nothingness Smith threw me into last night and I scramble for a handhold on the sleek, slippery floor. I manage to hook a leg up over the edge and pull myself onto the mirrored floor that used to disorient me so badly.

I let myself look behind me for one instant. The blackness is deeper than my dome is tall and I can imagine it swallowing my entire supernatural plane.

I feel a tingle near my feet and then my toes are hanging over the edge again. I gasp and scramble to a safer spot and stare at the edge of my reflective floor.

It's slowly, very slowly, disintegrating. Falling into the blackness. The pit is literally eating my world. This is what Smith has done to me.

White-hot anger spreads through me. Now I realize how much of me exists in this world—how much this world *is* me—and the empty shell I'll be if Smith steals it. I get to my feet and stride forward, looking for the door.

It's more than a door now; it's a wide, massive gate that stands open, sucking my dome into it. And then the horrifying truth crashes over me—the gaping hole behind me isn't eating my dome; it's the void left from my world being sucked through the door into Smith's world. And the destruction seems to be gaining speed.

I look at the gate, and then at the darkness behind me and I realize where this is leading. Smith's world will be the endless, powerful one; mine will be small and dark, and surrounded by the eternal void. A tiny prison in my mind that will hold me captive as surely as steel bars.

But Sierra was right; for the moment, I'm stronger. My world is bigger, and I still maintain my Oracle powers. I can beat him. I just have to figure out *how*.

I start walking to the gate and though it tries to retreat, it doesn't have as much room as before, because my world has shrunk so much. I pause for a few moments, then, remembering that I can affect reality here, I look up at a scene above my head. I stare at it so hard my eyes start to ache as I picture a future where I'm fighting Smith—fighting and *winning*.

Destroy it, Sierra said. The scene rolls down and I see myself wielding a huge hammer, high over my head.

That, I think with a grim spark of humor. I step into the scene and walk over to myself. I take a deep breath and then step into my own shoes and wrap my hands around the enormous sledgehammer.

I lift it with an unnatural ease. I turn and look back out at my rapidly shrinking dome. "My world, my rules," I say before tightening my grip on the hammer and stepping out of the scene.

For three weeks, Smith has been trying to convince me of the powers I *didn't* have—lying to me about my potential, and underreporting his own. But as I step away from the scene, the hammer still clenched in my hand, I'm on fire with the one secret he desperately wanted to keep from me; I am truly the master of *my* world. Here—especially in my awakened state—I can do *anything*.

I begin walking toward the gate. But I don't just walk; I glare at it and pin it into place. It's not easy, but the gate stays where it is, allowing me to approach.

I walk up to the curled steel and raise my hammer. But before I can strike, a niggling doubt enters my mind. The door has been getting bigger ever since that first time I saw it. And my world has been shrinking ever more rapidly.

Especially since I broke the glass yesterday.

I lower the hammer. If I smash the gate, it'll allow Smith to drain my world even faster. I have to go in and destroy his world first.

A deep grumbling inside Smith's world tells me I'm right as I walk through the gate and, for good measure, close it behind me. Now I'm trapped in here until one of us wins.

His world is so much bigger than when I was here last, a mere twelve hours ago, and I'm immediately disheartened at the work before me. But it's not only Linden's life I'm fighting for—it's my own, and through me, millions of people whose futures Smith would be more than happy to change. To destroy.

I heft my hammer over my shoulder and swing it at the nearest scene and the surface cracks like a television screen. The image inside distorts, then blackens, and I move onto the next, and the next.

At one frame I raise my hammer, but I see my mother, *walking* down our hallway. I hesitate and Smith's voice is suddenly all around me. "It's not like when you were here last, Charlotte. These aren't simply my dreams and memories anymore. I have enough of your world, enough of your power, that these are all possible futures. Will you destroy this possibility for your mother? Remember, you're awake, and everything you do in this world today will actually affect the future."

I pause, staring at the sight of my mother walking and my hands tremble.

"I could help it happen," Smith's voice says. "Fund that kind of research with the fortune we're going to make. There's no need for us not to have a symbiotic relationship. I'm happy to compromise and negotiate."

"I begged you not to make me hurt Linden," I yell. "You call *that* compromise?" And with a chunk of my heart breaking to pieces, I swing my sledgehammer, the head plunging right through my mother's face. Every breath is painful as the image fades from sight.

"It's a shame," Smith's voice said. "In ten years that surgery might have been available."

I say nothing. *Lies,* I remind myself. *He's never told me anything but lies.*

The next screen features a figure in white, standing next to a tall man who can only be Linden. I hardly recognize myself in the woman beside him. His love has made me more beautiful than I ever thought I could be. Happier. Complete. I have to close my eyes as I bring the hammer down on this one.

Sierra smiling and happy. My mother and a new husband. Me at my favorite college. Scene after scene I smash until my face is so wet with tears I feel them sliding down my neck.

But it's not enough. I look up at Smith's dark dome. I'm stopping the flow of my world into his, but it would take me years to go through every scene he could concoct in here. This is nothing but damage control—I have to find Smith. I have to destroy *him*.

I remember the last time I was here. It may be his world, but just like he has limited control over mine, I have some control over his. Until one of us takes over, we both *share* my powers. I look up at the ceiling and focus on a new scene. A scene of Smith sitting in his prison cell. Only seconds in the future. The scene draws near and I raise my hammer again, but instead of smashing the scene, I step into it.

Smith sits with his head leaning against the cell wall and watches me approach with emotionless eyes. I *know* he's here on the supernatural plane, which means that his physical body in the jail cell is helpless. Can I affect his physical self from here?

If I can make him regain consciousness in his cell, his projected self will have to leave my second sight. My hammer is still poised above my head and, reminding myself that I am nothing more than a compulsion in the mortal world, I bring the hammer down, aiming for his skull.

A hand reaches out from behind me to push the hammer off course, and I feel a jolt of success as I turn and see his retreating form. Not his physical self—the one here in the supernatural plane. The part of him that jumped here. When I threatened his physical self,

I pulled him out of hiding and he's here in this scenario with me, somewhere. He can't leave unless he can get out of this scene.

And there's only one exit.

The background changes and I whirl around, trying to look in all directions at once. His jail cell is gone—and the image of his physical self with it. Now it's a decrepit old manor house with dozens of shadowy enclaves to hide in. Dusty mirrors to bounce light from and throw me off. There's even a light wind to keep the ragged bits of curtains blowing—hiding any movement from Smith. It's a perfect place for hide-and-seek.

He wants me to look for him.

So that must be the *wrong* answer.

I peer behind me—the exit isn't small exactly, but it's guardable. Like a little kid stalking the base in tag, I pace back and forth, my hammer upraised. "I know you're here!" I shout. "Why are you doing this?" I ask, hoping that I'll be able to home in on his location.

A laugh from my right, a window shattering on my left. "To break you. And you're so close," he adds with triumph in his voice. "Why do you think all the victims have been your friends? Not friends even—*potential* friends in your otherwise lonely, pathetic existence."

I refuse to let his words make me sad. I won't. I have to find him.

"Why end with the boy you've been in love with

since you were in grade school? To break your mind and your resistance until you're nothing more than my puppet. Once you let me into your head, I combed your past—found people you cared for, even if you didn't really know it. This is all about you, Charlotte. All of them died because of *you*."

It's a lie, it's a lie. Smith killed them. It's not my fault. "Then why start with Bethany?" I ask, and I'm pretty sure that, despite the echo, his voice is originating from over to my right.

"To get her out of Linden's way. Did you think he really liked you, Charlotte? Did you believe?"

My heart cracks in two and my arms feel weak, trembling against the weight of the huge sledgehammer. *I can't . . . I can't . . .*

"So stupid. Stupid little girl."

His words make something flare inside me. He's made a mistake. Now I'm *angry*.

"I saw you," I shout. "The night that Clara was attacked. I saw you in your dumb coat running toward us. How could there be two of you?"

"It wasn't the physical me," Smith says, and now I swear it's coming from the left. I turn subtly in that direction. "I was in your second sight. I snuck in your head and you didn't even know it. I watched you change the vision. But, I admit, you did better than I expected, so once you started to lose consciousness, I hurried in to warn myself to leave."

Of course he wasn't saving Clara—he was saving *himself.*

"Why now?"

He doesn't answer right away. The scene wavers and I realize I've found a weakness. I remember him saying that he fed off the energy from the visions I couldn't fight. "I was getting too good, wasn't I? It was longer and longer stretches between visions. You were getting weak." And the logic crashes over me like an ocean wave. "So you had to do something big enough that I wouldn't be able to fight the vision. It was the only way you could survive."

"I do what I have to, Charlotte. You weren't ready when I found you. You were too young. That's the mistake I made with Shelby. With Sierra."

"So you started killing people to *feed yourself,*" I say caustically.

His sigh is almost strangled. "I tried other things, but Sierra was a good instructor. I almost missed my perfect window. Old enough to have truly come into your abilities, but not yet sworn to the Sisters who might have warned you about me. About people like me."

"You need me. You've always needed me," I whisper.

He's silent again and I know I'm right. He's nothing without me.

But I have to get him talking again.

"Weren't you worried I'd have a vision about *you*? Figure out who you were?"

"Worried? You have no idea how difficult it was," he snaps, and his voice is less echoing now. He's losing the energy and concentration to pull his little parlor tricks. He's angry that he can't get out. And angry that, at least for the moment, I'm winning. "I wore that mask day and night for weeks! I couldn't even risk *thinking* about my killings without the godforsaken mask on. The only times I didn't wear it were when I was with you. Then, if you had a vision about me, you would just see us working together."

I step to my right again when I hear something topple over and break.

"I am *never* going to pretend again," he shouts. "I will never hide, or run, or starve. Not because of *her* and not because of you!"

Then, from the opposite side, he's sprinting toward the edge of the frame. I visualize the hammer in my hand morphing into a long hook. I nab his feet and he sprawls onto the floor. I jump on him in an instant.

His elbow smashes into my nose and pain explodes on my face. *This isn't my physical body,* I remind myself, remembering the paralyzing pain of Smith's blows the night I saved Clara. *I can take it. I am stronger than he ever let me believe,* I tell myself, trying not to surrender to the excruciating pain.

I tighten my arms around Smith's neck as his fingernails rake at my skin. He flings his head back, our skulls connecting and, for a second, I see stars and

307

loosen my grip. He darts away, gasping for breath and when he turns there's a gun in his hand and he fires.

Heat blossoms through my shoulder and I look down to see blood. My sight swims but the sound of a second shot jolts me into action. I roll and he misses through some feat of sheer luck. I charge into him, throwing my noninjured shoulder into his belly, and he brings the butt of the gun down on my back with a crack.

Once, twice, three times and I feel blood trickling from where my skin breaks under his pummeling. Every part of me hurts but when I hear the gun click and realize Smith is going to shoot again, I know I can't simply avoid his blows. He's going to *kill me* on this supernatural plane.

And the only way to save myself is to kill him first.

As soon as that conclusion gels in my head, I feel the long stick that's somehow still clenched in my fist turn into a knife.

A very familiar knife.

Without hesitating, I swing the blade at him, hacking at anything I can find. I'm waiting—bracing myself—for another bullet, but my knife connects with something harder than skin, and Smith lets out a gasp of pain. The clatter of the heavy gun on the floor is the sweetest sound I've heard all day.

I don't know how soon Smith can make another weapon. So I keep jabbing blindly at him, accidentally stabbing the knife into my own thigh at one point and forcing myself to ignore the sizzling pain.

At last, I tear myself free. Almost blinded by agony and anger, I jump on top of Smith as he stumbles and I grip the slick, bloody knife in both hands and bring it down to his chest where it sinks to the hilt. Yank it out, trying to block out the bone-chilling, sucking sound it makes. Plunge again. Yank, plunge, yank, plunge, ignore the tears falling like rain as my innocence is truly stripped away, and Smith stops writhing, then stills beneath me.

THIRTY-TWO

I blink and even though my physical eyes can vaguely see the bright blue sky, I remain somehow in my second sight. But not on the dome of my supernatural plane; I'm in what I would normally classify as a vision, except that I don't feel the pressure in my head, or the storm in my brain.

I'm in the same scene I was in with Smith a few minutes ago. But this one is real—it's Smith, sitting in jail in the physical world. There are no specific indications, I just *know*.

I look over and for a second, I expect him to jump up and attack me.

But he sits, slumped against the wall, his eyes unfocused, just like before. I'm confused for a moment until I see that blood is pooling out of his ears. Not like in the memory of him with Sierra—not the trickle he somehow managed to live through. It gushes. Somehow, their connection years ago wasn't as strong. They both survived.

Not today. He's dead. For real. He tied our minds so closely in my second sight that he literally could not exist without me. By cutting him out of my world on the supernatural plane, I severed his life force.

The words my aunt said to me as I held the knife to Linden's throat rush back: *He's feeding off of you. He'll never be as strong as you are. You have to cut him off.*

She *knew* this would happen. That he would actually die if I defeated him. That must be why she was so worried when she heard I'd been to his world—she knew the connection was stronger this time.

But she spared me the knowledge beforehand. If I had known—truly known—I don't think I could have done it.

The vision fades and my physical sight takes over again. The sky is so bright I cringe against it after the darkness of Smith's world.

"Oh, thank heaven," I hear Sierra whisper, and then I see her face right above mine. My fingers fly to my shoulder where Smith shot me, but just like after the attack on Clara, I'm whole.

"Linden," I croak. My eyes fly to where he's lying in a snowbank, the bloody knife beside him. Although there's a red mark on his neck it doesn't look like I actually cut the skin. But the blood from the wound on his side has soaked through his coat.

"We have to help him," I say, crawling over. I pull off my scarf and wad it up and press it against the gushing cut. "Linden," I say, as his head lolls to the side. I pull his face toward me, leaving bloody fingerprints on his cheek, and he opens his eyes slowly. "Just look at me, Linden. Sierra, what do we do?" I shout, not taking my eyes from his.

"The ambulance will be here any second," Sierra says quietly, her tone back to the calm timbre I'm used to. "I called them just before you came to. As soon as you dropped the knife," she adds, and guilt churns in my stomach. She protected me—even at the risk of Linden's life. "I think he'll be okay," Sierra says, as though reading my thoughts.

I hear the faint sound of a siren. "They're coming, Linden," I say, and his eyes open again. "They're almost here. Stay awake."

Less than a minute later, we're surrounded by blue-garbed EMTs. I step back, letting them work. "Are you okay?" one of the EMTs asks.

"What?" I reply, wondering why the hell he even cares about me.

"You're covered in blood—is it all from him or do you have an injury as well?"

I look down at myself. I *am* covered in blood. It seems particularly fitting that Linden's blood covers my hands.

If he dies, I'll be a murderer.

"I'm not hurt," I say, and the EMT looks at me funny. I don't understand why until I vaguely recognize him from last night. I said the same thing then, over and over. I wonder what he thinks of me.

And realize I don't care.

"Can I go with him?" I ask, starting to panic when the EMTs begin to close the ambulance doors. *What if I never see him again?*

"Yeah, let's do that and we'll clean you up on the way, just to make sure."

I'm stepping up into the ambulance when it occurs to me that I left the knife just lying there in the snow. I glance back, but the spot where I dropped it is empty. With footprints leading right to Sierra.

I look away as the doors slam shut, too guilty for any gratitude to fit in.

They take him into surgery immediately.

I feel like my entire word has been ripped to shreds. Smith is dead and because of that I will never know for sure whether or not I killed Nathan Hawkins. Smith took that secret with him. I'll always wonder, always feel that heavy weight.

But I won't be able to live with myself if I've killed Linden. It doesn't matter that I was under Smith's control—he picked the right victim. If Linden dies, I'll be broken.

Linden's parents come rushing in minutes after the doctor talks to me. I tell them what he said, but when they ask me what happened, all I can say is, "I don't know," as endless tears trickle down my face. Linden's mother squeezes my hand and whispers something soothing, but I don't deserve her comfort. I don't deserve to even be in the same room as her.

It's over an hour before the doctor comes out. When he says Linden's fine, I'm as near to fainting as I can ever remember. "No vital organs were hit," he says, "just some muscle walls. A fairly shallow cut. He'll have a brag-worthy scar to show the ladies," he adds as he winks at me. I want to claw his eyes out.

Linden's parents and I go to his room where we sit and wait for Linden to regain consciousness. Every second feels like an eternity as I sit there staring at his pale form.

Finally his eyes blink slowly, like they did out in the snow. We all jump up and surround his bed, his parents each reaching for a hand. I feel like a traitor; I shouldn't be here.

But I have to be. I have to *know*.

A nurse walks in with a grin and shoos us from his side. She pulls out a chart.

"Well," she says in much too chipper a tone for my taste, "do you know your name?"

"Linden Christiansen," he says, and though his voice

is a little hoarse, it's strong.

She asks him a few more questions, his birthday, how old he is, what grade he's in. Then she asks him what he remembers about today.

I'm standing near the head of his bed in the opposite direction of where he's facing—I'm not actually sure he knows I'm here. When he starts to speak, I shrink even farther back.

"My girlfriend came over." My heart gives a tiny leap at the word *girlfriend*, even though I know I'll never hear it again.

"What's your girlfriend's name?"

"Charlotte. Charlotte Westing. We went for a walk. We left the sidewalk and then—"

I suck in a breath and get ready for my world to turn upside down. For everyone to turn their eyes to me in accusation and hatred. Both of which I completely deserve.

"I guess I tripped and fell on some kind of wicked rock or something. I don't know. But it was an accident," he says, and his voice is solid, sure. I would never have believed he was lying.

"Of course it was. It must have been a really sharp rock. The doctors said the wound was narrow and shallow. Almost like a knife." She laughs wearily. "Hopefully our days of knives are over. With the Coldwater Killer behind bars, I tell you what, we are more than happy to be back to just accidents where everybody lives."

"Amen," Linden's mother says quietly.

My knees are so weak they're barely supporting my body. *Why did Linden lie for me?* And how long can we both keep up the pretense? Lies never work, not in the end. Even if they fulfill their purpose, there's always a price.

The nurse explains that since it's already evening, they'd like to keep him overnight for observation.

"Can we stay?" his mother asks.

"Certainly," the nurse says. "But I'm afraid Charlotte will have to go once visiting hours are over. She's not family."

Linden's head swings around. I was right. He didn't know I was here. His eyes flash emotions so fast I can't even begin to read them. I wait for him to speak, then wonder if the kind thing is to say something first. But I can't make my mouth obey and in the end, I simply duck my head and walk out of his room.

I'm ten steps beyond the door before I hear someone call my name. I don't want to stop. Don't want to explain any of this to anyone. But I finally turn when I realize it's not Linden's mom or the nurse.

It's Sierra.

She walks up to me tentatively, as though I'm a skittish animal who will bolt if she moves too fast. I stare at her, this woman who I've never quite understood, but who has more empathy for me than any other human being in the entire world. We stand there for several seconds, inches apart. Then she lifts her arms—a small movement really—and the barrier between us shatters. I throw myself into her arms and sob.

THIRTY-THREE

Once again, every channel is interrupted by newscasts as reporters stare unblinkingly into the camera and report the unexpected death of the Coldwater Killer. The man who is in no databases, who carried no ID. Who, before he died, refused to identify himself by any name but Smith. The cause of death is cited as a spontaneous massive brain hemorrhage.

He's dead.

I killed him.

I guess you could argue that it was self-defense; in the end, it truly was him or me, even if technically my heart would have kept beating. But in my nightmares last night—each time I managed to get to sleep at all—I saw nothing but myself slamming that knife into Smith, over and over. The feel of the handle growing slippery with his blood; the *clack* of the blade ricocheting off his ribs; his life ebbing out of him in spurts of dark maroon. I wonder how long it will be before I can sleep peacefully again.

It's nine in the morning, yet I feel like it's the middle of the night. I'm so tired, but I don't dare close my eyes.

Sierra has left me alone so far. I think she's waiting for me to come to her. To let it be my choice. But not yet. I'm too exhausted. I lay my head down on the table and soak in the cool feel of the wood surface.

My phone rings and every muscle in my body clenches in fear when I see it's Linden.

"Hi," I say, just loud enough for me to hear. I'm not even sure it was loud enough for *him* to hear.

"Hi, Charlotte."

The phone is silent for several long seconds until we both talk at the same time. "Listen, Linden—"

"I wondered if—"

We both laugh and it's like nails on a chalkboard, making everything worse. "Go ahead," I say, if nothing else, to end the faux laughter.

"I'm being released at noon and my parents left to go shower and get some stuff for me. They won't be back for an hour or two."

I know what's coming and I want to cry. I hoped I could get away with pretending things were normal between us for at least another day.

"I hoped maybe you could come see me before I go home."

"Hey," I say, poking my head into his hospital room. He looks completely normal—he's wearing a T-shirt that's too big for him, probably his dad's, and he managed to get his jeans back. He's sitting on the bed, half reclined, and he looks like he could be at his house. On his own bed.

My face flushes red at that thought and I hide it by turning and pushing the door closed behind me. I face him again, but keep my back against the door, not ready to take another step forward. Not yet.

Linden smiles and I blink in surprise. It's not his usual winning smile; he looks sad. I expected anger, accusation, dismissal even. But sadness? I'm not sure what to make of that.

"Come here," he says, and pats a spot on the bed beside him.

"Linden, I have to—"

"Please," he interrupts. "Me first. Before you thank me for something I don't deserve."

As far as I'm concerned, he deserves *everything*.

"I was getting up the guts to talk to you about this when we went on our walk yesterday and everything . . . went wrong."

Understatement of the century.

He shifts on the bed, sits up a bit more. "Yesterday, when they showed that Smith guy who killed everyone, I freaked out a little, because I recognized him. I think it was the beginning of December, I was walking down an aisle in the hardware store when he stopped me and handed me a quarter. He said I had dropped it. I didn't think much of it except that he was weird and insisted that I take the quarter I was pretty sure I hadn't dropped. And his hair—I remembered his gray hair because he didn't look old enough for his hair to be so gray. . . ."

I nod tentatively, remembering having the same first impression of him. Vaguely I remember that it was brown in the scene of him with young Sierra. I wonder if whatever she did to him that day turned it gray. I swallow hard and force my attention back to Linden.

"Honestly I wouldn't have thought about it again except that every morning, for reasons I didn't understand—or question at the time—I put that quarter in my pocket. Carried it around all day." He laces his fingers together, clenches them, pulls them apart. "And that's when I started talking to you at school."

I'm confused, not following his logic.

"Charlotte, I haven't told anyone this, but I . . . Bethany and I were going out. We hadn't said anything yet—it was only for about two weeks and we were kind of enjoying our little secret." He looks sheepishly down at his lap, clearly embarrassed. "But since we're being truthful, I'd liked her for ages. Like, years."

I nod; I know *exactly* how that feels.

"We were together the night she died."

I suck in a quick breath of surprise.

"Sort of," Linden clarifies. "We *were* together and then I just . . . I left her. I didn't know why. But I did. When I found out she was dead, it was like somebody ripped a hole in my chest and took out my heart. But after I started hanging out with you, the pain was more bearable. There were times I wouldn't think about Bethany for an hour or two. And then it was a whole day. I was numb," he finishes, and looks up at me guiltily. "But I only felt that way when I was with *you* and so I kept calling. And texting. I didn't mean to be an asshole—I really did think I was falling for you. But it wasn't even that exactly, it was more like—I don't know how to explain it."

"A compulsion?" I suggest, the devastating truth pouring down on me like a ton of rocks.

Did you think he really liked you, Charlotte? Did you believe?

"Yeah," he says with a nod. "Exactly. And after I saw a picture of Smith, I started to put it together. I know this is going to sound crazy, but I think somehow he was controlling me"—he meets my eyes and the intensity I see there frightens me all over again—"the same way he controlled you with that knife."

To get her out of Linden's way. My mouth is so dry my throat hurts and I can't speak. I sit there frozen with fear, the ache of reality hitting me in the stomach.

"I didn't know you had anything to do with it, of

course. I just thought it was me. And maybe that's how he got some of his other victims. But when you pulled out the knife, I could tell it wasn't *you*. When your aunt talked to him directly, I knew, I *knew* that he was controlling you too. Looking back, that must have been why I left Bethany that night. He made me."

I nod and when I blink, a single tear slides down my cheek. Linden leans forward and brushes it away with his thumb.

"That's why I lied," he said. "I couldn't make you suffer for something you didn't choose, when I've basically been completely fake with you for the last three weeks."

"I don't care that it was fake, Linden," I say with a shaky smile. "I loved every minute of it."

I expect my words to make him feel better, but he looks guiltily down at his hands. "There . . . there's more." He digs into his pocket, then holds his hand out to me. I open my palm and he drops a coin onto it.

A quarter with a crack halfway down the middle. I study it and squint at a shimmering core in the middle that I'm pretty sure doesn't belong in a normal quarter. "It's the one Smith gave you," I say, and it's not a question. I put my hand into my own pocket and my fist closes around the necklace. I pull it out and open my palm.

The stone on the silver chain has a small crack in it too. And the same kind of odd glittery metal in the

323

middle. I didn't notice it when I grabbed it and shoved it into my pocket this morning. Just in case.

Every time you use the necklace with my spell in it, the door gets bigger, Smith said. This is it—the spell he somehow put inside the focus stone. Binding us together. *Every hour you spent using the necklace to come here strengthened my hold on you.* Now I know how.

"His mind-control thing is gone. When I woke up from surgery yesterday, I was overwhelmed with grief for Beth," Linden says, and gives me that sad smile again. "That's when I knew for sure that I *had* been controlled. And that it was over. That you did something to break it. Not just for you, but for me too."

He takes a long, shaky breath. "I know it's been almost a month, but to me, it feels like Bethany *just* died." He swallows hard. "I know this is a totally shit thing of me to do after basically making out with you for the last week, but I'm not ready to date anyone. I need time to grieve for Beth. And . . ." He pauses and blinks rapidly several times. "And I don't know how long it's going to take," he says, finishing in a whisper.

"I understand." It's the truth. I understand more than he could ever know. More than he *will* ever know.

He rushes on. "I thought maybe in a few months— if I'm ready and if you're ready, maybe we could try being friends and then . . . then see where it goes."

For one tiny instant, I think I can say yes. But only one. "Linden," I say, and I lay my hand on his knee, rubbing my fingers slowly up his thigh for the last time ever. Because even if he did decide he was ready—even if he *did* think he wanted me for real—I would always wonder if there was a lingering influence from Smith. He would know that once, when we were sixteen, I tried to kill him. And I would always have to hide that his girlfriend—his real one—died for the sole reason that the monster hunting me wanted her out of the way.

In my mind, I see the screen from Smith's world where I'm a shimmering bride smiling up at a handsome, slightly older version of Linden. Opening my mouth and forcing the words out now is just as difficult as that hammer swing. "I think we've had our shot."

For the barest moment, I see relief slide over his face and I know I've done the right thing.

"Thank you for telling me," I say as I rise from the bed. "It means a lot." I shrug, and force a smile. "And thanks for not telling *them*," I say, tilting my head toward the door—the doctors, his parents, the world.

"It's our secret," he says.

I hesitate. "I didn't know Bethany, really," I choke out, "but if you liked her so much, she must have been wonderful."

"She was," he whispers.

"I'm sorry you lost her."

He nods, and then he looks up and meets my eyes

and there's another emotion there that I'm not sure I understand. "I'm glad I found you. Even if it was only for a little while."

"Me too."

And he doesn't know, as I turn and smile down at him before opening the door, that my heart is splintering into pieces. That even those splinters are breaking in half, leaving almost nothing of my heart to beat life into me.

THIRTY-FOUR

I linger outside my aunt's room.

I'm filled with such a strange mix of curiosity, excitement . . . and fear. I'm not sure what to think of the last few weeks. I can't help but feel like I did *some* things right. Smith was targeting people specifically to get to me, so now I know that if I hadn't started breaking the rules, more people would have died.

He'd have killed dozens to get to me if that's what it took. Even if just to feed himself.

But did more people die than needed to?

Did Nathan die unnecessarily?

I finally ramp up my courage enough to lift my fist and knock lightly. "Come in," Sierra says in the same calm voice she always uses. It used to bother me. To scare me even, because I always assumed I would end up just like her. But now it commands a degree of respect. I've realized I'll never be quite like my aunt.

And that's okay. But there are a lot of ways in which I *do* want to emulate her.

I close the door behind me—something I rarely do. But I'm not going to skim the surface and make excuses this time; we're going to hash this whole thing out. It's time.

I'm surprised to find her sitting on the love seat in front of the bay window, coffee cup in hand. It's where I usually sit when I'm in here.

"You were waiting for me," I say before I really think about it.

She nods. "Charlotte, today there's nothing more important than you." She pauses, staring down into her coffee. "I heard you went to see Linden."

I nod. Now that I'm here, my tongue feels heavy and awkward. "We broke up."

"Even after he lied for you?"

"He said—" I hesitate. "He said he could tell I was being compelled by an outside force," I settle on. "He didn't want me to have to take the blame for something that wasn't my choice."

"That's very understanding of him."

I nod. We're both silent for a few seconds. "He had just gotten together with Bethany," I say in that whisper that is the only way you can speak when tears are so close. "Smith killed her to get her out of the way."

Sierra's eyes close for a long time, and when she lifts them there's an ocean of guilt there. "I'm sorry," she says quietly. "I'm so sorry I brought him into your life. Yours and Linden's. Everyone's."

"You didn't do it," I say, stepping forward with a lurch. "You didn't *mean* to," I amend. But I understand how she would feel that way. How Smith could make her feel that way.

"I'm still responsible," Sierra says, forcing a brave smile. "Come, sit."

I plop down beside her and even though there are still secrets to be shared, the walls between us have come down.

"Is your name really Shelby?" I ask, my head leaning against her shoulder.

"It was."

"Are you going to switch back now?"

She shakes her head. "I've been Sierra for so long I almost don't remember what it means to be Shelby."

"What did you tell my mom when you switched names?"

"The truth. That someone had tried to kill me and that I needed to go into hiding. I think she forgets a lot of the time too. It's just a name."

I reach out and touch a lock of her hair. "Will you grow the strawberry blond out?"

She gives me the most relaxed smile I've seen on her for a long time. "Probably."

"So after you severed your connection with Smith, did you go stay with my mom and dad?"

"Live with the newlyweds?" Sierra says with a snort. "Hardly." But she sobers. "Jason knew your mom, so I couldn't go to her. Couldn't even talk to her for years. I went deep into hiding, changed my name, and moved away just to be safe. When your dad got a job ten miles from the town I was living in, it was great because suddenly we got to see each other again. It had been just over five years and I thought I was safe." She pauses.

"He told me you guys knew each other as kids and that you were best friends."

"That's the truth. I don't know that he really understood what he was at that point. Feeders skip so many generations—ten, twenty, even—that I imagine he had to figure out everything on his own." She hesitates. "I have this theory that Feeders lie dormant until they're awakened by the presence of an Oracle. Like a carrier gene. And then they're drawn to them."

"He said he feeds off the energy from visions?" I ask.

"In the most literal terms, yes. These creatures prey off of Oracle powers. When you aren't able to fight off a vision, a trickle of power is released and a Feeder can survive for months—if just barely—on that trickle. He was very strong while we were friends because I secretly rebelled and rarely fought visions. And he practically lived in my second sight. I imagine he was dangerously weak when he started killing to get through your defenses."

"Where did they come from?"

She shifts so she can look at me. "When Oracles started to pull themselves and their powers out of the political sphere, you can imagine the rulers of the world were very upset." She shudders. "Legend says that they recruited Witches to experiment on Oracle captives and the result was a creature that could, in some ways, mimic the powers of *both* the witches and the Oracles, but at a terrible, terrible cost." She leans over and puts a hand on my knee. "They're despicable creatures."

"I saw a scene where Smith choked you and then you did something, and he was, like, knocked out." Sierra's face is pale, but she doesn't stop me. "He was bleeding from his ears, but obviously he lived. When I did it, Smith died." I swallow hard, reliving those moments in my head.

"Smith's connection with you was stronger than the one the two of us shared. He literally *couldn't* live without you. The trade-off is that he had more control. Would have eventually gotten full control."

"But he only got into my second sight two weeks ago!" I protest. "He was in yours for years."

"He didn't love you," Sierra whispers. "Taking over someone's mind is such a brutal thing. My guess is that he never had the will to truly take me over. He was strong enough, but he never went all the way."

"You were in love?" I ask, equal parts horrified and empathetic.

She doesn't answer. She doesn't have to. "My senior year, I finally started to realize what he was. What he was doing. I didn't understand the specifics, of course, all of that came later. But I knew it was wrong. We had the confrontation you saw, and I almost died. He broke some bones in my neck and I was in the hospital for a long time." She chuckles darkly. "In the end, it was the Sisters who shielded me, who helped me fix my supernatural plane, and eventually made all of the arrangements for me to go into hiding. I owe them so much." She adds in a whisper, "I joined them and decided to live by their rules, like I should have done from the beginning. I learned for myself that their way is the best way."

I fight the urge to squirm. Maybe it's the best way for *her*—even after all of this, I'm still not convinced it's the best way for me.

"I was so careful at first. But after five years, I figured he had to be dead. I slowly got in touch with your parents again—started to live. I don't know exactly when he found me, but I suspect it was through your mom," she says, and her voice is raspy. "My fault again." Then she's quiet for a long time and I don't push her. "I underestimated him and you paid the price."

I swallow hard. "He's been around a long time, actually. He made sure Mom and Dad's accident that I tried to stop still happened." My voice is shaky, but I tell her about the scene I saw in Smith's memories.

"Wow," my aunt whispers. "I had no idea." The flash of guilt in her eyes makes me realize that she's going to feel responsible for my dad's death the same way I have for the last ten years. In some ways, I've been exonerated. But now Sierra has a whole new issue to work through. I don't envy her. It's going to be a rough few months for both of us.

Sierra leans forward. "With their origins so steeped in witchcraft, these Feeders often enchant an item to create a connection between themselves and their chosen Oracle. Did Smith ever give you something? Something he told you to hold on to?"

"Yes." I put my hand into my pocket and my fingers brush both the coin and the necklace.

But they close around the coin.

Part of me doesn't want to give up the necklace. Not yet. It has saved me, but more important, it gives me access to my other powers. The ones I'm not supposed to know about. I'm not ready to give *them* back.

So I pull out the cracked coin and drop it into Sierra's hand without actually saying a word. She accepts it with a look of both interest and disappointment on her face. "Fascinating," she whispers. "It's not the coin at all but that shiny core you can see in the middle. He must have enchanted this himself." She sighs and then says, "I had hoped he might have given you a crystal pendant."

"Why?" I ask, trying to sound neutral.

"It's mine. I guess technically it might be yours now. It's what we used when I was younger. When my fight with Smith was over, the necklace was gone. I don't know if he took it, or someone found it. Honestly, I'm not sure even Smith understands how important it is. It's an exceptionally powerful focus stone that enhances all of the abilities we Oracles don't use anymore." She scrunches up her mouth. "That may not even entirely make sense to you."

But it does. It explains *everything*. How I was able to jump into my supernatural plane the night I cornered Smith, and take him with me. How I was able to fend off the attack in my vision the night Smith tried to kill Clara. That necklace saved my life the first night I went into Smith's world. But I say nothing.

"Will you tell me how Ja—Smith got involved with you?" she asks.

Part of me wants to say no. I'm ashamed and embarrassed that I was taken in that easily. But then, who would understand better than Sierra? So I start at the beginning—with the vision of Bethany's death—and I tell her everything. All of the things I now realize I should have told her before.

All the things I wanted to tell her two nights ago— that Smith wouldn't let me say.

"In the last few days, everything went crazy," I say. "I had these weird visions, of me covered in blood, of you and Mom dead, Linden. What were those?"

"The way a Feeder takes over your mind is by first getting in, of course." My face flushes; I did that completely on my own. "And then they have to break you. Smith obviously tried to do that by killing people you were close to, but I imagine he also attempted to just make chaos. To make you question everything until you literally went insane."

She says it so calmly, but I *was* on the brink of that insanity, and even now—in this comfortable room with Sierra's arm around my shoulders—it terrifies me. "I had a vision of me killing a friend of mine."

"He probably just made that one. Once they get in, a Feeder can exert *so* much power over you. I—should have prepared you. Taught you." She sighs. "Charlotte, I know you're not going to like this, but I need to get the Sisters involved."

"Why!" I'm not ready for this mysterious group. Not ready to join, not ready for them to know the things I did. Just not ready.

"One of the things I spent months doing after I cut off Smith is cleaning out my supernatural plane."

"What do you mean, *cleaning out*?"

"You cut off Smith's power, but your world still holds his dead world. One of the leaders of Delphi went into my supernatural plane with me and showed me how to destroy what was left and to restore my dome."

"But *you* know how; can't you show me how to do it instead?" I ask desperately.

"Not without a focus stone," Sierra says softly. "I'll have to borrow one from them. And I'll have to tell them *why*."

I clench my teeth and look away. The Sisters or my secret? Which is more important? After a few seconds, I dig into my pocket again and bring out the tarnished necklace. I hold it out flat on my palm and say nothing. Sierra stares at it and emotions I can't begin to interpret flash across her face. I don't know what I'm expecting. Anger? Betrayal?

She reaches, but just before her fingers touch it, I close my palm and pull it back, cradling the necklace against my chest. I can't give it up. Not now.

She stares at me, long and hard.

"It's mine now," I whisper. "He gave it to me."

I expect her to argue, to demand it back. But after a few seconds, she simply sighs and says, "Is there anything *else* you'd like to tell me?"

"No. Yes!" I take a deep breath and then just blurt out, "I don't want to be a Sister. Not yet," I tack on. After everything I've seen, everything I've done, I'm not sure I can live by their rules.

She stares at me, silently. Seconds pass. Maybe even as much as a minute. Then she nods. "You deserve to make that choice. But can we make a deal?"

I eye her, but don't say anything.

"Will you hold off on making that decision *for sure* until you're eighteen and you become eligible?"

I think about how much I've lied to her in the last three weeks. Maybe I owe her that. "Okay," I whisper. Then, "As long as you'll show me how to clean up my supernatural plane and not get them involved."

She smiles, but it's a sad smile. "Deal. However, before we start—and we're not going to start today," she says, looking very tired, "I want you to understand that when you let me into your supernatural plane, you're giving me the same access and power you gave Smith. I'm not going to hide that fact from you. Anytime you let *anyone* in, you give them a master key, so to speak. And there's no way to take it back without harming that person, like we both did with Smith. Although I trust her not to use it, one of the oldest Sisters has access to my supernatural plane from helping me eighteen years ago. If I were to destroy it, she's so fragile she would almost certainly die."

"Could I let *anyone* in?" I ask, rather horrified at just how much power I gave Smith.

"No," Sierra says quickly. "*That* is something I should have told you. Then you would have known immediately that Smith wasn't who he said he was. Even with an Oracle's permission, normal humans cannot travel to the supernatural plane. Only supernatural creatures."

"Like what?" I ask, sensing that she is alluding to more than just Oracles and Feeders.

She hesitates, and for a moment I don't think she's

going to answer. "Witches," she finally says. "Sorcerers and Mages. There are others."

My mouth drops open. "Are you serious?" I ask in a whisper. "And you know about them?"

"You will too," she says, but her voice is strained. "The reason it was even possible for all of this to happen is because I kept you in the dark. I'm turning on the light. All of my books," Sierra says, taking in her walls of bookshelves with a gesture. "All of the things you've wanted to know that I wouldn't tell you—the questions you asked that I refused to answer. I won't do that anymore."

My breath is coming fast now and I try to hide it by standing and walking very slowly to the nearest shelf and running my fingers along the ancient spines. She's offering me her *world*.

And I recognize that she's also offering me a choice. Not just assistance in fixing my supernatural plane. She's offering me knowledge that could change the way I lead my Oracle life. To follow my *own* rules.

And she knows it.

"Thank you."

The silence stretches as I look over the titles hungrily. I know which one I'll take first. I'm dying to read all of *Repairing the Fractured Future*. But I don't want to be a complete jerk by taking advantage of her offer right at this second. I'll give her a day or two to let it sink in.

Then I've got to start. I have a lifetime of learning to catch up on.

"I'm going to go sit with Mom," I say, not looking at Sierra. I have to leave this room or I won't be able to resist the temptation.

"Maybe I'll come out soon too," she says, and I hear a smile in her voice. Already things are getting better.

I head out, but pause at the door. "How did you know to come save Linden?" It's the question I've wanted to ask the most, but have also been the most afraid of.

She looks at me, her gaze intense, for a long time. The she sighs and her shoulders slump. "I had a vision," she says, as though admitting to a great failing. And after over a decade of never losing, I guess she sees it that way.

"Would you really have killed me?" I ask.

"I'm glad I didn't have to find out."

"But you'd already *seen* it," I protest, all too familiar with her unyielding stance on never changing the future. "You came because you saw it in the vision, right? You saw yourself come to my rescue."

Her long silence makes my hands tremble. "No," she finally says. "I came because I saw you *lose*. And I knew I could never let that happen."

I suck in a breath of utter astonishment. "You changed the future?"

Her cheeks redden and that's answer enough.

I nod and slip out of her room.

I have months—if not years—of healing in front of me. And there's still so much uncertainty. Will the cops and Feds lose interest in me now that the Cold-water Killer is dead? Will I ever remember what really happened the night Nathan Hawkins died? Will Clara wake up and have any chance at a normal life? Will Michelle keep our secret? I'm going to have to either get answers to these questions or learn to deal with never knowing.

As I walk down the hall, I let my hand slip into my pocket and squeeze the pendant. It's mine now, for better or worse. I'm going to study every book in Sierra's library. I'm going to learn from both the mistakes and triumphs of Oracles in the past. To decide for myself if and when the future should be seen.

Should be *changed*.

But I'm not going to fight anymore. None of it. Not my visions, not my abilities, not the powers of the pendant. Because the time may come when the world needs an Oracle again.

A *true* Oracle.

And I'll be ready.

ACKNOWLEDGMENTS

Perhaps this part would be better labeled *Part Author's Note, Part Acknowledgments*. If you're a dedication reader, you may have noticed that this book is dedicated to the survivors of the Sandy Hook Elementary School shootings. Before you get offended that I dedicated a book about killing teens to the families of slain children, give me a second. The shooting at Newtown was the first national tragedy that really hit me. Columbine happened when I was in high school, but I didn't know anyone from Colorado and as I was attending a school with fewer students and teachers combined than any single grade level at Columbine, it felt so foreign as to be unreal. I was in college on September 11, 2001. But again, I knew *no one* in New York City and though I was as horrified as the rest of the nation, it wasn't *personal*. But the afternoon the Newtown shooting occurred, the news that an entire classroom of kindergarteners (which is what they incorrectly reported the first day) had been killed came in less than half an hour before I went to the school to pick up . . . my kindergartener. I was overwhelmed by gratitude that when I arrived at the school, my five-year-old son would be *alive*—and mired in grief that so many parents could not say the same for their tiny children. The grief didn't go away when I found out it was first graders, it didn't go away the next week, it lingered and despite again not knowing anyone even indirectly involved in this tragedy, I was so shaken. About this time I got the green light on my proposal for *Sleep No More*. Now, the plot had been laid out long before the shooting, but once I got the green light, I found myself writing a story about a community dealing with deaths in their midst. As I did, I poured my grief into the narrative. And it became something darker and more personal than I ever expected. I spat this book out in thirty-eight days and when I was done . . . I felt better. I wasn't filled with that awful sadness. It wasn't gone, but it was no longer intruding on my daily life. It was a downright easy solution compared to the process everyone in Newtown still—I'm sure—faces. But it was the first time I felt that helpless grief and I had to put it *somewhere*! And that somewhere ended up being this book, which is why it is dedicated to those who had, and continue to have, exponentially more to deal with than I did.

Thanks go to my fab editor, Tara Weikum, who loved this story from the very first pitch, and to my agent, Jodi Reamer, who forgave me for taking it out behind her back . . . sort of. Erica Sussman, you are always there to lend a hand. Usually with the tedious details. Your line edits were priceless. To my publicist, Mary Ann Zissimos, for being an expert juggler. (And ARC-fort maker!) To my sister-in-law, Hollie, who was the first one to hear the story all the way through, and to my long-suffering husband, Kenny, who took all of the kids to the zoo on Christmas Eve so I could get six thousand words written.

APRILYNNE PIKE

Kimberlee Schaffer may be drop-dead gorgeous . . . but she also dropped dead last year. When she was alive, Kimberlee wasn't just a mean girl; she was also a complete kleptomaniac. Now she needs help with her unfinished business, and she's not taking no for an answer.

HarperCollins *Children's Books*

08/14

Don't miss the *New York Times* bestselling

WINGS SERIES

★ "Mixing a little bit of Harry Potter and a lot of Twilight,
Pike has hit on a winning combination. Yet it is her own graceful
take on life inside Avalon that is sure to enthrall readers."
—ALA *Booklist* (starred review)

HarperCollins *Children's Books*